Chelsea
HIGH

Chelsea HIGH

JENNY OLIVER

ELECTRIC
MONKEY

First published in Great Britain 2020
by Egmont UK Limited
2 Minster Court, 10th floor, London EC3R 7BB

Text copyright © 2020 Jenny Oliver
The moral rights of the author have been asserted

ISBN 978 1 4052 9504 8

www.egmont.co.uk

70298/001

Printed and bound in Great Britain by the CPI Group

For KY, SW & LG

CHAPTER ONE

I stopped so suddenly, I nearly got hit by a taxi. The cabbie honked his horn, swerving to avoid my bike, but I barely noticed. All my attention had been caught by the sight in front of me – the teeming mass of beautiful people lolling on the wide concrete steps of the red-brick building, all in grey and white uniforms, all the same as mine but infinitely better, the chequered flags waving from turrets and the million mullioned windows sparkling through the haze of bus fumes, all stained glass like a church. My heart lurched. Surely this couldn't be a school. It was a palace. A sightseeing dot on a map for tourists.

My eyes drank it all nervously in. The sun-kissed girls with big toothy grins who were draped like satin over the railings. The boys with their perfect shaggy hair, razor-sharp cheeks and ice-white shirts chucking rugby balls high in the air and laughing at stuff on their phones. My heart beat faster as they seemed to merge into one, a tangle of tanned limbs and glistening skin, posing for back-from-summer photos, shrieking, air-kissing, boys lifting girls into giant twirling hugs. All of them glowing like they'd been dipped in gold.

My every instinct was pulling my handlebars round, urging: *go home, go home*.

I thought about what would be happening at my old school right now. One of my friends would call a lazy 'Hi' as I ambled up the cracked tarmac path, toast in my mouth, hands trying to do something with my hair. On Mulberry Island, we saw each other every day regardless of whether it was school or holidays, so no one had a tan we didn't know about. No one had new hair, no one shone like gold and the old sixties building looked nothing like a palace.

But this wasn't my old life. And no one was waiting for me.

A huge black Rolls-Royce purred past me, so close it almost grazed my leg, pulling me back to the present. I felt everyone on the steps pause what they were doing. A chauffeur got out to open the passenger door, and I watched as none other than Coco Summers unfolded herself from the back seat – tall, blonde and impatient. I heard myself gasp. Model, influencer and selfie queen, Coco had maybe two million followers on Instagram, probably more. Her #cocostyle sold out within seconds. I recognised the slouchy silver backpack she'd just slung over her shoulder. I remembered how she once wore a grey woolly hat with a pink bobble that I owned, and then suddenly everyone had it. I was torn between a bubble of pleasure that we shared the same style and annoyance that she'd ruined my hat.

I stared, entranced, as she sauntered up the steps. Even if I hadn't recognised her, I'd have known she was special. Her caramel hair with its over-long fringe was perfectly, artfully dishevelled, her skin was luminous. She walked like she owned the world, and she had an aura that made it impossible to look away.

From the school steps, a glossy brunette whooped and tottered down the steps to hurl herself into Coco's arms before a guy with red hair and a deep golden safari tan leaped the bannister and grabbed them both, lifting them up as if they were weightless.

I had a panicked moment of tunnel vision. I couldn't fit in here. As the Rolls-Royce cruised away, I wanted to jump inside, to drive back in time to the warmth of the island, to my desk with its graffiti carved with a compass, to the register taken by Mrs Wellington who always had a cup of tea and three plain digestives, to the café after school where we drank hot chocolate piled with marshmallows or played basketball with the boys on a court ravaged by tree roots. To a place where no one twirled anyone, no one pouted, no one wore rucksacks worth over a grand to school.

I looked up with a jolt of desperation. The turrets loomed sharp as daggers. I saw the gleaming gold sign above the doors: Chelsea High School, the words *Vincere fecit* inscribed underneath. And beneath that, for anyone unfamiliar with the Latin: *Made to win*.

Go home, my rusty old bike seemed to whisper again.

But my home had gone.

CHAPTER TWO

In a bit of a daze, I looked around for somewhere to lock my bike. The chatter from the steps filled the air. I felt like I was in an impenetrable bubble, watching a cinema screen. I self-consciously flattened my hair as I took off my helmet and tried to catch a glimpse of my fringe in the metal of my handlebars to check it wasn't sticking up all over the place. The bike racks by the school were already full with spanking new Bianchis and other flash racing bikes, so I had to walk away, searching the side streets till I eventually found a spot much further up the road. I had to run back when I heard the bell ring – by which time the school steps were deserted. Everyone had vanished in a click of manicured fingers, leaving pigeons to peck at crisp crumbs and a forgotten school jumper slung on the railing.

I sprinted up the steps to catch the huge wooden doors just as they were closing. And then I stepped inside Chelsea High.

My eyes had to adjust to the darkness. As the fresco ceilings and gilded cornicing came into focus, I felt again like I'd come to the wrong building. This was a cathedral, not a school, and we should be silent in worship. Ahead of me, dark archways and low lighting led down endless empty corridors as doors slammed all around. The smoggy sunlight cast shadows like monsters across the gleaming parquet. I could hear my breath. I could hear my heart.

My old school came to mind again. The patches of damp on the plasterboard ceiling at Mulberry Island Academy, the Sellotaped window-pane cracks, my beloved locker. The railing I swung on to turn the corner every day. The smell of lunch cooking. The meadow with grass so long you could lie down and disappear. Eating Maltesers and talking to Jess about nothing. I would do almost anything to talk about nothing now. What a luxury – that careless boredom.

'No dawdling. First day of term. Start as you mean to go on.'

A deep voice echoed down the empty corridor.

Instinctively I stood up straighter, hitching my old rucksack higher, starting to walk forward. But I didn't know which way to go. I was completely lost. I vaguely remembered a map arriving in the post with all the other introductory papers in a brown envelope, but I had no idea where it had ended up. Everything at home now was just a mess of confusion.

I've lived on a houseboat all my life, and all my life I've loved it: the narrow cosiness, the cocooned security, the gentle lapping of the tangy water in summer and the harsh battering of the rain in winter. But this morning, the sharp rap on our front door had been like a crack splintering the boat's hull.

I watched my dad spill his coffee in his haste to answer the door. It was bad enough that he was dressed so differently today. He'd always been one for a bright shirt and, if he had to, a funny tie. 'Hook them with a laugh,' he'd say. This morning he had been wearing a pale yellow shirt, grey tie and suit trousers. Almost as if he was the one going to school.

My mum straightened up, visibly nervous as she said with vague dismissal: 'Time to go to school, Norah. Quick, off you go.' She'd put her arm round my shoulders and given me a distracted kiss on the top of my head.

'I don't want to go,' I'd muttered.

But my mum just waved the statement away, her interest diverted by the front door. She moved away from me, and my shoulder felt suddenly empty.

Dad stood to one side to let a humourless man in a dark blue suit pass on the narrow steps, arm stretched out to show him which direction to go. On a houseboat, there is only one direction.

My mum beckoned for him to sit at the small, round table where the remains of our breakfast had been cleared away. She had wiped the table and was now retying the black bow at the end of her plait, looking uncomfortable and fidgety in her long yellow and black patterned skirt, white shirt and bright yellow sandals. Dressed up but trying to look casual.

'Off you go, Norah,' she said. Insistent.

I didn't like the look of our visitor. No one in a suit had

ever set foot on our boat. Our visitors usually wore old baggy shirts and carried musical instruments or bottles of home-brewed beer.

'I've got to get my bag,' I said, watchful and hesitant.

The man in the suit was pulling out one of our mismatched chairs, scraping it on the floor, setting his black briefcase on the table. It wasn't my imagination that he gave the boat a disparaging once-over.

'Get a move on, Norah!'

The snap in my mum's voice surprised me. She'd never shouted at me before in my life. At my old school I would always scrape in just as registration ended. My best friend Jess would watch, bemused by how I could be late when she'd already squeezed a thousand and one things into her morning. As a family, we are always late. My mum doesn't own a watch.

'I'm going,' I said, hoping someone might notice the hurt in my voice.

But my mum and dad were already taking their seats at the little wooden table.

The humourless man in the suit was a lawyer. To him I didn't exist, a waste of time billed in five-minute increments. As I made my way to the door, my dad gave me a quick surreptitious wave, like displays of affection were no longer allowed.

Now, in the oppressive magnificence of the Chelsea High corridor, I was faced with another man in a suit. This one was

7

older, wearing what looked like a cape over his black jacket and a white bow tie. Even the masters had a uniform here. He came nearer, stopping right in front of me. He unfolded his arms, pushed back his cape and put his hands in the pockets of his suit trousers. 'Name?' he said.

'Norah Whittaker, Sir,' I said, palms sweaty. I'd never called anyone Sir in my life, but nervousness made it roll off my tongue. At my old school we called the teachers by their first names, and half of them were our neighbours. 'I'm –' I saw his eyes squint as he processed the information.

'Whittaker.' His voice whistled on the W. 'Well, well. We've been expecting you, haven't we, Ms *Whittaker*?' There was the whistle again. 'Not the best first impression.' He looked at his watch. 'Late on your first day.'

I shook my head. 'No, Sir,' I said. 'Sorry, Sir.'

He tilted his head like he was trying to get the measure of me. 'Your father was always late,' he said in the end. 'Shows a sloppiness of character. Wouldn't you agree?'

I swallowed, unable to reply. The reference to my father had caught me off guard.

For the whole of my life, Mulberry Island had been our home. The life my parents had led before they owned the boat was never mentioned. They talked only of life on the island – the river, the land, the community was ingrained in our blood. But just over a week ago I had learned the truth.

It still felt unreal. I had discovered, amidst the chaos – in hurried, snatched conversations – that my parents weren't native islanders. In fact, my dad had gone to this school; to Chelsea High. It was where he had met my mother. They had been rich. Were rich. Might be rich. I didn't know. His parents, the grandparents I'd been told were dead, were definitely rich, though. Very rich. It was them paying for the humourless lawyer who had arrived on our boat this morning. They were paying for everything. They were the reason our colourful old boat was now moored at one of the most exclusive docks in London, surrounded by stark grey floating palaces like sharks circling to eat us alive.

'Look at me when I'm talking to you, Ms Whittaker!'

My eyes shot back to his. I could see them, watery and angry.

'I warned them to steer well clear of you lot. Trouble. Always have been,' he sneered.

'Let's leave it there, shall we, Mr Watts?' A woman had swept up next to him, black pantsuit, cropped black hair, big pearl studs in her ears. 'I think Ms Whittaker understands the importance of timekeeping. Am I right?'

I nodded, a lump forming in my throat. It all suddenly felt too much, too overwhelming. If this woman (whoever she was) had hugged me at that point, I would have gladly hugged her back. But this wasn't Reception class. There would be no hugs.

Mr Watts straightened up. He folded his arms again,

pursed his lips and said, 'Late again, Ms Whittaker, and it will be detention.' He gave a curt nod to Mrs Pearce before striding away.

Putting her hand on my shoulder, Mrs Pearce ushered me down the dusky corridor. Our footsteps echoed. There were closed classroom doors on one side of us and big windows with mottled glass and a view out to an elaborate courtyard on the other.

'Don't worry too much about Mr Watts,' I heard her say softly. She was still facing ahead, as if what she was saying wasn't quite by the book.

With the threat of tears welling in my eyes, I didn't look her way. I focused on her shoes instead: Gucci loafers that clipped on the polished wood.

'I think he might have been . . . shall we say, a *disgruntled* class mate of your father's,' Mrs Pearce went on.

I looked up at her then, frowning.

She smiled, her kind eyes crinkling. 'He had quite a reputation here, your dad. On a sunny day it's still possible to make out where he wrote his name in weedkiller on the cricket pitch on the last day of term. An interesting choice, wouldn't you say? Writing one's own name rather gives the culprit away.' Mrs Pearce seemed to have the measure of my dad in an instant. 'A loveable fool' my mum always called him. 'A bloody idiot' seemed to be the kindest name currently on people's lips.

As we walked beside walls lined with oil paintings of past masters and gold-leafed boards listing the well-known names of old alumni, I tried to imagine Dad as a boy walking these same corridors, but it was too hard to visualise. Instead I thought about him sitting on the bench in the patch of scrubland we'd called a garden, next to our old mooring, dressed in his jeans and favourite shirt with hair swept to one side, an image of his usual self – except for his eyes, which that day weren't smiling.

'Come and sit down, Nellie Norah.' He'd patted the seat next to him. 'There's something I need to talk to you about.'

My immediate fear was that someone had died. That was the expression on his face. But no one had died. Except as he spoke, it felt like a death. A death of us, of what we had, of the life I knew and thought I would always know.

'The thing is, Norah,' he'd said, rubbing his chin, awkward, nervous, not quite able to look me in the eye. 'The thing is . . . I've made a little mistake. Well, actually, quite a big mistake.' He'd paused, glancing down at the weeds around our bench. 'The film company. All the financing. It was a scam, Norah. The McGinty brothers are not quite as honest as they seemed.'

I frowned, not understanding. 'It can't be a scam,' I said. 'We made a film. Everyone on the island invested in us.'

I remembered the party we'd held when we reached the financing target. My dad, grinning from ear to ear, thwacking Jess's dad on the back. 'We're gonna double your money,

11

Keith, you just wait and see. 'And Jess's dad holding up his crossed fingers with a nervous smile. 'It's everything I've got, Bill. Look after it.' As we sat on the bench, I saw the lines and wrinkles of my dad's downcast face.

'They're going to give the money back, right?' I said.

He didn't reply. Just sat up and stretched his arms along the back of the bench, as if he hadn't heard the question.

We sat side by side in silence. I kicked a dandelion with my foot. There are moments, I've realised, when you know your life is about to change, when everything around you gets much brighter, bigger, clearer. Right then I could see each individual petal of the dandelion, dazzling yellow, as big as a sunflower.

Mrs Pearce stopped at a polished wooden door. She seemed to steel herself for a second before pushing it open. Inside we were met with a wall of noise and laughter.

I stood, dumbfounded. If the entrance to Chelsea High was Victorian Gothic, then this was the Apple Store. The classroom was a gleaming cube of white, stripped back to stark white walls and achingly contemporary art. The pale grey floor gleamed like an ice rink. The light fittings were huge translucent orbs, and the windows had automatic blinds that responded to sunlight. People were everywhere, like ants. Phones were being passed around, music thumped, girls sniggered and swished their gleaming hair, boys lolled, kicking their feet against the expensive furniture. There was no compass-carved graffiti on manky old desks here, or hockey balls being chucked millimetres from the swanky art.

'Here we are,' Mrs Pearce said, ushering me into the mêlée. She clapped her hands together and shouted, 'OK, everyone, settle down. Settle down! Music off, phones away!'

Chairs scraped and bashed and huddles dispersed with lazy insouciance.

I looked around for a place to sit, but my eyes were distracted. All I could see was wealth – the labels on the bags, the top-of-the-range phones and iPads chucked on every smart white table, even the diamond studs in earlobes and the flawless make-up – sparking in me a shameful, envious insecurity. And then I noticed the people looking at me, the assessing glances. My cheeks began to pink.

Mrs Pearce was unwrapping her own iPad from a turquoise-leather pouch. 'OK, everyone, this is Norah,' she said, glancing from her emails to the class to me. 'She is joining us this year, so I hope you will all be your delightful selves and make her feel welcome. Freddie, feet off the desk, for Christ's sake. You're not in kindergarten.'

I stared at the scrutinising, disinterested faces in front of me. Aware of my hair, my skin, my bag, my shoes. Wishing I had put more thought into every item I was wearing. But of course my thoughts had been elsewhere.

'There's a spare seat at the back, Norah.' Mrs Pearce gestured vaguely to where the glossy brunette I'd seen earlier was leaning against the window sill, watching my progress. Her fingers thrummed on the table that belonged to Freddie, the boy with jaw-length black hair who'd had his feet on the desk.

I willed my feet not to trip as I walked across the shiny floor, trying to ignore the stares. As I put my bag down on the empty table, I reminded myself that this was temporary. Once the lawyer had sorted it all out, we'd be turning our boat round and chugging back to Mulberry Island. These people, this place was just a blip on my life's horizon. I could probably get through this without even having to talk to anyone.

The brunette was still watching me with narrowed eyes.

Then suddenly I was forgotten, as the door was thrown open and Coco Summers stalked into the room.

'Sorry I'm late, Mrs Pearce!' she called, breezing across the classroom in a cloud of blonde with her eyes glued to something on her phone. Without even pausing to register the fact I was standing by the desk getting my stuff out, she sat down in my seat.

I stood, not quite knowing what to do. My diary and biro were out on the table already. Coco had chucked her phone into her silver rucksack on the floor, her legs stretched out in front of her. It was only as she ruffled fingers through her blunt fringe and gave the room a cursory glance that she acknowledged me.

'Yes?' she said.

'I was . . .' I glanced at my things on the table, then to the front. Mrs Pearce was typing on her iPad, words appearing on the whiteboard screen behind her. I swallowed, pointing to the seat, wishing this wasn't happening. 'I was told to sit here.' Coco shook her head with a dismissive frown. 'I sit here.'

Mrs Pearce looked up. 'Oh, Coco,' she sighed, hands on her hips.

Coco looked bemused. 'I always sit here. You know that, Mrs Pearce.'

Mrs Pearce rubbed her forehead, then gave a half-smile. Coco grinned, wide and confident.

'Norah, if you could just find somewhere else for the moment, that would be great,' said Mrs Pearce. She peered around the room. 'There's one over there.'

In the corner was a spare double desk.

'I'm sorry, you'll be on your own,' Mrs Pearce said.

'It's fine,' I muttered, scooping up my things, wishing that had been where I'd sat in the first place. Anything not to have drawn attention to myself.

Mrs Pearce watched me until I sat down and got myself ready. I didn't have an iPad. I had a notepad and an old chewed biro. I didn't even have a phone. My mum had confiscated it after reading a message thread over my shoulder. *Surely these girls have something better to do!* she'd said, as the messages laid into me and my family, full of vitriol about the damage my dad had done and the shame I should feel.

The worst part had been when my friends had joined in. People I'd always assumed would give us the benefit of the

15

doubt. My mum hadn't wanted me infected by the news stories either. Like the time she threw away the bathroom scales – better not to know, she'd said. But I'd seen enough already. The camera crews, the so-called friends of my dad who had sold stories to the paper. I told myself they were just doing it for the money. When you've lost everything, sometimes your principles have to go too.

'First day of term, kids,' Mrs Pearce said. 'This is an important year for you, so no messing. Yes?'

No one really replied.

'Miss?'

'Yes, Emmeline.' There was a resigned tone in Mrs Pearce's voice as she looked at a girl with long black hair, huge eyes and a tiny stubby nose. The stuff on her table all neatly stacked in size order: MacBook, paperback, phone, neatly wound headphones.

'I think it's really demoralising to call us kids,' said Emmeline. 'I think it encourages immaturity because it expects immaturity.'

'You think so, Emmeline?' Mrs Pearce raised a brow while scrolling through the register.

'I do, Miss.' Emmeline flicked her smooth curtain of hair.

'And you don't think that perhaps I'm acknowledging the immaturity I see in the room and challenging you all to step up and overtake it?' Mrs Pearce mirrored the register to the screen behind her as she spoke. 'Rex Andrews?'

A guy at the front said, 'Here.'

'No, Miss.' Emmeline's hair swung as she shook her head. 'I think you should see us and treat us with the respect we deserve. We are adults.'

'Well, I think someone might have forgotten to tell Freddie and Rollo,' said Mrs Pearce.

The whole class looked at the two guys by the window who were silently cracking up at something on Freddie's phone, zooming in close.

Rollo, the mega-tanned redhead from earlier, glanced up when he realised he was being watched.

'Care to share, boys?' Mrs Pearce asked, leaning forward with her elbows on the table.

Freddie immediately put his phone away, unable to quite wipe the smile from his face. 'No, Miss.'

Mrs Pearce glanced back to Emmeline. 'Perhaps if you could get your brother up to speed, your cause would be more fruitful, Emmeline.'

Emmeline rolled her eyes and pulled her paperback out of the stack on her desk to start reading.

'Book away.'

She closed it with a sigh.

Mrs Pearce glanced back to her register. 'Verity Benítez?'

'Yeah.' The glossy brunette raised a dismissive finger a centimetre to signify her presence.

Someone's phone beeped. There was a scuffle of movement

as people went to check their bags.

'Phones away,' Mrs Pearce said without looking up from the register. 'Frederick Chang?'

Freddie saluted. 'Present and correct.' Mrs Pearce sighed. 'I've had enough of you already.'

'Ah, Miss, come on, you love me,' he said. 'I brighten up your day.'

'That's debatable, Freddie. Emmeline Chang?'

'Yes, I'm here.'

I watched as Coco read a message on her phone under her table and passed it to Verity.

'Rollo Cooper-Quinn?'

'Yes.'

Verity passed Rollo the phone. Rollo was big like a rugby player, effortlessly pleased with himself. He sat with the casual confidence of someone who knows they're chocolate-box handsome, chewing gum, eyes smiling.

'Coco Summers?'

'Here.'

Freddie grabbed for the phone but Rollo held it just out of reach, laughing.

Mrs Pearce clicked her fingers without glancing their way. She had some crazy surround vision. 'Phone,' she said. Coco swore. 'No swearing, Coco,' she added as Rollo gave Freddie the phone to take up to the table at the front.

Mrs Pearce took a moment to study the customised cover

of the slick new iPhone. Hot pink Perspex with the word *Coco* scrawled in gold glitter. 'You can have it back at the end of the day.'

'You can't take my phone, Miss; it's my business,' Coco said with big serious eyes.

'Do you want it back tomorrow instead?' Coco slumped back, fuming. Then a few seconds later bent down to check that her other, equally sleek rose-gold iPhone with a rabbit-ear jacket was still nestled in the pocket of her bag.

'Norah Whittaker?' Mrs Pearce looked straight at me at the back of the class. 'Whittaker?' Verity murmured.

She leaned over and whispered something to Coco, who laughed. Rollo leaned forward, keen to get in on the joke. I blushed. They knew, of course they knew. The whole world knew. It had been plastered over every newspaper in the country. 'Three arrested in alleged £15m film investment scheme'. It had been like watching it all happen to someone else's life. And as the headlines soon switched to 'Earl of Wesley's movie-fraudster son!' it *did* feel like someone else's life. These people were talking about my dad, who wore holey green jumpers, played banjo in the Mulberry Island band and ate carrots he'd pulled straight from the ground. Suddenly he was an earl's son.

There's a statue on a hill in Cornwall of a Roman temple. It rests high off the ground on a wooden frame, Underneath you can see each column tethered by a counterweight so when the wind blows the whole structure tips precariously to the left or right, yawing like a ship in a storm. That's how my life felt when I thought too much about it all.

Mrs Pearce looked from me to Coco *et al* and back again with an expression of pity. Then she looked back at her register and, with a slight frown, said, 'Ezra Montgomery?'

Everyone in the room looked up at the name. Mine was forgotten.

Mrs Pearce glanced around. 'Coco, do you know if Ezra's in today?'

Coco gave the slightest shake of her head. A gesture that seemed to surprise most people.

'Rollo?' Mrs Pearce asked. 'Have you seen him?'

Rollo shook his head too, suddenly a little less self-assured than he had been a moment ago. 'I only flew in last night, Miss,' he said.

I leaned forward, resting my chin on my hand, intrigued by the change in the room. The imperceptible tensing of Coco and her gang. Mrs Pearce was scrolling through emails, trying to find something on the unaccounted for Ezra. In the end she gave up and went back to the rest of her register.

'Rufus? Emir? Portia? Alejandro?'

Even the names here were different.

My mind wandered as Mrs Pearce read out the day's notices. A comment from the headmaster mocking the results of the previous year. *CHELSEA HIGH BREEDS WINNERS* came up in huge capitals on the screen. *If you're not an A student, you're not a Chelsea student.* My focus however was less on grades and more on how I was going to fit in around here. Or at least go unnoticed.

I would have to do something about my dress. Everyone else's was shorter, tighter, better fitting. Mine was like a giant boat in comparison. And my shoes. Why had I believed the information pack, why did I think that people would be wearing the regulation black lace-ups? Because I had foolishly assumed that at somewhere so grand, everyone would follow the rules. Not like at Mulberry Island Academy, where white shirt meant anything white and clean. Where my friends and I wore our tracksuits all day if we had PE in the afternoon.

There had been a melting pot of friendships at Mulberry Island Academy. Jess, for example, was my best friend, but she also had her canoeing friends while I had my drama friends. But we all knew each other and each other's siblings, regardless of style or interest. Here, you could tell from one cursory glance that the classroom was divided into hierarchical cliques. And Coco reigned supreme.

I was just watching Emmeline as she leaned over to whisper something to Coco, wondering how she got her hair so glossy – immediately annoyed at myself because I had never cared about glossy hair before – when the door opened. Everything around me went still, like the room was holding its breath. I saw Coco completely ignore whatever Emmeline was saying, her sparkling pink lips opening slightly and her eyes wide. She shifted in her seat, shrugging off Rollo's attention. A tiny crease developed between Rollo's brows.

I've spent my whole life studying the greatest actors and actresses in the world. It's all I want to be. So I understand facial expressions. I have whiled away many hours in front of the mirror perfecting the smallest quirk of a brow. If I make it to Broadway, I will die happy.

Maybe this was something I could focus on in the hours I spent here, friendless, before normality resumed. I could use these people and their expressions as part of my studies. Watching and learning, impassive, neutral.

But then I turned back and I saw him.

I know that my lips parted like Coco's, just less pink and less frosted, as he slunk over to Mrs Pearce's desk. Thick dark hair, olive skin, face all angular, body tall and sinewy. This had to be the elusive Ezra Montgomery.

'Sorry, I'm late,' he half mumbled.

'That's fine, Ezra.' Mrs Pearce smiled, all kind eyes. 'There's a seat at the back.'

She pointed to the only seat left in the room. The seat next to me.

I shut my mouth. I could feel myself start to blush for no reason other than the fact he was getting closer. Tall loping strides, nonchalant half-closed eyes, hand raking back messy hair. He took his time, walking down the aisle between the tables.

Coco was smiling. It was the softest I'd seen her since I'd arrived. She half stood up from her chair and called, 'Ezra, over here! We can squeeze up.'

He took in the lack of spare seats by Coco and his brow creased, like he was confused. That was enough for me to like him immediately.

'Over there's fine,' he said, pointing at the spare chair beside me, half smiling. 'Thanks.'

It was possible Coco blushed.

Freddie bounded out of his seat to give Ezra a natty little handshake. Rollo stretched across to follow suit – but their hands didn't touch because Mrs Pearce called out, 'Sit down, everyone!'

And then Ezra was chucking his black bag to the floor and kicking the spare chair out with his foot to slide effortlessly down in the seat next to me.

Coco seemed unable to tear her eyes away.

But, to be honest, so was I.

He was so close I could smell him. All shower fresh and fabric softener. Lashes like blackbird wings.

I saw a muscle in Rollo's jaw tense.

I sat rigid. Cheeks hot. Never in my life had I been so overwhelmingly aware of the presence of another human.

I tried to concentrate on my notebook, absently doodling round where I'd written *Chelsea breeds winners*, but my eyes

23

kept darting to the side. His top button was undone, his tie in his pocket. He wore a ribbed white T-shirt underneath his shirt. His black trousers were jeans. His black shoes were Nikes. His watch was cracked. I couldn't see his face again without tucking my hair behind my ears (which I did), but all my movements felt wooden and rehearsed. Perhaps I didn't have what it took to be an actress after all. I cast furtive glances across at the sharp contours of his cheeks, the line of his nose, the sullen dip of the corners of his mouth.

The room gradually settled back to normal.

Emmeline turned right round in her seat. 'Hello, darling Ezra,' she said, putting her hand gently on his. When she smiled, her whole face lit up with unexpected kindness.

I watched Ezra's mouth quirk up just slightly on one corner and his eyes spark. He put his other hand briefly over hers. 'Alright, Em,' he said. Emmeline turned back round, hair sloshing like paint down her back.

Coco was mouthing his name, trying to catch his attention. Ezra lifted a finger in a sort of wave. I watched him look around the room, his knee jiggling under the table like he was wired, excited, maybe nervous. He pushed his hair back from his face. Then, as Mrs Pearce was making us take notes about timetable changes and all I could hear was the gentle tap of twenty iPads, he turned to me and said, 'Can I borrow some paper?'

Caught staring at him, my flustered cheeks still prickling

with heat, I found myself saying, 'What? Oh. Yes, sorry,' and ripping off a sheet of notepaper so quickly it tore diagonally across the top. 'Don't have that one,' I mumbled, laying it on the desk next to me. It fluttered to the floor as I tore off another sheet.

He looked amused as I handed him the new piece and scrabbled to get the one that had escaped.

'Thanks,' he said.

I nodded, blowing my fringe out of my eyes, unsure how I'd made something so simple into such a trial.

'Any chance you've got a pen?' he added ruefully.

And I couldn't help but laugh, at his expression and the fact the ordeal was not yet over. I had one spare biro – I don't know where they all go; I think my mum takes them – and it was shameful. The end was chewed into jagged points and there was barely any ink left. Reluctantly I passed it over. 'Only this one,' I said, cringing as he took it.

'Thanks,' he said, then looked at it properly and laughed. 'That's a hell of a pen.'

I did a sort of apologetic shrug, and that was the end of our interaction. He turned away to scrawl down everything that was on the board while I replayed the incident over and over in my mind. My senses still tingled with awareness, at the smell of him, the closeness of his arm as he wrote, the two tiny moles on his cheek.

Then the bell went.

Everyone jumped out their seats. Scooping up her bag, Coco shot over to hug Ezra tight. Her face pressed close to his neck, she whispered, 'Hey, Ez,' as her presence filled the corner of the room with a rich, sweet-smelling cloud of coconut suntan lotion and Chanel.

Ezra put his hand lightly on her back. But where her eyes were shut tight, he kept his open, staring straight ahead. Then suddenly Rollo was there, splitting the hug apart with a quick punch on Ezra's arm, and next Freddie was laughing as Ezra caught him in a playful headlock while Verity leaned over the desk to deliver the kind of kiss on each cheek that was predominantly about keeping her make-up intact. If the girl had an emotion in her body, it wasn't visible to the naked eye.

The whole thing lasted hardly more than five seconds. And then they were gone, Ezra strolling out of the door with my half-chewed biro, me waiting, hopeful, for a backward glance. But he didn't look back.

CHAPTER THREE

The day didn't get better. I got lost in the maze that led from the original Gothic quarters of the school to a gleaming new glass extension, where the roof had a triangular-panelled dome like a giant observatory, the view reaching up to the wide blue sky and the gentle fluttering of plane-tree leaves, teasing in their freedom. But no matter the opulence, I would have swapped it in a second to be back at my old school, sitting in my old Drama class, the back doors open on to the wilderness pond, or sketching outside in the meadow for Art. The corridors here smelt box-fresh, the poured concrete floors glistened, giant art installations loomed down from the stark white walls like a fancy museum. In the corner was a coffee bar with low tables and lounge chairs, but the kiosk was bigger and more impressive than the whole of the Mulberry Island café. This part of the school was three storeys high, designed with a corridor running round the edge of the atrium, and open so anyone up above had a clear view down.

'Late, Ms Whittaker!'

I heard a familiar voice echo round the dome and looked up to see Mr Watts peering over the uppermost balcony.

'Sorry, Sir,' I called, rushing to find the stairs. Where they were, I had no idea. So when I finally made it to the classroom, panicked and breathless, Mr Watts made a point of glancing at the wall clock. As punishment for disrupting his class, he made me stand behind my white table and recite my thirteen times table backwards, which of course I couldn't do. Could anyone? My cheeks flamed like popping candy, my voice catching with nerves. Then when my humiliation was too much to bear and Mr Watts had proved his point, a skinny guy with thick brown quiffed hair and square glasses recited it number-perfect. The diagrams in my textbook blurred as I fought the press of hot, embarrassed tears.

Lunch was another minefield. No snaking queue and grumpy dinner ladies dishing out wet green beans and undefinable meat, no warm chocolate sponge pudding, no scuffed plastic water jugs and fake wood tables. Lunch here was like the food court at Wholefoods. There were various stations round the edge of the room and huge circular tables in the middle, all the different colours of the rainbow. In one corner there was a guy sizzling steak for burritos next to a Japanese woman rolling sushi. There was a shopping cart stacked up with baguettes, a sourdough pizza oven, a salad bar, and even a stall of fresh chopped fruit where you could make your own smoothies. I felt like Charlie walking into Willie Wonka's chocolate factory all wide-eyed in awe, while everyone else took it for granted, picking at their baguettes and texting as their pizzas cooked. It was hard to believe this would ever feel like the norm.

As I walked around the various food stands, I looked for a list of prices, not quite sure what I could afford. I had hardly any cash on me. I hadn't dared ask my mum because our money had been poured into the bogus film company and what was left had been frozen by the police. I paused by the baguette stand to ask the lady serving which was the cheapest.

She frowned. 'You don't have to pay, dear. You just swipe your card here.' And she held out a black card reader.

'It's free?'

'Well, not free,' she scoffed. 'It goes on your parents' bill. But that's for them to worry about, isn't it?'

People were piling their plates high. My unknown grandparents were paying my school fees. The thought of them poring over the itemised school bill, raising their brows at my expensive sushi lunch, was more than I could handle. So I went for the most basic cheese and tomato sandwich I could find and sat at the empty half of a giant blue table. The three girls on the other side didn't even look up from where they were huddled around their phones.

Instinct made me reach into my pocket for mine, for something to do. But I only found the replacement pager, given to me by Mum when she'd confiscated my phone after finding me in my room, deep in a wormhole of messaging, my unblinking eyes welling up. She made me delete all my

29

accounts after one glance at the screen. A girl in my year called Becky Brown, who I sat next to in History and whose dad owned the Mulberry Island pub, had written If ur dad doesnt die in jail, my dad says hes gonna kill him.

Naively, I'd tried to defend him. But when I did, more people joined in to side with Becky. I couldn't believe that people who I had known all my life could turn on us so quickly. They said that my dad had stabbed their parents in the back and now we were running away, rich cowards who'd lost nothing.

I felt sick. These had been my friends. Friends, with families my dad had helped in the past. He'd organised the river raft race to raise money for the leaking pub roof. He'd set up the Theatre Club when we'd all moaned about having nothing to do. There were always people sobbing on our boat about various issues, my dad listening with a Scotch and some words of wisdom. Yet suddenly there was no benefit of the doubt, no belief that he would sort this, that together we could make this situation better.

I'd screenshot the messages and sent them to Jess, who said it was just emotions running high. People were understandably upset. I knew that, but it didn't take away the sting. I just had to sit tight and wait for justice to win out, she said. But it was so hard. I'd nodded, watery-eyed at the screen, her words like a lifeline back to normality. When Mum looked at me wiping at my eyes with my cuffs, she walked out of the room with my phone. So now I just have my dad's old pager, from when he joined the lifeboats, to use for emergencies.

After wolfing down my sandwich, I wandered the grounds, pretending to get my bearings when really it was for something to do other than sit alone.

I walked the periphery, past a glass-walled indoor swimming pool and steaming outdoor one. I passed six tennis courts: two hard court, two clay, two grass, as if this was an international training ground rather than just school PE facilities.

The Mulberry Island tennis court was cracked diagonally from one side to the other like an earthquake had hit. The ball got wedged in it so often that any semblance of a game was laughable.

At Chelsea High the tennis courts ran half the length of the tree-lined back wall. Next to them were cricket nets and a gleaming pavilion. There was a path through the trees into a walled garden, partitioned with box hedges like a low maze and full of intricate topiary. Around the edge were benches where people sat soaking up the sun. I walked through to a large green space marked with an athletics track. To the left was a small grandstand and an L-shape of wooden buildings.

I quite like athletics. I'm good at running. I wondered what my version of good would be in comparison to here.

The sun was scorchingly bright and the air smelt so strongly of fresh-cut grass and a hint of river (I presumed the Thames ran along the back of the playing field) that I had to stop for a second and shut my eyes. The smell was so much a comforting reminder of home, the watery tang like an old friend or a warm blanket of safety.

Then suddenly all I could hear was the frantic sound of a whistle. I opened my eyes to see a black pony cantering straight at me.

It was so fast, bearing down, closer and closer, yet I was frozen to the spot. My hands lifted to cover my face. The hooves thundered. The whistle kept blowing.

I think I screamed out.

But no impact came.

I moved my hands to find myself face to face with the panting, frothing mouth of the pony. Its eyes were as black as its hair.

'What the hell do you think you're doing?' Coco yanked her helmet off, white hair flowing. 'Are you blind? I could have killed you. You could have killed us. Who takes a stroll on a polo field?'

'Sorry,' I stammered, the hot breath of the pony in my face. 'I didn't realise.'

'There are eight ponies on this field. How could you not realise?' Coco gestured to all the other ponies on the track. It did seem crazy that I hadn't seen them. But I wasn't looking. Who expected ponies at a school?

Verity appeared on a spotty grey and white one, hair

plaited, skin-tight white jodhpurs and a tiny pale pink polo shirt with a polo stick lying across her saddle. 'Do you know how much Coco's pony cost?' she asked.

I shook my head.

Verity leaned forward. 'Probably about as much as your grubby little daddy stole,' she said, voice as smooth as silk.

I felt like she'd whacked me with her stick.

Emmeline trotted over on a white pony with eyes like a Disney princess. 'Give her a break, Vee. She's new.'

Coco was still glowering at me. 'She's an idiot,' she said, and with one quick dismissive flick of the reins she was gone, black pony cantering back into play. Verity followed with a smirk.

The sun was so hot. The sweat trickled down my back as I stalked off the pitch. Adrenaline made my hands shake. Too late, a thousand witty clever comebacks shot through my head. If Jess had been here, she would have taken Coco down. They would have squared off and battled it out. Jess had never been afraid of anyone. It was only now that I saw how much I had depended on her. How lost I was on my own.

'Are you crying?' a voice said, more out of interest than sympathy.

I turned to see the times-table guy from Maths. Tall and skinny with his quiff and horn-rims. Hands in the pockets of his grey trousers, tie loose and top button undone, striped grey and blue braces, he came to stand next to me on the edge of the polo field.

'What?' I said, shaking my head. 'No, I'm not crying.'

'Good. I'm really terrible with tears. Though to be fair, I'd probably be crying right now if I was you.' He paused. 'Don't you hate people who say: *though to be fair*?'

I frowned, caught off guard by the conversation segue. It paused my desire to get as far away from the pitch as possible. 'Now you come to mention it, yeah, maybe,' I said, immediately liking the way his mind worked. This was the kind of nothing that we might have discussed staring up at the sun in the Mulberry Island meadow.

'"Yeah, maybe"?' he repeated. 'Case in point. My grandmother always says that one should be more succinct. Decisive. Get to the point. No "to be honest"s or "basically"s or "you know what I mean"s. I'm trying to wean myself unsuccessfully off them. Sloppy semantics, she calls it.' He took his glasses off and gave them a clean. 'I'm Daniel.'

'Norah,' I said.

'Yes,' he said. 'With the dad embroiled in the Ponzi scheme.' My delight immediately ebbed.

He went on, adjusting his glasses. 'It's a shame, because I actually quite liked the film. I saw it at the cinema. You weren't bad in it. And you know . . .' He paused. 'See? "And you know" is completely unnecessary in the sentence. It was the first time I'd ever been the only person in the cinema.'

I bit my lip, embarrassed, and unsure whether to take what he was saying as a slight or compliment.

The image of that first screening of my dad's film popped into my head. They erected a huge screen by the river, and everyone on the island sat out on fold-out chairs and picnic rugs. There was a bar in the corner serving hot dogs, fresh lemonade and beer. The film was a low-budget comedy-drama. It showed at a couple of the festivals to positive acclaim and had a limited cinema release; a trial run for the bigger, higher-budget films in the pipeline, but exciting nonetheless. I had a very small part in it, and had relished every last second of the filming, even the hours spent in make-up and the night shoots in the dark and wet, standing around for hours in big puffy coats so we didn't get cold. At the island screening there was a curtain call, and as part of the cast I was up at the front taking a bow. My dad gave a speech, beaming at the thunderous applause. It was a time when everyone still thought he was a hero.

But I also remembered four months later having to Google the words 'Ponzi scheme'. Discovering the two men who'd set up the production company – the McGinty brothers – had taken investment money off one load of people and then paid them back with money from another load of people, all to line their own pockets. My dad was the sucker the McGintys had picked to add credence to their fancy presentations, a guy these people clearly trusted with their lives as well as their life-savings. In retrospect, he was the obvious choice. His persuasive charm and popularity emanated as strongly as his unfulfilled, starry-eyed ambition to be a film-maker. Now it was apparent the big films were never going to be made, and the production company was just a sham. Borrow, borrow, borrow until there's no one left to borrow from: that was how the scheme worked. Until all the people on the little island idyll had no more money left to give.

To Daniel, I found myself saying, 'My dad had nothing to do with it.'

He gave me a look. 'I never said he did.'

Behind us was the noise of the ponies' hooves and the crack of the polo stick on the ball. The pervading smell was still of cut grass and sunshine. Daniel started to stroll along the edge of the field and beckoned for me to follow.

'In my dad's eyes, those films were bona fide,' I said as I walked, one hand shielding my eyes from the sun. My instinctive need to defend him had become so automatic, I had started to pre-empt any accusations. There had been nothing more devastating than seeing the unrelenting optimism drain from my dad, replaced with a sad, greying fear. 'He had nothing to do with the money side of things. He was as devastated as everyone else when, you know –'

But my lovely dad's innocence clearly bored Daniel, who just held out his hands and said, 'No need for a "you know" there. Do you see? Wasted words.'

Suddenly, we heard a scream from the polo field. Daniel stopped.

'Oh god, what's happened over there?' he said.

I looked across the field, quite relieved at the change of subject, to where the noise of stick cracking ball had been replaced by high-pitched shouting.

'Jesus, Coco! You're insane!' Emmeline was covering her eye with her hand.

'That was *so* not my fault.' Coco scowled. 'You cut right across me.'

Emmeline swore, her expression contorted in pain. 'My *face*, Coco. How could you smack me in the face and it not be your fault?'

The teacher blew her whistle and motioned for a halt in play. She shouted something to Coco, which was greeted with a slit-eyed pout, while gesturing for Emmeline to leave the field as she corralled the others.

Daniel jogged over. 'Jesus Christ, look at your face,' he said as he helped Emmeline slide down from her pony and took the reins. She had tentatively withdrawn her hand from the injury. As one of the grooms came over to take the pony and Daniel led Emmeline to the clubhouse chairs, he shouted back to where I was standing: 'Norah, do you reckon you could get some ice?'

'Erm, OK,' I said, head filled with questions that clearly weren't appropriate to ask as Emmeline winced through pain and tears. Like, did he mean from the kitchens? Would they wait here or were they going to follow me? As I half jogged back to the main building I found myself quite pleased to be assisting. There was a flutter of pleasure at having some useful connection to the water-haired Emmeline, especially in defiance of Coco.

But by the time I'd located the kitchens in the maze of corridors, battled with a reluctant dinner lady for a bag of ice and then navigated my way back to the field, out of breath, the whole polo landscape had changed. I stopped up short, panting to get my breath back. It was like nothing had happened, and the drama was over. Grooms were walking the ponies off the pitch, the girls were sitting on benches out the front of the clubhouse, pulling off their boots, raking back sweaty hair, chatting, laughing.

Rollo and Ezra had appeared along with their grinning sidekick Freddie, all of them mud-splattered from rugby. Ezra leaned against the wall, hunched over his phone. Rollo sat on the bench beside Daniel, long legs splayed out in front of him, lazily throwing and catching a rugby ball with Freddie who didn't seem like the kind of person ever able to sit still. The ice dripped through the holes in the bottom of the plastic bag as I watched, frozen, too intimidated by the presence of the whole gang to step forward.

Coco was inspecting the bruise, lifting Emmeline's chin to the light with her finger so she could get a better view of the purpling creation blossoming over Emmeline's right eye. 'I think you should be thanking me,' she drawled. 'It looks amazing. And your mum's going to hate it.'

Emmeline pulled her head out of Coco's grasp. 'It really bloody hurts.'

'Don't be a baby,' Coco said with a laugh.

The boys sniggered.

The icy water dripped to the concrete floor. I'd expected to return to Emmeline and Daniel alone, and for the injury to be more serious, more in need of ice. But right now that wasn't the case at all, making a mockery of my keenness and effort.

I was on the verge of quietly tiptoeing away when Daniel saw me. 'Emmeline, your ice,' he said, gesturing in my direction.

I blushed as everyone turned to look.

Emmeline frowned, clearly surprised. 'Thanks,' she said, walking over and taking the bag. 'That's really kind.'

'It's fine,' I said, wanting the moment over, feeling in their eyes like a lackey or a desperate hanger-on.

Emmeline reached into the plastic bag and took a couple of pieces of ice out, rubbing the cubes straight on to her face with a wince.

'Jesus, Em, not like that.' Coco stalked over and snatched the bag. She nudged Emmeline on to the bench and, tipping some water from Rollo's water bottle on to a spare T-shirt, she heaped a handful of ice on to the cloth and wrapped it up to make a compress. They had their backs to me. 'It smells like Ezra,' said Emmeline.

Ezra glanced up from his phone. 'Hey that's my T-shirt.'

Coco said something that made Emmeline giggle. Ezra held his hands wide, aghast at the audacity of his T-shirt being used in such a way. Verity sashayed over to laugh at how silly Emmeline looked with the T-shirt on her face, while Daniel grinned as he sucked on an unused cube.

I was dismissed simply by their lack of acknowledgement. I had never felt so firmly at the bottom of the pecking order.

As I passed the stables and the grooms working on the polo ponies' gleaming coats, I had to laugh. Not only did I come from a school where the idea of playing polo was laughable, I came from a school where the social structure was flat. There was no hierarchy; we all just sort of got on. Everyone was kind of friends with everyone because we had to be. We knew each other too well, each other's families too well. We might not have been crazy about monosyllabic Amy Snyder and her weird boyfriend Jez who built robots in his basement, but we still said hi to them and their friends if they were in the Mulberry café because sometimes they were pretty funny to be around, and at the end of term Amy could be counted on to host a party on the wasteland at the back of her dad's used-car dealership. It wasn't the most glamorous of settings, but it was isolated and backed on to the river. They'd tied a rope swing to the remains of a broken bridge where you could plunge right out almost to the centre of the freezing water. Jez had built a barbecue out of an old oil drum and Amy's dad turned a blind eye to the bike jumps we built, the bonfires and the music. We just all existed, together.

I could hear the sound of Coco's laughter as I walked back through the little manicured courtyard, and had to fight the urge to turn round and watch them all strolling back to the main building. As a gang, they had a magnetism that made the other people furtively glance up or outright stare, jog over with a beaming grin or just be happy to follow in their wake.

My dad's words from the previous evening, as our boat had spluttered down the Thames to its new fancy mooring, were playing like a mantra in my head. 'Don't worry, this won't be forever.' I had stood next to him as he steered the boat down river. Ahead of us lay a string of bridges: Barnes, Hammersmith, Putney. We ticked them off one by one. The water was darker there, meaner. Tidal. Ready to sweep us out to sea if we weren't careful. Before that day our boat had never moved. It had lived quite happily in the silt and sludge on the banks of Mulberry Island, by a patch of weeds we called a garden with terracotta pots spilling with gnarled geraniums and dandelions. In among the flowers we put all the old knickknacks we fished out of the river, anything from dolls' heads to dinosaurs, flashing roadwork lights, plastic pug dogs and round red floats. Once we'd even scooped up an urn of someone's ashes, but we threw it straight back in again.

But now there were no more willow trees and bramble-covered verges, just building after building blocking out the sky. Wandsworth, Battersea Bridge, Albert Bridge. The river banks were traffic now, cranes, adverts, restaurants, penthouses with wraparound views, and lights. Everywhere there were lights. And wealth. My dad had slung his arm over my shoulder as I stared back from where we had come and whispered with a crinkly-eyed smile, 'Before you know it, Norah, we'll be turning round and going back the other way. Fingers crossed the old boat can make it.'

As I walked back into the overbearing ornateness of the Chelsea High building, I wanted to go back right now. It was hard being invisible. It was hard being always on the defensive and trying to act like you didn't care. It was hard having no phone, no contact with the outside world. And however much I pretended it wasn't, it was hard suddenly finding yourself on the lowest rung on the ladder, hating yourself for wondering desperately what the view was like right up there at the top.

CHAPTER FOUR

When I got home to the boat my dad was hovering by the front door, clearly waiting for me to arrive. Odd. He was usually far too engrossed in something else to realise it was that time of day already. He jogged out on deck to greet me, still in his yellow shirt but now wearing his jeans, taking the weight of my bike as I hauled it up the gangplank steps. He seemed a bit jittery. Maybe excited that I was home. After all, it had been a day of lawyers and trial preparation.

'Good day?' he asked, arm outstretched to give me a hug. Grinning and without pausing for an answer he added, 'Bet it was great, wasn't it? Bet you really enjoyed it.'

'It was OK,' I said, slightly wary of his enthusiasm. I wondered if he was being deliberately upbeat.

'Good, good,' he said, brushing a bit of lint off my shoulder and tucking my hair behind my ear. 'Good stuff.'

I flicked my hair back to exactly where it was. 'What are you doing?' I said.

'Nothing, nothing. Can't have you looking less than perfect, that's all.'

I frowned. I always looked less than perfect. My dad had

moved on to neatening up the pots of geraniums on our deck, dead-heading as he waited for me to lock my bike to the guardrail. I remembered what I had been meaning to ask him since my run-in with Mr Watts that morning. 'Dad, did you know someone called Watts when you went to school?'

'Sorry?' He seemed more focused on ushering me inside than listening.

'Watts?' I repeated.

'What?'

'No, a person. *Watts!*' I laughed, bashing him on the shoulder.

He sniggered at his own mistake, then ran his hand through his hair, thinking. 'Oh, *Wattsy*. Oh god, we had some fun with Wattsy,' he said, then made a guilty face. 'Maybe too much fun. Not my finest hour. Probably a bit brutal. Don't tell me he's there?'

I raised a brow. 'He teaches me Maths.'

My dad made a face. 'Sorry, kid.' He held the door wide for me and then, with his previous nervy distraction, said, 'Come on, in we go.'

As you walk down the steps into our boat you can see straight through into the kitchen with its log furnace and island unit of colourful tiles. Pots and pans hang from a rack on the ceiling along with a big plait of garlic. The lounge area is in front of the kitchen, but shielded from the front door by a bookcase to make it cosy.

My mum was standing by the kitchen counter, watching from a distance as I came down the narrow entrance corridor. The moment I saw her, I knew something wasn't right. She had changed her clothes. She looked stark in a black sweater and skinny jeans. She had simple black sandals on and her make-up was flawless. I'd never seen my mum without bright red lips unless it was very early in the morning, and even then she was usually up and ready before me. But she didn't usually look quite as painted as she did right now, with flicks of blue eyeliner and perfectly blended sweeps of blush. I frowned. It was like she was armoured up.

I chucked my bag into the little cupboard by the door where we kept our shoes. There was a different smell on the boat. Heavy and thick. It was hard to tell if it was nice or not, like walking into a florist.

'Norah, honey, guess who's here to see us?' My dad said, hand on my shoulder, steering me round the bookcase. He was sweating slightly; I could see the beads on his brow.

As I walked into the lounge, two people stood up from the sofa. Two beige people. Like two butter toffees.

'It's Granny and Grandpa!' my dad said, as if we holidayed with them every year.

My eyes widened, not quite sure what to do. All I'd wanted was to collapse in front of the TV with a bowl of Honey Monster Puffs. I swallowed, forcing my mouth into a semblance of a smile.

'Hi,' I said.

Now one of the toffees was hugging me in her overpowering flower-smell hug, her powdery cheek up against mine.

'Oh, my darling,' she said, almost breathless.

The other toffee had his hand out for me to shake. Rough and cool and deep-grooved. 'Norah,' he said, as if he wasn't quite sure of my name. 'Nice to meet you.'

'You too, Sir,' I said, a hangover from school.

The old man laughed, adjusting his chequered tie. 'No need for sir.'

They looked so out of place among our things. Their neatness made our comfy old sofa with its patterned throws knitted by my mum seem painfully shabby.

My dad laughed, awkward and on edge. 'Tea?' he said. 'Let's have tea.'

I sat down on the arm of the comfy chair in the corner by the sofa, watching as my dad nervously shuffled about in the kitchen. This wasn't the dad I knew. The one who sang in the Mulberry Island band while strumming his banjo. Who jumped up on the open-mic comedy nights and brought the house down with his off-the-cuff one-man show. Who once lazed on a frayed sunlounger and recounted the story of the time he almost made it big in the movies. 'I was this close, Norah, this close to getting the main part,' he had said, his fingers a millimetre apart, staring up at the clouds. 'The movie was going to be the next Laurel and Hardy; it was going to be massive. It had big studio backing. Big buzz. Big everything. Name-in-lights stuff. I would have been a star, Norah. It was the dream. It was my bloody dream. Course then the director walked and the whole thing collapsed like a stack of cards. It was all over like that.' He had swiped his finger across his neck. 'One minute I was gonna be as famous as – who's the most famous person you know?' He had lain clicking his fingers, thinking, and when I didn't answer quick enough he'd said, 'More famous than that person. I was going to be the most famous actor in the world and the next minute I was flat in the dirt.' Then, as if the memory of that lost chance of stardom was too painful, he had jumped up and slipped straight into a character and we had played the double-act game we always played. We were Daddy Warbucks and Annie. ET and Elliott. Marvelling at our own theatrical skill.

I know you're not meant to have a favourite parent. And I don't, not really. But if I had to be stuck on a desert island with one of them, it would be my dad every time.

'And we're hoping we might see you a little more regularly,' my grandfather was saying, reaching forward for a gingernut that my dad had put on a plate. Never in my life had I seen a biscuit on a plate on this boat. More often they were demolished straight from the pack as soon as they were opened.

Everyone was looking at me. I was flitting in and out of paying attention.

'Yes,' I said, which seemed to appease most people, except my mother who pursed her red lips together where she stood glued to the edge of the kitchen counter, wiping down the surface that was clearly already clean.

'We thought –' My grandmother was looking at my grandfather, her white hair swept back in flouncy waves, her eyes darting uncertainly behind pale pink wire spectacles. 'Every Sunday.'

'Don't do this,' Mum said, chucking the cleaning cloth into the sink.

My dad shifted on the spindly wooden chair he'd brought over from the kitchen table to perch on, proffering the biscuits as a distraction.

'Do what exactly, Lois?' my grandfather said.

My mum screwed up the top of the gingernut packet my dad had left on the counter and put it in the biscuit tin, clearly annoyed. 'Regiment everything.'

My grandfather scoffed.

I focused on the biscuit I was nibbling as awkwardness radiated through the air.

'You can spend time together,' my mum went on, as if she hadn't heard him. 'But don't timetable it. That's not how we work.'

The old man raised his bushy grey brows and sat back. The sofa was squashier and deeper than it appeared, and he flopped further into it that he was expecting.

Some grumbling ensued while my grandmother propped his back up with more cushions, and I tried really hard not to snigger. My dad was making big eyes at my mum to make her say something conciliatory. She shook her head and carried on tidying up the kitchen.

After a few seconds of awkward mutterings all round, my mum finally said, 'OK, we can try for Sundays.' She put the milk back in the fridge. 'Just let's not set it in stone.'

My dad clapped his hands as if that was that sorted. The toffees looked at each other, dubious as to whether they'd had a defeat or victory. But my grandfather nodded, pulling the sleeves of his shirt down so the cuffs edged neatly out of his jacket, making up for the momentary lack of order.

My grandmother edged forward on her seat and, smiling at me like I was five, said, 'And how was school, Norah? We're so delighted that you're following in the family footsteps at Chelsea High. You know, not a single generation has missed out since it was founded in the seventeenth century.'

'I didn't know that,' I said, trying to mirror her enthusiasm.

'Did you enjoy your first day?' she asked, her hands clasped together so I could see all the diamonds dazzling on her long, thin fingers.

My mouth stretched into a polite smile as I pondered the question. How was school? Mean. Rich. Unreal. I thought of the polo and evil Mr Watts. Then I remembered the look on Ezra's face at my ugly, chewed biro and laughed slightly when

49

I said, 'It was fine.'

My grandparents shared a look.

'Did something funny happen?' my grandmother said, leaning in, keen for the joke, but also unsure.

'No,' I said. Looking her straight in the wrinkly eye. Like hell they would be included by me. They weren't having that as well as my Sundays, my dad's weak acquiescence and my mum's bad temper. 'Nothing at all.'

My bedroom has always been my favourite room on the boat. It's on the second floor, along from my parents' bedroom, and it's tiny – the exact size of a single bed – but magical. Like living in a cocoon. All the walls are wood-clad and bare except for a couple of shelves cluttered with my favourite knickknacks. My clothes are all folded in a cupboard under the bed. But the best thing is the giant window at the head of my bed that stretches across the entire wall, so as I'm falling to sleep I can stare out at the water and the stars. My parents' room is much bigger, but I wouldn't swap mine for the world.

In bed that night, however, I wasn't looking out at anything. Instead, I was sitting at the other end of my bed with my head pressed up against the wall, listening to my parents rowing under their breath.

'They're paying all that money, Lois. For the lawyers, the school, this mooring. It's fair enough that they expect something in return,' said my dad, voice hushed and emphatic.

I thought of my grandmother's strained smile as she sipped her tea, her pearls and her neat gold-buckled shoes, and I thought: *This is your fault. Both of you*, I added, throwing in the grandfather as well: his beige jacket, his brown striped shirt and navy-checked tie with the crest of some club or other embroidered in the centre. They were the reason we'd had to up-sticks and re-moor. They had paid for this new berth, among the best in London apparently, but what good was that when out of my bedroom window, where once I had seen nothing but blue sky, the view was now of a sleek minimalist grey barge where a woman in a bright pink polo shirt was always vacuuming? It was their money paying for the flashy lawyer that we didn't really need, but they'd put their collective foot down. The family name had been dragged through the mud enough. I had heard my dad mimic my grandfather when he thought I wasn't listening, *'By god, son, I sit in the House of Lords.'* And now they were responsible for my parents – who never argued – arguing.

My mum sighed softly. 'I don't want them having Norah. I don't want their influence in her life.'

'I know, I know. But what other choice do we have. Your parents?' Dad said, tone almost mocking.

My mum made a noise somewhere between a scoff and sigh. I'd Googled her family, after everything had come out about my dad. Under normal circumstances I'd have asked her outright, but everyone was too distracted, too brittle and wound up. She'd always said she'd never got on that well with them, that they lived in Australia and called once in a blue moon – always when I was at school. They weren't big on family, she'd said. According to Google, however, their last address was a super-yacht in Cannes. There was a grainy newspaper shot of a woman who looked remarkably like my mum, just fractionally older: face taut, lips plumped, lounging on deck in a gold swimsuit. She had a cocktail in one hand and with her other was snapping an angry reciprocal photo of the paparazzi stalking her. I had just glimpsed the headline, 'Camilla Wentworth celebrates fifth divorce in style!' when the whole messaging debacle kicked off and my mum confiscated my phone. Further investigation was on my mental to-do list for the future. I wasn't sure I needed any more surprises about my extended family at the moment.

Through my bedroom wall on the boat, I heard my mum sit up and take a sip of water then put the glass back down. 'I just hate being in debt to them, Bill. I hate it. I wish I'd never let you say yes to those films. I think about it, lying here, all the time. Why didn't I read the contract?'

'And what would you have done?' my dad said, his voice a little lighter, laced with humour suddenly. 'What would you have spotted?'

'Nothing,' she said after a moment, admitting defeat.

I listened, chewing my lip. It was unfair to blame my grandparents. Without them we would have nothing right now. It was just my mum and dad were so endearingly kind and trusting that I didn't want them to have to go through any of this. I didn't want to see weakness in what I had always seen as their greatest strength.

'We're useless. The pair of us,' my mum sighed.

'Useless, but I love you,' my dad replied with a laugh.

There was a pause, I held my breath. Then I heard her laugh too, and allowed myself to exhale. To relax. I snuggled into my blanket, safe in the knowledge that barring any boat-related emergencies (which weren't out of the question in houseboat living), if they were laughing, then for the next nine hours everything would be OK.

CHAPTER FIVE

By Friday I had a handle on the route to Chelsea High at least, which in retrospect was achingly simple. I'd even found a bike rack that always had a space, tucked away down a side street just before the main school entrance next to a tiny café called Sorrentos, the type of place that's so old-fashioned it's a surprise it hasn't shut down. The outside wall was all crazy paving with the name *Sorrentos* written in white calligraphy on the window. A neon sign jutted out with the word *restaurant* written in green above a striped awning smattered with pigeon poo.

For the first time, today I was early for school. To my surprise I saw Coco and everyone clustered together with cups of tea in Sorrentos' window. I'd have expected to see them somewhere flashier, like La Serre on the corner with its Art Deco train station lights, white tablecloths and snooty waiters. But, as a tribe, they were hard to predict. Obviously this was them slumming it, ironically huddled into ripped green and white lino booths with fake flowers on the table, Freddie munching on a grilled-cheese sandwich with strings of mozzarella falling from his lips. Coco was holding court, fingernails tapping on a can of Diet Coke as she recounted some story. Verity was doing an asymmetric French plait in her hair as she listened. Emmeline and Daniel were squeezed into an adjacent booth with a few other people I vaguely recognised.

Overnight, the bruise over Emmeline's eye had morphed into a giant purple swirl, a filigree tattoo that she seemed pretty proud of, hair tied back tight to show it off in its grotesque majesty. Daniel was sitting on the end of the bench seat, elbows on his knees, catching up with Ezra while Rollo stood behind them, really laughing at something someone was saying on the phone. Emmeline was reading, but shut the book to listen and smirk at something Coco was shushing the group to say.

I tried not to stare, but I couldn't help it. I'd never locked up my bike so slowly. Coco was toxic, but her jokes were still funny. I couldn't help wanting in.

It was lonely at the moment being me. I'd never been lonely before. There had always been something fun to do, someone to talk to. Bands playing at The Mulberry pub where my dad played banjo and I was roped in on the drums when Old Percy couldn't make it. Sometimes my mum would sing some cool jazz with her wafty skirt and flowing hair, me and Jess and the others watching on the deep leather sofas with Diet Cokes. In the early summer we all pitched in to help with the mulberry picking, the big purple fruits staining our fingers and lips.

There was always a massive party after the harvest, when lovely Mrs Jackson would make mulberry and coconut pies that we ate that evening by the river with festooned lights twinkling between the branches. Summer days were spent fishing, rowing, canoeing. The river raft race had become an annual event, and everyone competed in teams on their badly botched-together rafts. There was a charity bingo night (funnier than it sounds), and Theatre Club every Wednesday run by my dad and Wilmot Heath an old daytime soap actor. They were a hilarious double-act. Wilmot had me and all my drama friends in hysterics with his stories of soap-opera life, but he gave amazing lessons in the craft, as did my dad. We hung off their every word. I really missed those evenings, in the shabby room above the pub with plastic chandeliers, everyone messing about, practising, improvising, working till long after the session was meant to end. Wilmot had invested a lot of money with my dad, and he'd had a part in our first film. I wouldn't be welcome in his class any more.

I missed my old school with my actual friends – people who, even if I'd had a phone, I was too nervous to contact. I'd been burned once and I couldn't face it again. I missed cooking with my mum. TV with my dad. Building things, fixing things. My dad always on to the next surefire way to make money. The schemes: the coffee van, getting up at five a.m. to stand outside the station in the rain; the boat-building business; the window cleaning. The new app. Somehow everyone on the island got addicted to this dreadful game that he'd paid a Computer Science undergrad to create, everyone online competing with each other, all supporting. I missed my home.

I glanced at them all in Sorrentos again, thinking how my old friends would be doing this very thing in the Mulberry café, but instead of grilled cheese they'd be eating salt-smattered pretzels and cinnamon buns made by the old German owner, Hans. Or, as the weather was still good, they might be walking as they ate, to sit by the river. Jess would be out in her canoe. I wondered who remembered to buy her a raspberry cinnamon bun now that I wasn't there.

I wouldn't know. I had zero access. My dad's phone had been taken by the police and my mum didn't believe in them. I'd tried to log on to Instagram in the school library to discover social media was banned from the entire network, so I'd sent Jess a quick email instead – except when it came to writing it, everything seemed either too important or too banal to ask about over email, so I'd ended up just telling her a couple of stupid things about life at Chelsea High. As I was about to log off, I'd Googled the trial, then shut it down immediately. The words in black and white were making it all too real, too terrifying.

The court case was due to start on Monday. I'd asked my dad what he thought of the lawyer as we ate fruit and cereal that morning from the unusually well-stocked fridge. I assumed the grandparents had left some money.

'Eye-wateringly dull,' my dad had said between mouthfuls. 'Exactly what a good lawyer should be. And to Granny and Grandpa's delight, he's ex-Chelsea High stock.'

'I bet he is,' my mum said, stabbing viciously at the green flesh of the kiwi fruit she was scooping out with a teaspoon. 'Norah, I don't want you becoming a lawyer, do you understand?'

'I thought parents were meant to push their children to become lawyers and doctors and things like that,' I said.

My mum shuddered. 'You can only be a lawyer if it's for human rights or women, or something similar. Understand? At that school, they'll try and tell you it's the only way, but it's not.'

There was a moment where I knew we were all silently taking in the flash mooring, the lawyer, the school, the fruit, all paid for by my dad's estranged father. Who himself was a lawyer. It made our way look distinctly like the failed way.

All week I'd been looking forward to Friday. Not just because it marked the glorious freedom of the weekend, but because my entire morning's timetable was Theatre Studies.

At Chelsea High there wasn't a drama department, there was a whole theatre. One kitted out with a bar and a huge backstage area, a snazzy wireless intercom system, dressing rooms with mirrors with lights, an orchestra pit, full lighting rig, rehearsal rooms – everything.

The theatre on Mulberry Island was Grade-Two listed, our shows sold out, there were write-ups in the paper about us, but we didn't have a patch on this.

I sat on one of the flipdown seats in the rehearsal room waiting for Chelsea High's Theatre Studies teacher Mr Benson to arrive. I was aware of Coco and everyone along the row from me, whispering and giggling about something. Mr Benson scurried in five minutes late with a Thermos of coffee. He was a big man with a brown beard and matching thick brown glasses, plus the same black cape and bow tie as Mr Watts and the other masters but with the addition of a green fleece gilet. His demeanour was of someone always trying to catch up, permanently harassed.

He put his coffee down and flipped through some notes. 'Right,' he said, scanning what was written down. 'Who can tell me the first rule of improvisation?'

I knew but I didn't answer.

He glanced up over his glasses. 'Anyone?'

There was a shuffling silence.

'The first rule of improvisation is: Always agree!' It was my dad's rule for life.

Mr Benson went on, 'So you say yes to any question and see where it gets you. Better than that, you say, "Yes, and . . ."'

We were put into groups of three and each group was given a black bag. Inside the bags were different fictional scenarios written on pieces of paper. The objective was to see how long you could sustain a viable improv, saying yes to everything in order to keep the scene rolling.

'You need to be open, free, engaged and willing,' Mr Benson called out.

I saw Coco roll her eyes and Verity giggle. I turned my head so I couldn't see her. I didn't want her to find it stupid; I didn't want the experience undercut. This was pretty much what I lived for.

To begin with, I was partnered with Daniel and a girl called Tabitha from my English class, who had Pre-Raphaelite amber curls and peaches-and-cream skin and was so posh I could barely understand a word she said. But she was funny. I liked her. She wrote an ode to Shredded Wheat during our class on Keats' poetry. Coco barely tolerated her but she was still part of that circle, if only a peripheral member. Tabitha was funny in Improv too, happy to make a fool of herself, to get fully into character, limping across the stage as an old witch with a stick one minute, swaggering back as a surfer dude the next. Daniel, on the other hand, was dreadful. His movements were all wooden, his cheeks flushing red with every word.

'God, I hate this,' he said, tipping his head back to the high concrete ceiling.

The room was industrial and dark, like the National Theatre. All modern and brutalist. Not to everyone's taste, but I loved it. You could smell the coldness of the concrete in the air, the freedom, like an echoing warehouse. You could scream and shout and sling a can of paint around this room and it felt like no one would care.

'Why do you do it then?' I asked.

'Oh, he has to,' said Tabitha.

'Why?' Daniel was standing with his shoulders slumped. He sighed and rolled his eyes my way. 'Because my mother is Helena Rhys.'

'*The* Helena Rhys? Oh my god.' My hand went to cover my mouth. 'I had a picture of her on my wall growing up. *Manhattan Rooftops* is one of my all-time favourite films.'

'Yes,' Daniel replied with a theatrical sigh. 'I'm doomed to a lifetime of drama, in both senses of the word.'

As the improv went on, Mr Benson perused the groups, hands behind his back, pausing to listen, occasionally to laugh. When he got to us he watched silently for a while, then swapped Daniel for Freddie. I rolled my eyes as Freddie jumped into our space, all jazz hands and look-at-me attention-seeking. But the moment Mr Benson gave us a scenario, the goofing around stopped and Freddie got into character in an instant. When Freddie acted, he was nuanced, funny and unexpected, and his face was weirdly elastic. I'd never seen anything like it. He could pull any expression out of the bag. The three of us worked amazingly together.

Then suddenly Mr Benson pulled in Ezra.

My body tensed, my senses on high alert to the fresh

washing-powder smell, the frayed cuffs of his sleeves where his hands were in his pockets, the laces of his Nikes, the fade of his black jeans. I couldn't concentrate with him there, let alone act, too aware of my movements and overly self-conscious. But Ezra and Freddie worked off one another like they'd been doing this a lifetime.

Ezra's style was cool and confident but reserved, like he was holding back, surveying. That made him funny. As he moved his body visibly relaxed, as if he, like me, was happier in character. It was that which made me loosen up enough to go with it, to slip outside of myself; the realisation that it was irrelevant at that moment who I was in the everyday. This was what I was good at, and there was a space for me to fill.

Out of the corner of my eye I caught Coco trying to see what was going on as Mr Benson stood by us, chuckling. At one point he paused the class to make them watch our intrepid-explorers-in-a-booby-trapped-cave scene. Even Coco and Verity's sneers couldn't detract because everyone else was laughing. I loved it. Every second. Every moment I was me but not me.

CHAPTER SIX

Torrential rain that afternoon cancelled games. Everyone had to stay inside and study, huddled in cliques in our form room, the air building with boredom. Sixth-form prefects hunted stragglers down like prey, depositing them with overblown authority back to the rooms where they belonged.

As the grey rain poured outside and hot breath fogged up the windows, there was talk of a party at Verity's house that weekend.

'Oh god, you should see the dress I was sent by Stella, Vee, it's amazing.' Coco was painting her nails a dark teal between swipes of her iPad where she was vaguely reading *Wuthering Heights* for English. 'This book is insane. The guy's a beast.'

It was only when Verity said, 'My mum wants me to wear Dolce and Gabbana – they asked her and, you know, she loves them, so it's fine with me, I guess,' that I realised the Stella that Coco was referring to was Stella McCartney.

Coco gave a shrug as if that seemed OK with her without looking up from her nails. 'I'm definitely wearing the Stella. Emmeline, what about you?'

'Oh I don't know.' Emmeline retied her hair. 'My mum was

so livid about the bruise and what it's going to look like in the photos I think she'd rather I didn't go at all.'

'It's only Tatler,' said Coco. 'And they won't even put you *online* with that thing on your face.'

Emmeline raised a brow. 'Thanks, Coco.'

Verity laughed.

Outside the rain poured against a dirty concrete sky. Freddie was drawing pictures in the condensation on the window. My eyes glazed over the words I was meant to be reading in *Wuthering Heights* as I imagined what a party at Verity's house with Tatler taking photos might be like. Certainly not a bonfire on a wasteland behind a used-car dealership, that was for sure. In my mind it was all floor-to-ceiling glass windows, swimming pools and swishy designer dresses, and I knew I was barely scraping the surface.

Coco blew her nails dry with a smirk, then snapped a pic of the perfectly blue-green talons. 'Let's see what my public think, shall we?' she said, posting it to her two million followers. A second later she refreshed the screen and said, 'Yep, *c'est bon.*' Then she gave up on *Wuthering Heights* and twisted round in her seat to talk properly with Verity.

Behind them Rollo and Freddie had their heads on the desk, sleeping. Daniel was up at the front in a Rubik's Cube competition with the geekiest guy in class, Peter Fellowes, who had short blond hair and pink skin too tight for his body. Daniel seemed the only person able to flit with ease between the groups, as if the pecking order held no sway.

The door to the classroom flew open, shocking everyone to attention.

'And stay in there this time!' shouted a black-haired sixth-former with a mean mouth and narrow shoulders.

Ezra slunk into the room with a half-grin and a shake of his head. He sat down in what had become his standard seat – when he made it in early enough for registration, which had only been twice so far this week – next to me.

Coco immediately twizzled round in her chair. 'Ez, we were just talking about Vee's party Saturday. You're coming, aren't you?' It was the sweetest I'd ever heard her voice. She toyed with the end of ponytail as she waited with big doe-eyes for his reply.

'It's black tie,' said Verity, glancing briefly up from her phone.

Ezra frowned. 'Why?'

Verity shrugged. 'My mum says.'

Ezra made a face like black tie was a deal-breaker.

'You have a really nice suit,' cooed Coco, leaning forward, elbows resting on her crossed knees so she could get even closer to him.

I was pretending to read my copy of *Wuthering Heights*, but I'd read it before and this was more interesting. Especially when I thought I heard Ezra huff a laugh under his breath.

Rollo was sitting up now, rubbing sleep from his eyes.

'He'll be there.'

Ezra's eyes flicked my way.

I shot my attention back to the page.

'We can pick you up on our way through if you like,' Emmeline offered.

'You've got to be in black tie, though, Ezra,' said Verity, bored now of her phone and chucking it in her bag. 'It's for the photos.'

Ezra nodded like he just wanted the topic to be over. 'Whatever.'

Coco was still facing our way, mouth half open like she wanted to say more but couldn't think what. The rain turned to hail and lashed like a whip at the windows. No one took any notice, except for me. I loved weather like this, lying cosy in my little cabin bed watching the hail stones smash into the rain-flattened water.

Rollo went back to sleep. Verity started painting her nails the same colour as Coco. Emmeline got a mirror out her bag and inspected her bruise. Daniel plonked himself back down next to her, hands whirring round a Rubik's Cube.

'Good book?' Ezra's voice asked as I stared transfixed by the speed of Daniel click-clacking.

I checked he was talking to me. He was. So I nodded, feeling the sudden pressure of a possible conversation with him, a rise in my heart rate because he had asked me a question and a burning desire to be able to play it at least vaguely cool.

He tipped his chair back so it rested against the wall, his hands behind his head. 'You haven't turned a page since I sat down.'

'I'm sure I have,' I said, feeling my cheeks start to flush.

He shook his head, eyes smiling. 'No,' he said with certainty.

He was right. I hadn't read a word. I'd been too busy eavesdropping – fascinated by them all, by him. But he seemed pleased with his observation, presumably because he had nothing else to do. There were no books on his desk, no iPad, no phone.

He didn't let it go. 'You definitely haven't turned a page,' he said, expression one of cocky certainty.

There was a fizzing in my veins from his undivided attention, and it made me brave, emboldened. I put the book flat on my desk and made a show of turning the page.

He laughed.

I just pretended to read, feigning absolute concentration while my eyes jumped from word to word. I was unable to focus simply because he was watching. I could see his fingers thrumming on the desk. Long fingers, really short nails. My eyes were drawn to the skin of his wrist, the pale tan line under his watch with the broken face, the jut of the bone.

'Still no page turning,' he said with a lazy drawl, like he knew exactly why I wasn't concentrating on the book.

I frowned, trying to come up with a decent answer. 'I've

read it before. Anyway, why are you watching me?' Turning it back on him seemed the best solution to hiding my own embarrassment.

'Something to do.' Then he added with a smirk, 'And it's polite to take an interest in one's desk mate.'

I closed my book. His brown eyes crinkled in amusement, waiting for what was going to happen next. I could feel myself wanting to smile. I was still fizzing, still emboldened, the rest of the class had blurred away.

'What's my name?' I asked, tilting my head in challenge.

He opened his mouth to speak, paused, then shut it again. His eyes narrowed as he thought, his lips twisting in frustration, then he shook his head, finally admitting defeat. 'I don't know.'

I arched a brow and went back to *Wuthering Heights*, making a show of turning the page this time. Inside I was itching not to mess this up. If this was back at my old school, Jess would be next to me cheering me on. I imagined emailing her about it the first chance I got. She'd be impressed I'd made it this far, because I was usually hopeless with any sort of flirtation. I blushed too much. I don't know why I wasn't now. Maybe events over the last couple of weeks had toughened me up, or maybe if I looked in the mirror I'd have a bright red face and just didn't have any friends to hand to tell me.

Someone at the front, where all the grungier rich kids sat, had put some music on. Rollo shouted for something better.

They ignored him, but the tunes got a little more mainstream and everyone was happy except Emmeline, who put her headphones on.

'What is it then?' Ezra asked, tapping the thumb on the desk in time to the beat.

I looked up. 'What is what?' I said, although I knew exactly what he meant.

'What's your name?'

'Norah,' I said.

He laughed.

'Why is that funny?' I asked, laughing because he was. His grin was infectious.

'Norah?' he said, shaking his head, his dark hair falling over his eyes. 'Come on! It's a funny name. Norah.' He laughed again, holding his hair back with his hand.

I scoffed, incredulous, but still enjoying myself. Half amazed that he seemed to be too. 'What's *your* name then?' Even though I'd known exactly what his name was from the moment I'd laid eyes on him, I didn't want to give him the satisfaction of presuming I knew.

The question seemed to take him by surprise. 'Ezra,' he said, with a quirk of his arrow-straight brow.

'And you laugh at *my* name?' I replied. I could feel my adrenaline rising every time I made him smile and with it the telltale sensation of a blush. I tried to cover my cheek by resting it on my hand.

He held his hands wide with mock affront. 'Ezra is a good solid Hebrew name.'

'It's weirder than Norah.'

He shook his head, definitive. Then he smiled and stretched. His jumper rose up slightly to reveal a strip of tanned skin at his waist. 'So you're new?' he asked, almost on a yawn.

'Yeah.'

His hooded eyes were assessing. 'Nice to meet you.'

I wondered if he had any idea that I'd been in his Improv group that morning. Or whether he'd just looked straight through me that whole time. 'You too,' I said.

He did a kind of smirk of approval. Then he leaned down, pulled his iPhone and headphones out of his bag and tipped his chair back against the wall with his eyes closed.

I was half sad, half relieved our chat was over. I didn't think I could take the pressure much longer, but when I nestled into the corner with my book, I held tight to the exciting little thrum in my chest. I glanced at the clock to see how much time was left till the bell and saw Coco glaring at me. Green, mean eyes immediately stilling my thrum.

CHAPTER SEVEN

Finally, it was Saturday. My mum had a stall at Portobello Market selling vintage clothes, and it felt like my only remaining touchstone of normality. She co-owned it with a woman called Jackie who had short curly white hair with a pink streak like a pretty skunk and a poodle called Percy that wet himself when he got excited. We were forever hoiking him off the clothes and steering him away from people eager to pet him. Many a customer had walked away with a sprinkle of pee over their shoe without realising. He wasn't the best for business, but howled if he was left home alone. To Jackie he was the closest thing she had to family – bar my mum and me.

Right now, I'd never been happier to see Jackie. The familiar over-made-up face, skin tight with Botox and rouged to the max. She had a trout pout and her collagen lips were slicked fluorescent pink. She was wearing leopard-print leggings and a gold blouse with a pink and orange faux-fur coat, huge and fluffy like a yeti. Even though the sun was out it was permanently cold on our pitch, especially at five in the morning. Percy ran circles round me, leaving spirographs of wee on the tarmac.

My mum was wheeling a rail of vintage evening dresses across the road from the van, awkwardly trying to button her bright green mohair coat at the same time as it flapped open in the wind. Jackie was hefting men's jackets on to one of the scaffolding poles that made up our stand, shaking her head at a man who wanted to buy a stack of top hats for half her quoted price. I was smoothing out the tablecloth ready for all the accessories.

Setting up is always fun. There's a sense of purpose, a thrill about what the day might bring. Dealers scurry around like ants, squabbling over who got their hands on which piece first, working with quick sleight of hand, flick-flick-flicking through our rails as we're putting the clothes out and suddenly ten or fifteen of our new dresses are over their arms and they're peeling off notes from wads of cash, naming sums of money that are miles off Jackie's estimates. There's always ruthless haggling and big dramatic sighs at prices. The ultimate theatre.

It's the taking down at the end that's the killer. It's so slow and tedious and all the van drivers are honking because someone's double-parked and they want to get away quick smart. Jackie always insists on all the clothes being loaded in a very specific way so she can unload easily at the other end. She also owns what she calls an antique shop, but is more of a junk warehouse. She stores everything in the lock-up room at the back.

Big Dave from next door's army surplus stall waved as my

mum approached, dragging the rail of clothes behind her. He definitely fancied her. All the blokes here did. She was forever evading their massive hugs and wet cheek kisses.

'Trial start Monday?' he shouted.

My mum nodded as she yanked the rail up over the kerb.

'Thought I might go down and have a gander,' he said.

It only occurred to me then that anyone could view a court case. Even I could go if I wanted. A scene from our production a few years ago of *To Kill a Mockingbird* popped into my head. I wondered if anyone from Mulberry Island would be there, baying for whatever blood they could get.

'I think Bill's part will be over quite quickly, Dave,' my mum said. 'He's just there to give evidence.'

Big Dave made a face like that fact surprised him. He was a true crime addict and subscribed to all sorts of magazines about unsolved murders. It really annoyed him that everyone had jumped on the true crime podcast bandwagon, as if this sudden wave of popularity diluted his hobby. He was nice and all, but I could see his casual chitchat about the case, as if it was a new documentary on Netflix, was winding my mum up.

'So how's he going to prove he wasn't in on it then?' he said.

My mum paused, hand on the rail, 'He's not, Dave. That's what the lawyer does.'

When Dave went to open his mouth again, she did a massive sigh, and pushing her unusually messy hair out of her face, she snapped, 'Can't really talk right now. There's loads that needs doing.'

'Right, got ya.' I've never heard my mum shut down a conversation before. She usually stays listening for hours, nodding and smiling at jokes that aren't remotely funny., It's why she's such a good stallholder. You'd never guess how many shoppers are just people on the hunt for a chat. The purchase is a decoy. They buy a vintage crocodile-skin belt just to offload about their dreaded family holiday or failing marriage. Jackie and I are terrible at that side of things. I usually go and buy the coffees while Jackie hides at the back rearranging the handbags.

Now Jackie and I exchanged a look. My mum was replaiting her hair, fingers working with sharp annoyance. As she was tying her hairband, the wind blew and caught the edge of the vintage dress rail that she hadn't locked into place, dragging it round to the side and tipping it into the men's trouser rail.

'Oh for god's sake,' my mum shouted, hauling it back up and into place, stamping hard on the tiny wheel brake.

'Lois, why don't you go and get the coffees?' said Jackie, walking over and placing a hand on my mum's shoulder.

'Because there's work to do,' my mum said, voice curt.

'And we'll do it,' said Jackie. 'But I need a coffee. And Norah needs a hot chocolate.'

My mum looked at us both and sighed again. 'Fine,' she

said. Wrapping her big orange scarf round her neck so it covered half her face and snatching up her bag, she stalked off in the direction of our favourite Portuguese café round the corner.

Jackie watched her cross the road. 'She looks dreadful,' she said. I bit my lip. I didn't think she looked that bad. Jackie exhaled with a shake of her head. 'He's a pain in the arse, your father.'

I felt my hands clench. Wanting to remind her that she hadn't thought that when he'd danced her round the boat on Christmas Day and she'd called him a charming old rogue before accidentally spilling her mulled wine down his back.

'How much is the coat, love?' a man in a woolly hat shouted, pointing to the beige trench on the mannequin at the front.

'Fifty,' said Jackie.

The man whistled as if that was way too high a price.

'No one's forcing you to buy it,' Jackie called back, shaking her head as he walked away. She turned to me, picking up as if there had been no interruption. 'Never invest in anything that doesn't have walls, Norah. That's what my old man used to say.'

I'd heard that every time my dad had tried to convince Jackie to invest. But she'd stuck to her guns. 'Not that I have anything to invest anyway, Bill. Not sure you can fund a film with a load of old rags.'

I was unable to quite believe she'd called my dad a pain in the arse. How quick her loyalties turned. We stood on opposite sides of the stall in the icy wind tunnel of the market, the tips of my fingers turning white as all the blood rushed to protect my organs from the chill. In winter we have torches because it's so dark, and have to scrape the ice off the jewellery cabinet. I wear three pairs of socks and two sets of thermal underwear.

Today, despite the chill under the bridge, the sun was low over the buildings, the sky poster-paint blue. Big Dave had moved off to talk about a new Amazon Prime crime drama with Barbara who sold costume jewellery on the main drag and had an African Grey parrot in a cage on her stand. Barbara had got the parrot from a rescue centre, half bald from having plucked out all his feathers. African Greys live for eighty years, so it was difficult to know how many homes he'd had before hers. But anytime anyone said, 'Ahh, a parrot,' he'd say, 'Go away, I'm not in the mood,' clearly learned from one previous miserable owner. Customers would guffaw, goad him to say more while clogging up the stall. If they were lucky he'd shuffle about on his perch and say, 'I've had enough, I'm going to bed.' Barbara was forever trying to teach him to say, 'Why don't you buy some of this lovely jewellery?' but he wouldn't comply.

Jackie came over to stand next to me, holding out a bag of pastries. 'Croissant?'

'No thank you,' I said, arms crossed, eyes fixed on the moody parrot.

'Have I done something to upset you?'

'No,' I said, stamping my feet to keep warm, deliberately not looking at her.

She narrowed her purple-shadowed eyes at me. 'Norah, you listen to me. Your father is a grown man. He got himself into this mess and now he's facing the consequences.'

I felt moisture collect in my eyes. 'He didn't know!' I spat.

'I know that,' she said, her face softening as much as it could with all the Botox she'd had. 'But it doesn't mean he's not a complete idiot for getting himself sucked into the whole debacle. He's always been blind when it comes to a get-rich-quick scheme, and this time it's backfired royally.' She thrust the croissant bag at me. 'It's a fine line between ignorance and guilt.'

I grappled with that statement as we were both pulled in different directions by dealers querying prices.

We were popular today because Jackie had done the house clearance of someone's recently deceased gran in Vauxhall. 'Norah, you should have seen the place,' she'd said when she came to pick us up in the van at four thirty that morning. 'Absolutely ghastly. Curtains orange from cigarette smoke – filthy it was. Rats under the floorboards. I could hear them running about between the walls. But in her wardrobe . . .'

She'd whistled, bombing through the dark deserted streets of London, her eyes shining. 'She had the works. Yves Saint Laurent, Biba. Ossie Clark. Mary Quant. All pressed and folded in old Tesco bags in the back of the wardrobe. Don't think anyone knew they were there. She had the most perfect white Chanel suit – you've never seen anything like it. Never been worn, I don't reckon. I've kept that for myself. One day I'll be able to squeeze into it. Not likely, seeing as I've already eaten half a packet of Jaffa Cakes this morning.' She had laughed. 'I got the lot for two hundred quid and we'll make that back on a couple of the handbags this morning.'

And she was right. I sold three of the Mary Quant shirts to the woman who buys the vintage for Topshop, and my mum came back and flogged a beautiful Ossie Clarke dress to a stylist friend of hers.

There was always this lovely window – sometimes ten minutes, sometimes half an hour – after the first frenzy of the dealers and just before the public arrived. Today, Jackie settled herself down in her pink fold-out chair. She was knitting a scarf out of a giant ball of lumpy angora wool. My mum, who usually read the paper around this time, just sat staring into space.

Between eight thirty and nine o'clock, the build-up of the public started. Some keen thrifters arrived at seven but usually, on a Saturday, most people sauntered round with a coffee from nine, cooing over frilly tea-dresses and nineteen-twenties satin nighties, which were our bestseller for boho girls looking for a bit of floaty, flirty kitsch for a party.

I was just wrapping a powder-blue silk slip dress when I heard someone shout my name.

'Norah?' said the voice, unfamiliar in this scenario, so I couldn't place it. 'It's Norah, isn't it?'

Coming our way was Emmeline – her eye even more monstrously dazzling – Daniel and Tabitha.

I moved away from the stall to meet them, trying to keep my two worlds separate: Jackie and my mum in their crazy coloured coats, the yapping, peeing Percy, me in a big old red and white baseball jacket and fingerless gloves, while they were all in little lace-trimmed jumpers and skirts, holding Starbucks with their names scrawled casually on the side. Our difference was conspicuous enough. I had no make-up on either, and my hair was scraped up in a top knot, a bit greasy. Saturday was my who-cares day. I was a general dogsbody on a Saturday, and that was fine with me. I didn't have to think.

'Is this your stall?' Emmeline asked, between unexpected kisses on my cheek, her shiny hair falling forward like a curtain.

'My mum's,' I said, pointing to where Jackie and my mum were huddled in the corner pretending to consult the receipt book that I knew full well never needed any such consultation, little grins on their faces as they covertly watched all the air-kissing.

'We love this stall,' Emmeline said, stroking the fabric of one of the mannequin dresses, and I thought how weird it was that our paths had crossed in the past without me knowing.

They moved further into the stall to start leafing through the rails. I hovered, nervous. Wishing they hadn't spotted me here, or that I'd tried a little harder with my appearance at four o'clock this morning.

My mum brushed past me with the excuse of straightening a skirt on one of the mannequins. 'Calm down,' she whispered. Then to Emmeline and Tabitha, she said in her normal voice, 'So, ladies, anything I can help you with?'

Emmeline sucked on her Frappuccino. 'I wanted something to wear for a black tie and neon party tonight.'

'Me too,' said Tabitha. 'Although I'm not sure I suit neon. What are you wearing, Norah?' she asked, all plummy and clueless as she perused the silk scarves.

There was an awkward silence.

I shook my head. 'I'm not going.'

'Why not?' said Tabitha, frowning in posh confusion.

I cringed at the fact I had to spell it out. 'I haven't been invited.'

Emmeline studied one of the dresses with embarrassed scrutiny.

My mum was taking it all in.

'Well, that's me sorted!' said Daniel, breaking the tension as he pulled on an acid yellow jacket, all baggy and double-breasted. A monstrosity from the eighties.

'You might laugh,' said Jackie, hands on her hips. 'But I warn you, that's vintage Versace and two hundred quid.'

Daniel flipped the collar up and admired himself in our shabby mirror. 'Fine with me.'

I'd heard rumours that while Daniel's mum was a hotshot actress and his father an art dealer, Daniel himself had made a killing importing light-up yo-yos to the UK when he was twelve and now ran a successful import-export business from his bedroom.

Jackie covered her eyes with her hand in disbelief, her rings clattering together. 'Wish I'd had money to burn at your age.'

Daniel continued to examine himself in the mirror. 'Oh, it's a blessing and a curse, believe me,' he said with exaggerated melodrama that made Jackie – who never laughed – laugh.

Just then Coco appeared arm in arm with Verity. 'Where have you been?' she asked. She was dressed in a cropped grey tie-at-the-front shirt and frayed blue jeans, her expression masked by gold-rimmed sunglasses as she stood accusingly, sucking on the straw of a bright green drink. 'We've been round this place about five times looking for you.'

Emmeline looked a little panicked. 'We were just talking to Norah.'

Coco stopped sipping the green drink and frowned. Then she saw me. 'Oh,' she said, with a dismissive glance over the top of her sunglasses before stalking over to flick through the rails. 'What are you buying, Emmeline?'

'Not sure. I like this.' Emmeline held up one of Jackie's new Mary Quants.

Coco scowled. 'I don't like that at all.'

I could feel Jackie next to me bristle. They skimmed through the racks some more.

Daniel was getting his card out of his wallet to pay for the jacket.

'You want me to wrap it?' said Jackie.

'No, I think I'll wear it,' he said. He caught sight of Verity making a face as she hovered on the threshold of the stall. 'Why are you looking at me like that, Verity?'

'Because,' she said, her lip curled, her arms crossed tight over her pristine white sweatshirt.

Daniel raised a brow. 'Because what?'

'Because it's dirty.'

Jackie looked up from keying the numbers into the card machine. 'It's not dirty.'

Verity rolled her eyes in dismissal and got her phone out.

'She doesn't do second-hand,' said Daniel to Jackie by way of explanation. Jackie scoffed as she ripped off the receipt.

Emmeline was whispering something to Verity.

'Who?' said Verity.

Emmeline gestured for her not to be so loud. 'Norah,' she said, hushed but completely audible.

'Who's Norah?' said Verity, all dismissive confusion.

Coco went over to join them. 'What are you saying?'

Everyone was watching now. The sun had peeked out from behind the bridge and cast a light over their posse.

Verity frowned, as if this was all an annoying distraction.

'Em was asking if some Norah person could come to my party. I don't even know a Norah. Do we know a Norah?'

My mum stepped forward. 'This is Norah,' she said, pointing to me, her jaw set rigid.

I closed my eyes. Cheeks flaming. Verity was at least civil enough to look vaguely sheepish.

Coco waved it away, uninterested in the emotion. 'Let's go. I'm late already,' she said, taking a sip of her green juice.

Tabitha slipped the satin nightdress she'd been intently studying back on the rack, clearly embarrassed by the exchange.

My mum narrowed her big blue eyes, as if seeing Coco properly for the first time. 'You're Lavinia's daughter, aren't you?'

Coco paused, lips round her straw, frowning in surprise at the reference. 'Yes.'

My mum laughed. 'I should have known.'

The comment was met with wide-eyed silence. Coco pouted, not quite sure how to react.

There was a small moment of triumph on our side, until Big Dave's voice boomed into the mix.

'It's Southwark Crown Court, isn't it, Lois?' he yelled from the kerbside, scrunching up his yellow T-shirt to scratch his belly. 'Just for Jim at the burger van, he wants to follow Bill's trial on the web.'

I winced. My mum inhaled through her nose.

Coco's lips stretched into a cat-like grin.

'Lois!' Dave shouted again. 'Southwark, yeah?'

Peering round the stall, my mum said a little wearily, 'Yep, Dave. Southwark.'

Coco licked her lips. 'Lois, is it?' she said. 'I'll make sure to tell my mum you said hi.' Then, with a little smirk, she hooked arms with Verity and called, 'We're going, guys, catch us up,' to the others. And they sauntered off, their heads close, sniggering under their breath.

'We'd better go too,' Emmeline said, glancing at me and then at Daniel.

I nodded.

'Sorry about, you know –'

I waved it away. And they left, Tabitha scuttling after them.

'Well, they're lovely, aren't they?' my mum said, all saccharine sarcasm.

Jackie snorted.

My mum glanced her way. 'And that jacket? Versace my arse.'

My jaw dropped. 'It wasn't Versace?'

'Could have been.' Jackie laughed. 'Could be anything. The label's long gone.'

'Jackie!' I said, incredulous. We did stuff like that all the time, but never to people we knew. And even then we would always give a hint that there was doubt about the authenticity.

'What?' she said, holding her arms wide. 'He could afford it.' Sitting down, she unscrewed her Thermos. 'Shall we have a hot chocolate?'

My mum plonked herself down with a sigh. 'What am I going to do about Dave? Shouting like it's bloody *Judge Judy* or something.'

'He'll get bored soon; don't worry about it. Norah, hot chocolate?' Jackie said, proffering a mug in my direction.

I took it, wrapping my hands round the warmth and moving away to stand on the threshold of the stall to look out. I cringed when I replayed the Verity/Coco chat over in my head. But I was also having trouble aligning myself. We were the rich ones now. My mum was one of them; she'd gone to that school. She had *been* them. It was a fact completely at odds with the laid-back, bohemian, land-loving, hand-to-mouth existence her and my dad had exalted prior to this move. We ate food we had grown, we bartered aubergines for goat's milk, tomatoes for eggs. We shopped of course, but we also made stuff – bread, juice, clothes. I could sew practically the same age as I could write. We've made furniture, boats, treehouses. And not because we had to but because we wanted to. Because it was fun, because it was our way of life. But it was all starting to feel like we'd been there

85

under false pretences.

Was it easier for my parents to be unconventional because they had a cushion of convention? A soft bed of money waiting to catch them if they fell? How real was that? And here was Jackie, tripling the price of some horrible eighties jacket because she could tell Daniel had money to burn. Didn't that make us as bad as them? At least Coco and Verity were screwing us right out in the open. I liked Daniel. Surely a person's character should come before money and stereotype. Like with my dad. Why did everyone jump to conclusions based on what they'd read and heard, rather than considering the man they knew?

But then I ruined my own argument. When I glanced back at my mum and Jackie in their big colourful coats with their plastic mugs of cocoa, and their knitting and their crossword, I saw them through Coco's eyes and I was embarrassed.

What did that say about me?

CHAPTER EIGHT

Sunday was my first visit to the grandparents. They'd suggested I come alone, which infuriated my mum. 'They're trying to brainwash her,' she raged.

'I don't think so, Lois,' my dad said. 'I think it was so you and I could have some alone-time before the trial.'

My mum scoffed. 'Bill, your parents have not done this for us. They don't have a selfless bone in their bodies.'

I sat across the breakfast table, eating Rice Krispies, thinking how my mum and dad's alone-time used to include me. Or rather, they never used to *need* alone-time because we had such a lovely time together.

My dad cycled with me to my grandparents' house, along the river and through the backstreets of Chelsea. The buildings and pavements gleamed like someone polished them each morning. Even the plants in the neat little front gardens seemed like they'd been given a shine. Everywhere I looked there were vast swathes of ice-white Georgian terraces where women with fur coats, dark glasses and little dogs tripped down the steps, or vast red-brick apartments with polished gold signs and chauffeurs waiting outside in idling Bentleys.

A low-slung sports car roared past us, painted a bespoke metallic gold, narrowly missing our bike wheels. The wealth was daunting. I felt conspicuously shabby as I cycled my old bike past Cadogan Hall – 'God, that's where I used to sing choir,' my dad shouted without turning back, as if suddenly his forgotten youth was coming back to him – then into Belgravia, which was even richer, and then up to Knightsbridge, the sun warm and the air soft with the last of summer.

My dad stopped in front of a large Georgian mews house round the back of Harrods. I gawped at the impressive Harrods window displays, the polished brass buttons and top hats of the doormen, the tourists coming out laden down with dark green glossy bags as I locked my bike to a lamp post. While I marvelled, my dad was jogging up the steps of the mews house opposite to ring the bell. His movements were instinctive, as if he'd done it a million times. This had been his home, I realised. Taking in the gleaming railings, the huge flower display in the window, the door number etched in the glass above the door, I couldn't begin to comprehend it. My mind compared it to the cracking wood of the door on the boat, the sun-blistered paint, our old weed-strewn patch of garden. How could he be that as well as this? How could I be?

The door was opened by an aloof-looking butler in a black suit.

I could feel my hands shaky with nerves.

My dad grinned. 'Alright, Harold,' he said, giving the

butler a quick pat on the arm as if he saw him every day.

I saw the surprise on Harold's face. Then he broke into a smile. 'Bill!'

'Keeping well?' my dad asked.

'Very well, Sir,' said Harold.

My dad's grin widened. 'Good to see you, old man.'

Harold did a sweet little blush and a nod.

I watched as they chatted briefly. It was calming to know this Harold guy was here, that I'd seen the smile beneath the shuttered exterior. But I was still dreading what the next few hours might hold.

My dad, however, wasn't hanging about to settle me in. I could tell by the way he furtively glanced over Harold's shoulder that he was keen to leave before he saw either of his parents. He gave me a kiss on the top of my head and said, 'Be good, Pumpkin. You'll be OK, yeah?' And he was cycling away before I had a chance to ask him to stay.

Harold led me into the house. 'This way, ma'am.'

I followed, shaky hands stuffed in my pockets. The hall was painted the same sludge green as Harrods, dark to the ceiling. Pictures in gold frames covered the walls, some covered in tissue paper to protect them from the sunlight. I wondered if they were ever unwrapped. Everything smelt of the same furniture polish Jackie used in her shop, but here it smelt intimidating rather than cosy. A giant vase of white lilies sat on a gleaming wooden side table. I watched it teeter gently as it was nudged by an ancient old Labrador crossing the hall, eyes white with cataracts like fog over a lens. Harold steadied the vase as the dog slowly plodded on, then gestured for me to follow in the same direction.

'Hello, old thing,' I heard my grandfather say to the Labrador.

Harold cleared his throat. 'Roger, Miss Norah is here.'

I saw my grandfather, sitting in a chair by the empty fireplace, look immediately embarrassed that I'd heard his affection for the dog. He stood and walked over to me, his arm extended. We exchanged a rigid handshake, his grip like an army major.

'Thank you, Harold,' he said. He was dressed no less casually today than when I'd met him on the boat: stripy cricket-club tie, thick cream shirt and blue cardigan, burgundy corduroy trousers and monogrammed slippers.

Harold nodded, hands clasped behind his back. As he left the room I heard my grandmother's voice call from somewhere in the house, 'Tea in ten minutes, Harold.'

My grandfather gestured to the cream and flowery sofa in front of him. 'Take a seat, Norah,' he said. Then there was silence, neither of us knowing what to say. Both of us, I think, waiting for my grandmother to come in and take charge.

We were saved by the weary dog stretching in front of the fire. My grandfather patted him gently on the bum. 'Poor Ludo here isn't in the best shape. Blind as a bat,' he said. Then he paused and added, uncertain whether it was the right conversation topic, 'Descendant of your father's dog, actually.'

'I didn't know my dad had a dog.'

'Oh yes, he adored him.'

'He's always been a cat person,' I said. It felt combative, as if we were competing for who knew my dad best.

My grandfather looked down at his clasped hands. 'I don't know much about cats, I'm afraid.'

The dog searched for someone who would give him a stroke. I knelt down on the pale green carpet to scratch him between the ears.

My grandfather watched, smiling. The dog almost purred. I laughed and realised we were OK while we had this animal to focus on.

'Your father won the dog in a bet, as far as I could gather,' said my grandfather. 'Some tomfoolery at school and he comes home with a puppy. Called him Lucky. He was Ludo's father. Didn't do anything with him, of course. Muggins here had to do all the walking and the feeding,' he added, pointing to himself with a raise of his eyes heavenwards. I smiled.

'Oh, hello, Norah.' My grandmother's voice cut in from the doorway. 'No need to sit on the floor; we have chairs.'

I shot up into my seat, smile forgotten.

A look passed between her and my grandfather – a wince and a shake of the head on his part - and she seemed suddenly all in a muddle, as if she'd been planning to be all relaxed but had messed it up at the first hurdle.

'Sorry.' She waved a hand. 'By all means sit on the floor and pet the dog.'

But my bum was now firmly glued to the chintzy sofa, all the cushions around me impeccably plumped. My grandmother took a seat in the chair next to my grandfather and smoothed her skirt, with an air that something had been ruined. It was a pale bouclé tweed that I knew, because it was Jackie's Holy Grail, was almost certainly Chanel. It was all very awkward. They both looked so old and crestfallen, I almost felt sorry for them. I had to remind myself I was here under duress.

My grandmother gave a little cough, then nudged her glasses up her nose. 'So how is school?'

I gave her the same answer I gave on the boat. 'Fine.'

'Do you play sport?' she asked with a small fixed smile.

'No,' I replied.

My grandfather said, 'What *do* you enjoy, Norah?'

'Acting.'

My grandmother sucked in her breath.

After that no one said anything for a while. All was silent, except for the occasional loud snore from the dog. I thought about my dad cycling away. How happy he had been to leave me with them and flee. I felt more like a bargaining chip than a daughter.

Luckily Harold arrived with the tea, which gave my grandmother something to do. She busied herself with 'How do you take it?' questions, tea strainers, sugar tongs and milk jugs.

I caught Harold's eye as he was walking away. He winked. It made me think of him being nice to my dad as a child, and stopped all the negative thoughts from creeping in. We couldn't turn against each other when we were all we had.

I was presented with a teacup of weak, milky, loose-leaf tea – we stew ours in mugs till there's no life left in the bag – and a plate with a slice of Battenberg cake.

I looked around for somewhere to put them down, and my grandfather jumped up to bring me a side table, knocking a vase of fat pink peonies in the process. I realised we were all as nervous as each other.

'Thank you,' I said. Setting everything down, I picked up the cup to take a sip.

'The saucer will catch the drips,' my grandmother prompted, gaze on the saucer I'd left on the table.

My grandfather shook his head as I apologised and put the cup down. My grandmother was flustered again. She snapped at my grandfather, 'Well, we've just had the carpets cleaned.'

'It doesn't matter, Evelyn,' he snapped back under his breath.

It was so tense. I could feel nervous laughter bubbling up in me.

My grandmother was pink-cheeked. She went to sit down with her tea but, tripping on the dog's paw, spilt some in her saucer. 'Oh bother,' she muttered. Reaching to get a napkin, she knocked the tea table and tipped the whole Battenberg cake on the floor. I watched her lips tremble as the yellow marzipan crust snapped and little squares of pastel-coloured cake rolled all over the carpet. The blind dog seemed to have no trouble sussing out where it had fallen. He creaked his way over and started scoffing it off the floor, drool like slug trails on the carpet.

It was all too much for my grandmother, who put her hands to her face and cried, 'Ludo, bad dog. No! Oh, damn that dog. For goodness' sake.' Then, covering her mouth with her hand, she fled the room.

I watched my grandfather, wide-eyed and not quite sure what to do. My tea cooled on the side table. The dog was snuffling across the carpet searching out more crumbs.

My grandfather met my eyes with a look as weary as the dog's. 'My apologies, Norah. I'm afraid it's been a very trying time for your grandmother. She rather hoped this would be a roaring success.'

He leaned forward, patched cardigan elbows on his corduroy knees. 'I had warned her that it may take time, but she was so very determined . . .' He opened and shut his clasped hands to round off his point.

'Do you think –' I pointed to the door, wondering if someone should go after her.

'No, no. Best to leave her to calm down on her own.'

In our house we would definitely go after someone if they left close to tears. I wondered if that's what they'd been like as parents, leaving my dad to mull over his bad deeds alone.

I felt guilty that my grandmother had left, that my presence had made her so on edge. I looked down at the big flower pattern on the sofa. I could have tried harder, been less monosyllabic, but I resented them. I resented *everything*. I resented that we were suddenly tied to them because of their money. And I suppose, if I was honest, I resented them because they knew about the part of my parents' life of which I knew nothing. They were in on the joke. They knew the younger, richer, posher versions of my mum and dad. It's hard not to feel the fool when someone you love keeps you in the dark. It's hard not to resent them and everyone else who knew.

My grandfather rubbed his hand over his face. 'It's a mess. A godawful mess. Not least because, while we're all worried about the outcome of the trial, we're furious with him, Norah, for denying us a grandchild.'

I swallowed, realising then that they were excluded from our joke too. They too felt the fool.

'We're flesh and blood, you and I, Norah. And yet I don't know you at all. Not one thing. Except perhaps that you think school is fine.' He raised a brow like he was quite certain I had purposefully been a monosyllabic brat. 'We've been through some mighty fine fiascos with your father, but this really does take the biscuit.'

He slumped back, resigned, in his armchair.

I shifted in my seat, glancing at the door. Wondering if my grandmother would come back any time soon.

As I looked around the room – at the empty fire grate and the polished fire tongs, the watercolours on the walls, the soft folds of the curtains – I saw the photos on the windowsills and on top of the piano. Pictures of babies and young kids with younger versions of my grandparents. I walked over to look, the carpet fluffy under my feet. There was my dad in a team photo, posing in his Chelsea High hockey uniform, sticks crossed at the front. The one behind was in a restaurant, on holiday somewhere, my teenage dad all tanned and holding up a drink with a cocktail umbrella, my grandmother smiling with her now familiar awkwardness as he pulled her into a hug for the camera, clearly used to a life of more reserve. It was hard to imagine my dad growing up with these people.

I reached to the photo at the back. It was a shot of a Chelsea High gang posing outside the main gates. Not dissimilar to one that might be taken now of Coco and co. I skimmed over the faces, all the big teeth and artfully dishevelled hair, and saw my dad at the back, standing on the top step, arms thrown wide, grinning ear to ear.

'That was their end of term,' my grandfather said, giving me a shock. I hadn't heard him stand up. He took the picture frame out of my hands and peered at the photo. 'I think Bill might be the only Chelsea High student to be expelled two minutes before the end of term.'

My eyes widened. 'He was expelled?'

My grandfather put the photo back. 'Not only did the fool write his name in weedkiller on the cricket pitch, he abseiled the main tower and spray-painted the old mullioned windows black.' He went back to sit by the dog. 'He certainly didn't get the genes from me.'

I grinned.

Whenever I had quizzed my dad about the past he'd just waved the questions away. 'Long time ago, Norah. Different life.'

But as I looked at my grandfather, the hint of a smile on his face at the memory, I wondered if maybe the answers would be different here. If I wanted to fill in the blanks, this might just be the place to do it.

'What were the other fiascos?' I asked, a little tentative as I sat back down on the sofa.

He looked across at me with tired eyes, the dog's head resting on his slippers. 'I beg your pardon?'

'I said, what other fiascos? You said you'd been through some mighty fine fiascos with my dad.'

He thought for a second as the dog shifted at his feet. It was clear they weren't memories he'd considered for a while. 'Well,' he began, 'when he was a boy, by golly he was a tinker . . .'

I settled back and ate my Battenberg. It was sweet and

sugary in my mouth as my grandfather told me about the time they were chopping wood in the forest behind their house in the country – my eyebrows lifted at the existence of such a thing – down near Devon. At six years old my dad had climbed to the top of the tallest tree, waiting for the chainsaw to knock him to the ground.

'He was crouched up there like a koala. We only spotted him because he lost his nerve when the chainsaw started cutting. What on earth would have happened if he'd had the bottle to cling on, I don't know. But no one could go up because the tree was completely unstable, and he couldn't come down because he was too damn scared. My goodness!' He rubbed his forehead with his hand. 'It makes my heart go, even now. Talking the little blighter down. Of course his mother was making the matter worse. Beside herself.' My grandfather raised his bushy brows to warn me that those words weren't ones I shouldn't repeat.

I smiled down at the remains of my cake.

The old wrinkly face seemed less stern. 'Your father shimmied down like a little monkey in the end when the nanny appeared with a chocolate cake and a very stern telling-off. She was a fierce one, by jingo.' He shook his head, picturing that naughty little six-year-old. But the nostalgic image seemed to collide in the air with where we were now: the trial, the lawyers, the lies. All less sweetly resolvable.

He glanced to the door. 'I should probably go and check on

Evelyn,' he said. The moment for jollity was over.

'Yes,' I said. 'And I should probably go.'

He didn't try and stop me, which I appreciated. Instead he nodded. That had been enough for today.

Harold appeared from thin air to show me out.

'Are you alright to cycle home, Miss?' he asked.

'Yes,' I said, stepping into the warm, fresh air. 'Can you call me Norah, please?'

'I can, miss.' Harold huffed a laugh at the slip of the tongue. 'Norah.'

My grandfather appeared unexpectedly at the door as I was buckling my helmet. 'Will we see you next week, Norah?' he asked, and I wondered if I heard trepidation in his voice – a nervousness as to whether he had done enough to counter the earlier tension.

'Yes,' I said, without thinking.

And he nodded, on his lips what could have passed as a smile.

The door shut. I started to cycle. Then I paused and looked back, intrigued by my certainty that I would return. Against my better judgment, I had enjoyed myself. Not all of it, of course, but part of it. It intrigued me – my father's past, the fact I was part of them. Enough to want to find out more. Up at the window I caught my grandmother watching before she pulled back.

'How did it go?' my dad asked as I freewheeled down the gangplank to the boat. He was sitting with his bare feet up on the rail, my mum next to him with her sunglasses on, both of them soaking up the sun.

I immediately begrudged them their alone-time. They seemed at odds with the real world, sitting here all calm and peaceful when the trial started tomorrow. The picture of false contentment.

'Fine,' I said.

'Please, Norah.' My mum looked at me over the top of her sunglasses. 'You know the rules. Anything but *fine*.'

In the past I would have told them everything in minute detail. But the words wouldn't come out of my mouth. I didn't want their opinions to cloud what I was trying to process. In this sea of change, I was being washed up on one side and them on the other. And until I could make sense of it all, school, and stories like the ones about my dad told in that old and crumpled voice, belonged right now to me. As did the nuances of the day: the cake tantrum, the blind dog's saliva trail, the twitch at the window, the smell of the polish – that was all mine, to keep close until I knew what to do with it. Till all that was up in the air decided where to fall.

'It really was fine,' I said, breezy, walking past them through to the kitchen to pour a glass of water. 'We had tea and talked about school.'

CHAPTER NINE

All anyone could talk about was how amazing Verity's party had been. It felt like the whole school had been there, along with stilt walkers, fire jugglers and a magician who levitated Coco a foot off the ground.

'I'm not telling you how he did it,' she said, all coy, perched on Ezra's desk with her back to me and blocking my view of the room. Rollo was leaning up against the window, and Emmeline was sitting on Daniel's knee because Freddie had pinched her seat.

There was a message on the board to say Mrs Pearce was running late for registration.

I'd been sitting at my desk for what felt like hours already.

The black car had come for my dad at 7.45 a.m. Tinted windows. Electric. It had pulled away silently from the kerb.

My mum had gone with him. Hair tight back, make-up neutral, wearing wide grey trousers and a cream sleeveless tank top from M&S – not her normal fare at all. She looked like a businesswoman. I barely recognised her.

I'd left as soon as they had, not wanting to stay on the boat alone with only the woman on the posh barge next door for company. I'd never seen anyone on there except her, polishing and vacuuming. Then it occurred to me that she was the cleaner. There was no new community here for us to join.

The inside of our boat was a mess. Presenting a polished front to the public meant everything behind the scenes got forgotten. There were heaps of old clothes that my mum was mending for the stall on the sofa, washing piled up in the basket and dirty dishes in the sink. I did the washing up before I left, arms in soapy suds, wondering who would be in the gallery at the court. Would all my old friends' parents be crowded in? People who I spent my childhood playing round their houses, picking strawberries with, eating their crisps at pub tables, swinging from ropes across the river. All of them now broke.

I was really starting to hate money. Hate what it meant and how it divided us. Made us broke and broke us.

I watched the cleaner vacuuming next door – the stark white immaculate interior – and thought of the contrast with the haphazard island boats. Our neighbour Phyllis's barge had an Astroturf roof and a menagerie of ceramic animals that sat round tinfoil ponds while gnomes lounged in deckchairs fishing for nothing. As children, we would be fascinated by all the little critters. There was old Percy's colonial steamboat, built in the style of the ones on the Mississippi. He was getting on a bit now and didn't have the energy to paint his fretwork, so he paid me and Jess to do it, served up glasses of dandelion and burdock while we painted, and told long tales about how life on the island used to be when he was a kid. And there was ex-Olympian Maxim, Jess's canoe coach. They'd go out at sunrise and come back to the boathouse with a Jamaican spiced bun baked by Mrs Jackson who lived on a huge blue Dutch barge. Mrs Jackson would pass them out to them every Friday morning when they canoed past, and I would wait at the canoe club so Jess and I could walk to school together stuffing warm, sweet bread into our mouths.

Now all their futures were in the balance because of us. It *had* to be made right. There was no conceivable alternative. They were my family and I wanted them back.

We *would* be back, I had convinced myself as I pushed my bike along the jetty, away from the cold lifeless minimalism of next door.

Now as I sat, excluded by Coco with her shadow cast over my desk and watching her arms gesticulate as she talked, I found it harder to picture the grand island reunion. The money was still gone, no matter who was to blame.

Mr Benson came into the classroom with a handful of fliers. He'd swapped his zip-up fleece for a yellow woollen V-neck and red bow tie under his black cape. Everyone paused to watch as he stuck one of the fliers on the magnetic board at the front of the room.

'School play,' he said. 'Auditions Friday.'

As soon as he left, Freddie jogged to the front to grab the piece of paper.

'What's the play?' Rollo shouted.

Freddie made a show of staring right up close to the flier and then coughing to clear his throat. Adjusting his faux bow tie, he said in a voice exactly the same as Mr Benson's: 'This year, despite my burning desire to perform some meaningful Chekov, the bloody headmaster has demanded commercial. So I thought, he wants commercial? I'll give the miserable old moaner commercial. I'll give him singing and dancing like he's never seen before . . .'

Even Ezra was smiling at the impression.

'So this year, kids, we're doing the cheesiest, most musical of musicals I could get my hands on. We're doing *Grease*. Like it or lump it. Please don't put yourself forward if this is an exam year or if you have heavy sporting commitments – that's you out, Rollo.'

The room applauded. Freddie took a bow. The door opened again and Mr Benson said, 'I heard that.'

Freddie blushed.

'Just wait till auditions, Frederick,' said Mr Benson.

Freddie skidded away, head hung, grinning, back to his desk.

I stared at the flier on the wall, my body tingling with excitement. I love nothing more in the world than a musical, and *Grease* was an all-time family favourite. Last year, all of us had snuggled under a blanket at the Mulberry Island screening when everything was still perfect. Jess had come with us, as she did every summer, because her mum worked night shifts as a nurse and her dad ran the screening committee so was too busy to picnic. It had been magical – *Grease* projected on to a huge white screen hung between an enormous horse chestnut tree and the corner of the sailing club, the river still as glass behind, the mulberry bushes twinkling with a million fairy lights, all of us with picnics on the hill. Fresh strawberries and pink lemonade; Jess, me and my dad singing along at the tops of our voices when the songs came on, my mum shielding her eyes with mock shame.

I drifted back to reality as Coco was saying, 'Well, it'd make sense for me to play Sandy. What do you think, Ezra? This is definitely our year to lead.'

Friday couldn't come quick enough for me. I was desperate to audition and have something to take my mind off the bleak reality of home. I didn't even mind that Coco had already stamped her mark on the lead role, mentioning it to Ezra every chance she got. It seemed inevitable. But then when Friday came, as I was walking through the atrium to the theatre for the auditions, I paused at the sight of a black shiny limousine pulling up at the side entrance of school. Through the railings I could see a driver get out and wait by the car door. Coco flew down the path in a cloud of blonde hair, out of the gate and into the plush back seat. The driver got in and the big car glided smoothly away.

'Where's Coco going?' I asked Daniel and Emmeline, who were coming up behind me.

Daniel shrugged.

Emmeline said, 'Oh, she's always off somewhere. It'll be something to do with some company she endorses on Instagram.'

'But it's school,' I said, feeling a bit naïve about how popular Coco was, how demanding her extra-curricular work. 'She'll miss the auditions.'

'She'll work something out,' Emmeline said, all casual.

I thought how I had been counting down to this moment all week. How huge it was for me, how infinitesimal to her. The adrenaline had kept me awake last night. Not even Mr Watts in Maths had been able to put a dampener on it when he'd handed me my red-pen-scrawled homework with a tut of disappointment and said, 'Sloppy work, Ms Whittaker. You were clearly distracted. You need to focus, otherwise you're wasting my time as well as yours.' He knew my dad was in the dock. Of course I was distracted.

The auditions had become a beacon to block out the greyness of home, my dad pulling his tie out of his collar and flopping down on the sofa, running his hand over his face and saying things like, 'I don't think I can handle another day, let alone weeks of this thing.' Last night he'd thumped the arm of the sofa and said, 'Christ, I just want my life back!' then sat with his head in his hands. Every night was a shock. Before all this I'd never seen him less than smiling. Silence shrouded the boat like night, thick and black, broken only by a routine phone call from my grandfather, when my dad would go outside and talk to him for hours. My mum sat quietly sewing, so I did the same, tailoring my school dress so it would fit me better, nipping it in with little darts at the waist, hoiking up the hem a couple of inches.

I realised that was why Daniel was frowning at me now. 'Well, look at you in your natty little outfit,' he said, looking me up and down.

I felt myself blush, thankful that we'd reached the auditorium.

Everyone was sitting in the rows of theatre seats as Mr Benson rifled through sheets of paper to find the right music for Ms Venn, the music teacher and audition pianist. He spilt his coffee, misplaced his glasses and finally, yanking off his cape and fleece and rolling up his shirt sleeves, said: 'Right. Yes. *Grease*. Big musical numbers. Lots of energy. I need a committed cast – there will be a lot of rehearsal time after school. If you can't attend, then don't audition. I'm assuming you've all seen the film. If you haven't, it's a basic boy-meets-girl. Girl doesn't align with boy's socio-economic standing although –'

Daniel stood up. 'Boy is cool. Girl is not. In the end they

get together. There are lots of songs. Got it?'

Everyone giggled.

Mr Benson pulled off his glasses. 'Thank you, Daniel.'

Daniel sat back down next to a grinning Emmeline.

I glanced around at the other auditionees. Next to me was Tabitha of the Pre-Raphaelite hair. Next to her were a couple of other people I recognised from our Theatre Studies class. Then Freddie, Verity and Ezra.

I was surprised to see him there, considering the rules about not auditioning if you had sporting commitments. Earlier in the week, during one of my bored lunch-break walks of the school, I'd come across a wall of trophy cabinets. The bright sunshine splintered light as best it could through the small mullioned windows of the dark empty corridor, and the cabinets were lit with a dim strip light glinting off the old gold cups and medal shields. There were cabinets for everything: rugby, swimming, cricket, rowing, hockey and more. Rollo was in nearly every one of the most recent team pics, standing with his foot on a rugby ball or propping up a rowing blade. But next to him was a face I hadn't been expecting – Ezra.

I had barely recognised him. The smile was too wide, the cheeks too glowing, the body too solid, the hair too neat. But there was no denying the same slight slope of the eyes. In one of the hockey photos he was holding up a cup with Rollo, who hadn't changed an inch. They were clearly high on the adrenaline of a win. The faces of the others seemed to smile more at the duo than the cup itself. I scanned the names: Rollo Cooper-Quinn and Ezra Montgomery. I pressed my nose against the glass, staring at the delight-filled face. The shorn hair, the rosy cheeks. It was him. A healthier, happier version of him.

In the theatre, Mr Benson seemed to have zeroed in on exactly what I was thinking because he narrowed his eyes at Ezra. 'Are you sure you've got the time to do this?'

Ezra nodded. 'Yes.'

'What does Mr Simpson say about it?' Mr Benson asked, referring to the hockey coach.

'Nothing. I'm not playing this year.'

Mr Benson frowned. 'Really?'

A couple of other people turned to look as well. As if this were big news.

Ezra shrugged.

Mr Benson gave a surprised nod, then looked back to his clipboard. 'Right then. OK. Anyone going on the ski trip needs to tell me now, because the dates clash with the dress rehearsal, which is the week before end of term. You can go; I just need to know.'

Half the room put their hands up. Mr Benson rolled his eyes. 'Maybe I'll just move the dress rehearsal.'

As soon as the trial was finished, we'd be leaving. In my head I always hoped that was going to be before Christmas. But I didn't want Mr Benson to tell me I couldn't audition. It was too important to my sanity to walk away.

Daniel handed me the stack of song sheets that were being passed down the row. 'I can't sing to save my life,' he muttered.

I grinned, passing the stack of papers to Tabitha. 'Can you sing?' I asked.

'Oh yes,' Tabitha said with her usual plummy enthusiasm. 'I'm lead soprano in choir.'

Emmeline leaned forward. 'I forgot to say, I loved your mum's stall, Norah. I'm definitely going to come back and buy one of the dresses.'

'Yeah,' Daniel agreed. 'My jacket's a real winner.'

'I thought it was for the party?' I said.

'It was but I love it. It's my go-to.'

I smiled, feeling suddenly less on the outside.

'You'll stand up row by row and sing four lines each.' Mr Benson was talking. 'From that we will go to individual pieces. Everyone understand? Freddie? Are. You. Listening?'

The first row started. There were some terrible singers.

The room was huge and echoey and did no favours to anyone who suddenly got shy and lost their nerve. The silence as the solos started seemed to close the room down to nothing, like a spotlight shining on every fault and insecurity.

I was getting nervous. My heart rate rising. I tried to quash it with thoughts of going home, cruising back along the river through thickets of overhanging chestnut trees. Maybe we could hold off till Christmas so I could finish the play, if I got in. Perhaps there'd be a frost on the grassy banks and shards of ice in the water. I wondered what I would do with this world I was in now, these people. Would I just box them up in my head and wonder at what might have been? Wonder how any possible friendships might have played out? Would I stalk Ezra online in years to come, to see who this heart-thrumming boy had become? Would I still visit my grandparents in the house with Harrods as its nearest supermarket?

Once a world opened up, was it possible to sew it back together again? Would I lie on my back in the Mulberry Island meadow wondering at this different life, or would it be like a holiday, fading to the recesses of memory after a fortnight back home?

Emmeline gave me a nudge. I looked up. It was my turn. Ms Venn huffed and picked it up again when I apologised for missing the cue. She kept repeating the same bars till I sang. Four lines of the song, *Hopelessly Devoted*. The lyrics about desperately not wanting to forget the one you love. The words summing up everything I had left, and everything I wanted so desperately back.

Then I stopped. No one sang after me, because Mr Benson had held up his hand. 'Well I never, Norah. Come and stand over here, please.'

I looked around, surprised. Mr Benson beckoned again. Emmeline winked at me as I squeezed my way through the seats and went to sit up the front. I was blushing with so much pride that I didn't really listen to the others as they sang. But by the end of the first round there were about fifteen people sitting up the front, including Tabitha, Freddie, a couple of Lower Sixth, more of our year whose names I wasn't sure of – and Ezra. Verity, Daniel and Emmeline hadn't made the cut.

The play was already carving us up differently.

Ezra glanced across at me. 'Nice voice,' he said. Then, as if to show he'd remembered, 'Norah.'

'Thanks,' I replied, internally fizzing. 'Ezra.'

He laughed.

All I could focus on were his perfect teeth and sparkling eyes that crinkled shut like a cat when he smiled.

I wondered what it must be like to be Coco and be able to talk to him normally.

Everyone else left as we went on to individual auditions. Mine was less good than my four lines because my nerves had kicked in, but it was passable. Tabitha was a little too choral, but funny. Ezra was excellent at the acting, a bit shaky on the singing but good enough; kind of gravelly, like he'd be better with a guitar in hand. Freddie was all-round brilliant, a regular jazz-hands musical theatre star. We were just listening to a Lower Sixth girl hit her high notes when the big double doors at the back of the room flew open and Coco stalked in. Verity was beside her, and Rollo jogged in behind like a Labrador fresh from rugby practice.

'Sorry I'm late, Mr B.' Coco waved a hand, clutching her

phone like a lifeline, hair big and back-combed and sprayed in unicorn colours. 'I had a promo thing. It was really important profile building.' Mr Benson sighed. 'It's too late now, Coco. I'll hear you tomorrow. Come and find me at lunch break.'

'Unfair.' Coco pouted. 'You'll already have made your mind up. It'll only take a sec. You know I'm good anyway.' She sashayed up to the front, ignoring the final Lower Sixth who had had to pause mid-audition. 'I was talking about it today, all the journos were really interested. *Tatler, Hello!* Everyone.'

Mr Benson sighed. 'Coco, just pick up a song sheet and sing.'

Coco grinned, whipping a spare song sheet from a chair. She nodded at Miss Venn. 'Alright Miss V. Let's go.'

Miss Venn started playing. Coco positioned herself like a star, giving her multi-coloured hair a quick scrunch. Rollo stretched himself out in one of the seats at the back and did a little whoop like he was cheering on a rugby match. Ezra was smiling. Coco had that effect on people.

Then she sang.

To my dismay she was good. Not incredible, but much better than I thought she would be. Like one of those girls on *The X Factor* who wow because of the whole package rather than just the vocal range. And Coco definitely had the whole package. I couldn't bring 'media' to the opening night – unless they were following my jail-bait father.

I immediately felt bad for even thinking that. Dad would be in the dock right now. I pictured him in a square booth like you saw on TV, staring plaintively out at the jury, but he was probably just behind a desk with his boring lawyer beside him. My stomach clenched at the idea of it. Of my mother watching, hands fidgeting. I thought of him trying to crack the odd joke – get the steely jury on-side. I imagined him made small by questions he maybe wouldn't understand or would be tricked by. I thought of the McGintys bringing my dad on board with their watertight promises. They'd come over for dinner a couple of times – told loud confident stories in booming voices and hearty laughs – and then, as we'd filmed the first low-budget movie, they had sat nodding and clapping on set when we wrapped a scene. They were slicker than my dad. Wilier. Slippery as fish. What if they tricked him again now? What if they incriminated him for a lesser sentence? Did that kind of thing happen in real life, or just on the TV? I closed my eyes, couldn't think about it. As if by thinking it, it might come true.

I didn't care suddenly if my dad had lied about going to this school, his family, his money. I just wanted it all to be over. To see him, to hug him, to be hugged by him. For him to kiss the top of my head and say it would all be OK.

More than anything, I wanted someone I loved to say it would all be OK.

Coco had finished. 'Yeah?' she said to Mr Benson,

expression cheeky. 'Enough to bag the lead?'

Verity and Rollo cheered.

Mr Benson looked down at his notes. 'I'll put up a cast list by the end of tomorrow.'

'Come on, Mr B.' Coco sidled over to try and see what he'd written. 'Who else has sung better than that? You know it's mine.' She nudged him playfully on the arm with a flirty little smile. 'You can tell Coco.'

Mr Benson just shook his head like he'd had quite enough of Coco for one day and started packing up all his papers.

The bell rang.

At the end of the aisle, Ezra got up. Coco fell quick into step beside him, squeezing her arm round his waist. 'I think it's absolutely going to be you and me, don't you?'

He shrugged. 'Maybe.'

She lifted up his arm and draped it round her shoulder. 'It's in the bag.'

Rollo jumped up from his seat. 'Aced it, babe,' he said.

He enveloped Coco in a huge hug that lifted her from the floor, which had the effect of knocking Ezra's arm from her shoulder. Coco seemed annoyed but covered it well. They walked together, Coco picking up the pace slightly so she was level again with Ezra, Rollo following suit. But then Ezra reached his hand into his pocket and got his phone out, holding it up to his ear and making a gesture like it was something important and he'd catch them up. Coco paused, eyes a touch hurt. Then she left the theatre with Rollo, through the double doors at the back. Ezra left via the side entrance. As did I. It was closer to the Art block for my next lesson.

In the corridor, Daniel was walking past with his portfolio on the way to Art. 'Hey,' he said to me. 'Nice audition.'

'Thanks,' I said, eyes still on Ezra. Almost immediately on exiting the theatre he'd put his phone away and walked, hands in his pockets, in the same direction as Coco and Rollo, but down a parallel corridor.

'Are Coco and Ezra a couple?' I asked Daniel, distracted by the goings-on.

'Used to be,' he said, gaze following mine in the direction of Ezra's back. 'Why? You like him?'

'No!' I said, far too quickly.

Daniel laughed. Infuriatingly, I blushed.

We reached the glass doors of the Art department. Daniel pushed them open with his back and paused so I could walk through. 'Thanks,' I said.

'*De rien.*'

'I don't know what that means.'

He rolled his eyes like I knew nothing. '*That's OK* in French.'

That wasn't school French lesson stuff. That was casual, roll-off-the-tongue French holiday chat. I imagined Daniel's summers spent languid on the Côte d'Azur or winters up the mountains in places I couldn't pronounce.

Mrs Pearce was standing by the floor-to-ceiling windows of the Art block, beckoning us all to our places. Her cape discarded on her chair, she was dressed in a long patterned skirt, grey woollen waistcoat and bright red boots. Her jet-black hair was slick to one side. Style-wise she reminded me of my mum. Uninterested in the rules. Strong but fair.

I had never thought of my mum as strong before. Perhaps because she was always overshadowed by the presence of my dad.

Last week we had started drawing a hanging still life in the vein of the Spanish artist Juan Sánchez Cotán. Mrs Pearce had hung an apple, a cabbage, a carrot and a lemon from individual strings from the ceiling. They were still there, looking a little less fresh than the previous week.

'They're rotting, Miss,' a girl, Genevieve, called from across the other side of the room, her lip curled in distaste.

'That's good!' Mrs Pearce took a sip from her steaming mug of coffee. 'This is an exercise in looking at the overlooked,' she said, walking between our easels. 'Raising the humble to a position of majesty.'

'It smells,' said one of guys. He jabbed the apple with his pen so it knocked against the vegetables like one of those executive desktop games.

'Cut it out, Rex,' Daniel said, annoyed, already adjusting his sketch to allow for the shrivelling fruit.

I glanced at Daniel's picture.

'You're really good,' I said in amazement.

'I know,' he replied, pencil outstretched, measuring up the proportions of the lemon. 'You're watching a master at work.'

Picking up my pencil, I wondered why Ezra and Coco had split up. It made Coco's arm-lifting interplay seem less like a mutual decision. I thought about Rollo giving her that hug. 'Is Coco with Rollo?' I asked.

'You ask a lot of questions,' said Daniel, concentrating on rubbing out part of his cabbage.

'Only two so far,' I said.

He chucked the eraser back on the easel and stretched his arm out to take new measurements of the hanging vegetable. 'What did you just ask? Coco and Rollo? No, they're not together either.' He squinted at his pencil and the cabbage, then marked it out on the paper.

'Rollo adores her, which is unfortunate. Coco can smell it a mile off.'

'So?' I asked.

Daniel was measuring again. 'So she keeps him where she wants him.'

'Miss Whittaker, will your pencil be touching your paper this lesson?'

Mrs Pearce was suddenly standing behind me.

I felt my cheeks go red and hurried to do some hasty shading of my apple as Daniel chuckled under his breath.

On the other side of the room, the base of Rex's easel clattered to the floor.

'It wasn't me, Miss,' Rex said, jumping back, hands in the air.

As Mrs Pearce went over to sort things out, Daniel paused to study his work, arms crossed. 'It'll really cause some trouble if you get the lead in *Grease*,' he said suddenly. I felt a sudden rush of adrenaline. 'I won't get the lead,' I said.

He shrugged. 'No, probably not.'

My adrenaline sagged.

'But it would certainly be interesting if you did,' he added with an amused grin before going back to his lemon.

I stood staring blankly at the lines on my paper. Only lying in bed at night had I allowed myself the odd second to think I could be in with a chance. I wanted the lead more than anything. I wanted to play Sandy. I wanted lines to learn and an all-consuming part to perfect. I wanted another person's mind to embody, so that I didn't have to focus on mine. And most of all, I wanted my dad to be sitting in the audience, watching, clapping, singing along – free.

But now I wanted something else. If Coco and Ezra weren't together, I wanted Ezra to get the opposite lead. Something I could barely contemplate. My cheeks burned and my heart thumped at the thought.

The status quo of their gang was already altered by the bubble of the play. If I could belong in this glossy, glittering, covetable world, then maybe what I had left behind wouldn't seem so important. So all-consumingly sad. It might start greying in my mind, while the possibilities here were playing out in traitorous Technicolor.

CHAPTER TEN

I was late home because Mr Watts gave me a detention for still not being able to recite my thirteen times table backwards.

He made me stay behind and write it out a million times. I realise now why everyone knows it so well. After an hour of writing the thirteen times table over and over – believe me, you don't forget it.

It was dusky outside as I left, the sky still blue but outlines blurry. A breeze bringing in autumn.

They were all in Sorrentos, squished into a booth, the light inside all cosy and yellow as they laughed. I felt a stab of jealousy. There was Coco on her phone, sipping San Pellegrino mineral water through a straw, Daniel and Emmeline laughing at something, Rollo taking huge bites of grilled cheese. No Ezra.

Then I saw him up ahead, unlocking his bike from a lamp post. I hung back, watching as he slung his bag on his back. For a second he looked back, hair hanging half over his eyes. I wondered if he saw me as I quickly glanced away, trying to shrink into myself. But when I looked back, he was already pedalling away, slowly at first along the pavement, then dipping down to the road and cruising off as fast as the black cab trying to overtake him. When he got to the crossroads he freewheeled the corner and was gone.

I cycled the same route more slowly, reluctant to go home and dreading another night of silent melancholy. I itched for my phone when I was there, just for some escape. It was completely at odds to when we'd been on the island, my phone forgotten in my room because there were always people at our boat, hanging out on our squishy sofas or pausing for a chat on the bank that turned into drinks and dancing with the fairy lights switched on.

When I walked through the door, I wasn't met with the bleak scene I was expecting.

My dad was at the stove, frying pan on the hob, novelty gorilla-body apron on, massive smile on his face. 'Norah, honey, you've been ages! I'm making pancakes. Banana and blueberries or just blueberries? Or scrap the fruit all together and just chocolate chips?'

I looked around the spotless boat, feeling bemused. Had the sleek barge cleaner come and sucked the last few weeks away with her Dyson? I'd been expecting hushed whispers and serious phone call debriefs. Not my dad in his green tracksuit bottoms and red T-shirt holding up a bag of chocolate drops and a banana. It made my heart relax. It made me dump my school bag, kick off my shoes, perch up on the counter and say, 'Blueberries, banana AND chocolate.'

He clapped his hands together. 'Excellent choice, kiddo. How was school?'

'OK.' I reached for a chocolate chip. 'I auditioned for the play.'

'Good girl. Anything good?' He poured in the tub of blueberries.

'*Grease.*'

He paused mid-stir to stare wistfully out of the window before belting out the words to the *Grease* overture, doing some cheesy moves while singing into the wooden spoon. He did it without an ounce of shame, only stopping when he flung batter at the kitchen window by mistake and leaned forward to swipe it off with his finger.

'One of the classics,' he said, catching his breath.

Grinning, I watched him light the gas and pour some oil into the pan. 'How was today?' I asked.

'Do you think you'll get a good part?' he said, slicing the banana into the mix.

I frowned at his complete dismissal of my question. 'Maybe, I don't know.' Noticing suddenly his overly bright cheeriness. The possible fake stretch of his smile.

'True talent will shine, Norah. Cream always rises,' he said, and ladled batter into the pan.

I used to always nod in agreement when he said that. But today I just stared at him. I wondered if he still believed his time would come. Maybe he saw the trial as his best audition yet. Was that why he wasn't taking it seriously? It was all a game, a stage, a showcase of his talents. Did he think the curtain would close at the end and it'd all be over?

I suddenly wanted to lean over the counter and shout, 'You could go to jail! Don't you realise?'

Something I hadn't even really let myself consider.

But then I watched him flip the pancake with a flamboyant flick of the wrist and shut his eyes to catch it, as was his party trick. When it fell bang on centre, he looked my way for a reaction, his smile ear to ear but his eyes pleading.

I couldn't be the one to ruin it. So I smiled, like I always did. But I was smiling out of pity and I hated myself for it. Because I knew then that he knew. His freedom was at stake, but it was too terrifying for someone like him to accept. The showman no longer able to show.

My dad went through his full *Grease* repertoire as the pancakes bubbled and browned in the pan.

My mum came out of the bedroom at the far end of the boat and walked barefoot up the corridor.

She looked like she might have been crying.

I watched her look at Dad dancing with his spatula.

I gave her a look that asked as best I could about how the day had been. She shut her eyes and gave a soft shake of her head.

I wanted my phone so I could Google the details of the trial, but equally I didn't want to know. I wanted my mum to walk over to me and whisper, 'It's not that bad.' But she didn't. Instead she went to stand by my dad, to smell the warm scent of the pancakes with one hand on his shoulder.

I could feel a lump in my throat, a misting over my eyes and a tremble in my bottom lip. In the past she would have been at my side in an instant, enveloping me in a patchouli-scented hug. But when I caught her eye I saw her almost glare at me, warning me to pull myself together.

My dad was still singing, oblivious. I looked down at the surface of the kitchen counter, trying to quell the press of tears. It was our job to protect him. Our job to hug him and tell him it would all be OK. There were no concessions any longer for being the child.

I looked back up. My mum was grinning as my dad took her hand and twirled her around the kitchen, his spatula between his teeth like a red rose. Then he grabbed my hand and brought me in too, the three of us dancing, while outside the twinkling lights of the Albert Bridge mirrored the garishness of our smiles.

CHAPTER ELEVEN

My dad always talks about that feeling when you just know. When you ask a question, close your eyes and you just *know*. He would talk about that feeling before he went to an audition: never when he came out. 'This one, Norah, it's got my name on it.'

Bizarrely, while he was never right about himself, he always nailed it when it came to my mum. 'I can feel it in my tummy, Lois; this is your day,' he'd say, and she'd go to a car-boot sale and stumble across a box filled with someone's granny's jewels, gaudy beads and brooches the sellers sniggered at, deeming them worthless, which would fund our island life for the next few months.

As I looked at my mum now, calmly poised with her coffee, I was beginning to wonder if maybe it had nothing to do with my dad's gut instinct and everything to do with my mother's quiet, unsung talent.

Outside the sun was dazzling bright over the water. One of the big dredgers was making its way up the Thames, piled high with rubbish.

'Today's going to be a good day,' my dad said, spooning

Weetabix into his mouth. 'I can feel it in my tum. That part's got your name on it, I reckon.'

I humoured him until the lawyer arrived to pick him up.

'Believe me,' he said as I hugged him tight goodbye, 'it's a good day. We're going to have a good day in court.' The lawyer stood stony-faced at the door. 'And that part, it's yours.'

At lunch break, as I stood in the crowd waiting outside the staff room for Mr Benson to come out with his cast list, I was wishing my dad's gut would be right, my fingers crossed in my pocket.

Daniel was next to me, nonchalant about his own role in the play but giving me side-long looks. Freddie was doing a sort of tap-dancing jig that was making Rollo smirk, his arm slung casual but possessive over Coco's shoulders as she perfected a selfie on her phone.

It was warm today. Coco had her hair piled up in a messy bun and she fanned herself with her iPad. Verity was leaning against the wall. Ezra's arms were crossed over his chest, shirt-sleeves rolled up to over his elbows. Emmeline flicked the pages of a book perched on the window sill. They lingered with effortless grace, all of them still bronzed from the summer, the longevity of their tans mirroring the length of their holidays.

Mr Benson was a stark contrast. Pale skin, coarse beard, red cardigan buttoned up wrong under his cape. He came out holding a cup of coffee in a branded Chelsea High mug, *Making Winners* written on the side. Everyone was suddenly less languid, moving fast to get the optimal view. The piece of paper in his hand was pre-pinned; he was clearly prepared for a quick getaway. At the Drama noticeboard he had to physically move Freddie out of the way.

'This is ridiculous,' he said. 'All of you – go! Wait round the corner and don't come back till I've gone. You're a mob. Go!' he shouted again when nobody moved.

The mass started to slowly shift towards the corner like a giant octopus. No one wanted to be the one to leave if no one else did. Ezra, Freddie and Coco hung back as if naturally exempt from the order until Mr Benson stared them down. Ezra held his hands up in a pretence of uncaring and sauntered off with the rest of us. Coco rolled her eyes, as if her precious time was being wasted.

We were round the corner for maybe a second before Freddie shouted, 'It's up!' The whole mass changed direction, swarming forward like locusts. Mr Benson had scurried back to the staff room.

It was all hoots and whoops. I couldn't even get close, but gleaned from the shouts that Freddie was playing Kenickie: one of the lead boys and part of the T-Bird gang. A guy called Nick French was Sonny, another of the T-Birds. Tabitha was Frenchie, part of the girl gang the Pink Ladies, as were two girls in the Lower Sixth whose names I didn't know. I saw

Daniel peer at the board then stand back, a bit confused.

'What?' I shouted over the din.

'I'm Assistant Director,' he said.

'Wow.'

'I know, right?' He looked pleasantly perplexed.

'Can you see my name?' I asked, pushed and pulled by the crowd.

And then suddenly the mass around me stilled. As if after spotting their own name they all looked up to the top of the list to check out the leads.

Coco slapped the piece of paper with her hand and went, 'What?!'

At the same time Ezra went, 'Yes!' because his name was next to the male lead, Danny Zuko.

Daniel turned to me with a mischievous grin on his face. 'You've got it,' he said, voice a whisper.

My heart was beating in my throat. Adrenaline coursed through me. The effect was immediate, like I was raised off the ground looking down on them all.

But that's when I saw her.

The crowd parted to let Coco through. She stalked towards me like an Amazonian warrior. I could understand suddenly why Mr Benson had scarpered.

As she took her sweet time, I wondered if with every high in life there must come a low.

I wondered whether my dad had foretold his own good

day, and if he had, what catastrophes might follow.

Verity was standing to Coco's left, sucking on a lolly and scowling. Emmeline was just a little further away with Freddie, watching with a frown.

I crossed my arms, then uncrossed them so as not to look defensive. Whatever happened, I would be going home and telling my dad that I was Sandy. She couldn't take that away. Could she?

'Congratulations,' Coco said when she was close enough for me to see the blend of contouring on her cheeks, the little gold Chanel crossed Cs in her ears. 'I'm sure Mr B didn't make a mistake but I'll double-check.'

The mass was watching. A sea of white shirts, grey dresses and maroon ties. 'I'd have liked to have seen your audition,' Coco went on. 'You must have been mind-blowing. What was she like, Ezra?' She glanced to where Ezra was standing chewing gum, hands in his pockets.

He narrowed his eyes as if assessing whether he wanted a part of this or not. Then shrugged, noncommittal. 'Alright.'

Coco fixed her eyes back on me. 'Maybe you could show me now? Show me what I need to live up to.'

Behind her Verity smirked.

I heard myself laugh nervously, felt my cheeks start to flame. 'No,' I said, trying to catch someone's eye. This was preposterous. But no one would meet my gaze.

Coco angled her head as if she hadn't heard. It was exactly

like when she'd been on her pony, except this time it was her angry breath I could feel on my face. 'Why not?'

'Because I don't want to.' Even to me it sounded like lame reasoning.

I could sense her brewing. Just getting started.

God, I wished Jess was here. In instances such as these, she would back me up when I started to crumble. She was the strong one, the one with the death stare that nobody messed with.

Over Coco's shoulder Daniel made a face like I was being crucified and he couldn't bear to watch.

Coco's brow creased. 'Well, are you sure you're cut out for this?' She had the list in her hand, was holding it up so I could see my name, *N. Whittaker* next to Sandy.

I wanted to tell her that I had been in a feature film, but I could guess her reaction. She'd scoff and ask me how many cinemas it had showed in. Then it would all descend into remarks about it all being a front for money-laundering or whatever, and matters would be made worse. So I didn't say anything.

She changed her voice as if talking to a baby. 'Because you're going to be singing in front of a lot of people, N. Whittaker. A lot of important people. People who will be there on my recommendation, and I don't want to let them down. If you can't sing in front of little old us, then maybe . . .' She paused, shrugged, flapped the paper so it brushed my nose. 'Maybe this isn't quite right for you.'

I ran my tongue over my lips, waiting. I knew she wasn't done, and it seemed pointless jumping in before she'd finished. I held her gaze, praying she couldn't hear my heart thumping in my chest or see the sweat on my palms.

'It's certainly not a failing to admit that you can't do something,' she said, voice soft as caramel. 'That something might be a little too big for you. Me, I can sing wherever I am. Because I'm a professional.' At that she bit her lip for a second, then with a massive smile on her face broke into an impromptu version of *Crazy in Love* – so uber-confident that what should have been excruciating actually had the crowd clapping and cheering around us.

When it was over, she threw back her hair and laughed. 'A real actress, Norah, can turn it on like *that*.' And she clicked her fingers.

The others watched. The Beyoncé moves had tipped the crowd in her favour. I could see Ezra, slightly to the side, impassive but intrigued. They were watching, waiting, needing me to validate Mr Benson's choice.

I ran through my options. To sing now would be on her orders alone, and that would make me look weak and feel weak. Worse, if I messed it up – which was likely because I was panicked – she'd have even more ammo. But not singing at all was somehow making my casting appear unjustified.

And the longer I stood silent, the worse it was getting.

'It's not looking good,' Verity piped up, twisting her lolly gleefully between her lips. 'Maybe you should have a word with Mr Benson, Coco. Don't you think, Ezra?'

Ezra just shook his head, like this was all beneath him.

'I think you should,' Rollo pitched in.

Coco winked, and Rollo grinned like he'd been offered the Crown Jewels.

'The thing is, Norah,' Coco said, 'Mr B often likes to champion the underdog. It's his thing, you know. Challenging privilege and all that. So, it's not that you're not a fine singer. I'm sure you are. But he's only doing it to try and even things out, yeah? Which would be great, if this wasn't going to be in front of so many people. Every year we give people the best. And I think we all know that you're not the best. You wouldn't want people feeling sorry for you, would you?'

She was messing with my head. I couldn't see Daniel any more. At that moment I hated her.

'I think you should be the one to tell him, though, that you think he's made a mistake,' Coco purred. 'That you know deep down you're not lead material.'

'Coco,' Ezra cut in, voice almost a sigh.

But she carried on as if no one had spoken. 'It takes courage to admit the truth,' she said, and she smiled. It was the same stretched fake smile that I had seen on my mum's face as she danced on the boat last night.

In that moment I didn't know deep down if I was good

enough. But I did know that I was going home that night and I was telling my dad I had got the lead and I was going to see on his face a genuine smile. One that lit up his eyes and made him forget whatever had happened in his day. In our family at the moment, you didn't give up the good bits, however hard you had to fight to keep them.

So I opened my mouth and I sang. Against my better judgment, I proved myself to her.

I could hear my voice, quiet but purposeful, softly fill the corridor like feathers in the wind. They all paused.

Coco angled her head like a bird of prey, masking her surprise with a cool assessing sneer.

I could imagine Jess with one brow raised in disbelief that I had caved to the pressure. But this place did that to you. Its grand corridors and imposing lighting, huge windows and dark-stained floor, its air of history and privilege, wealth and entitlement, its matching uniforms and the beautiful, bronzed faces of the elite.

I was stopped by the sound of stark, slow clapping. Mr Watts had come out of the staff room.

'That's enough, thank you,' he said. 'Detention after school, Whittaker. "Why I must not sing in the corridor". I might remind you that this is a school, not the bloody *X Factor*. Now, the rest of you, clear off or you'll all be in with her.'

Coco stalked away, sniggering, arms linked with Verity.

Outside, she paused so I almost bumped into her. Verity hung off her arm, eyes running over me with bored disinterest.

'You were OK, I'll admit it,' Coco said, lips pursing in what was meant to be a humble pout. 'Not too bad.'

The sun glinted off the marble flagstones and intricate box-hedge topiary that lined the path.

I waited.

'So I'm prepared to see how it goes,' she said with a shake of her hair, as if she'd just granted me the role herself.

'OK,' I said.

'Good,' she said, and did a little movement with her lips that could have been nothing or it could have been a smile. It was too quick to catch. Whatever it was it made me wary. 'Let's go, Vee,' she said, tugging slightly on Verity's arm so they turned as one.

I stayed where I was, watching them go.

'Oh!' At the steps Coco paused and turned, her hand on the door. 'I forgot to say –'

I raised my eyebrows waiting to hear.

Coco took one step back towards me. 'My dad has a lawyer friend who I think is part of your dad's trial. He said there'd been some really positive progress,' she said, eyes soft and voice flat with sincerity.

'Yeah?' I said, incredulous. Waiting. She didn't fool me.

She nodded, smiling encouragingly, as if everything that

had gone before had never happened. 'They say he's definitely going to rot in jail.'

I saw Verity hold in a snigger as Coco squeezed her arm and they sashayed away.

I had known what was coming. I wasn't stupid enough to think she was suddenly sweetness and light and on my side. But I hadn't expected someone I barely knew to find such pleasure in the destruction of my family. I was walloped. Struck rigid. I didn't make it to the loos before the tears were rolling hot down my face. I had to hide in the cleaner's office where the mops and buckets were kept and shelves were stacked with industrial blue tissue paper. I ripped open one of the cellophaned packets of tissue and blew my nose. The paper felt like sandpaper on my skin.

It was only as I was wiping away tears of shock and fear and white-hot fury that I saw the phone next to a kettle and some tea-stained mugs. An old black landline that didn't look like it had been used in years. I stared at it in disbelief. A lifeline.

My hand hovered over the receiver, fearful that someone might come in and catch me. Then I realised I didn't care.

I knew Jess's mobile number by heart. As it rang, I crossed my fingers she wasn't in the gym doing an extra training session, unable to hear her phone because it was in her bag. Then I heard her voice. 'Hello?' she said, confused by the unknown number.

'Jess, it's Norah.'

'Norah?' I could hear her surprise. 'What's wrong, are you OK?'

'Yeah, I'm fine,' I said, picking at the strip of cellophane I'd torn off the blue-tissue packaging. It was really calming to hear her voice. 'I just have to talk to someone about what's just happened.'

'Why what's just happened?' It sounded like she was chewing on something.

'Are you eating?' I said. 'Where are you?'

'At school, on one of the benches outside. I'm just having my lunch because training ran over.'

It was all so familiar. I pictured her on one of the lichen-stained picnic benches out the back of school by the basketball court, with her sandwiches and Hula Hoops, probably a Diet Coke as well or a Capri Sun.

'Go on then,' she said, through a mouthful of sandwich.

'Oh, Jess, it's so horrendous here,' I said, plonking myself down on the twirly desk chair by the phone. The shame and upset dissipating as it became a story for someone I knew would appreciate every minute detail. And Jess did. She gasped and gagged and made me laugh as I told her all about Coco, the cord of the phone twisted round my finger, my face remembering what it was like to really smile.

Then I heard the bell ring at her end. A second before the one rang at Chelsea High to signify the end of break.

'I have to go,' she said.

'Me too,' I replied, sad it was over. 'What have you got now?'

'Double Art.'

'Oh, I'm jealous,' I said. 'I have Geography.'

'Is Geography as bad there as it is here?'

'Worse.'

I heard her stand up and scrunch up her lunch rubbish. 'Well, good luck with your "Why I must not sing in the corridor" detention.'

'Thanks,' I replied, reluctant to put the phone down.

'I really have to go now. Bye, Norah.'

I hung up, back to being alone. But as I chucked my scrunched-up bit of blue tissue in the bin, I realised how much better I felt. I was recharged. Even the rest of the Chelsea High day didn't seem so bad.

CHAPTER TWELVE

After detention I cycled home faster than I've ever cycled in my life. Weaving in and out of traffic, round pedestrians, up on the pavement, wrong way down a one-way street, till I was clattering down the jetty to the boat, skidding to a halt and jumping off as a man in one of the barges shouted, 'No cycling! What's wrong with people?'

I wanted to tell my dad my news about getting the lead part in the play. I wanted to make his day better with my casting coup, to give him the injection of happiness that talking to Jess had given me. I had sat watching the clock all afternoon, thinking how this little nugget would counter some of the stress he was having to deal with in the day.

When I reached the boat, I saw my mum sitting on the deck in her pyjamas: a buttercup yellow T-shirt and pair of threadbare brown temple trousers she'd got on a trip to Jaipur when she used to work in corporate fashion. She was just finishing a cup of tea when she saw me. Her eyes were tired and glazed.

'There's dinner in the oven,' she said, standing up and heading into the soft yellow glow of the boat. 'Your father has gone out.'

That meant he was in the pub. My shoulders sagged.

The man who had shouted at me a second ago about the cycling walked past me on the jetty, and sighed when he had to toss a piece of our broken bunting back on to our boat.

My place of safety and harmony was fast becoming a place of sadness and shame. The garish colours of our flaking paint, the silly pot plants dying in their old tin cans, the frayed bunting. Almost overnight, our old stuff had lost its charm. Compared to the flash minimalist barge next door, we were an eyesore.

I threw my bike at the railing in fury. Caught it just before it slipped into the river. Then I sat in my mum's still-warm chair and I waited for my dad to get back. Clutching tight in my chest the news that I knew might make him smile, if only for a minute.

I woke up as my mum was trying but failing to lift me.

'What's going on?' I was all confused, dreaming of school plays on the island, Coco slow-clapping in the audience.

'You're too heavy for me.' My mum laughed softly.

'What time is it?' I asked. The sky black, the waves lapping.

'Late,' she said. 'I didn't know you were out here. Norah, you're freezing.'

I shivered then. 'Is Dad back?'

'No.'

I followed her back into the boat, my steps jarring from

muscles frozen into place. 'What's going on, Mum? Is it really bad?'

She flicked on the kettle, making hot chocolate to warm me up. 'It's not good,' she said.

'There's very little evidence to prove your father is telling the truth.'

'But he *is* telling the truth,' I said.

'I know,' she replied. 'We know your dad's a good person. But the law likes facts. And there's a lot of different versions of events going round that court room.'

I looked down at the floor, not wanting to ask the next question, but having to. 'Is he going to jail?' She winced, as if by asking I had broken a silent code. Without looking at me, she poured hot water into the chocolate and said, matter-of-fact, 'The world would be a very unfair place if he does.'

The first run-through of *Grease* was in the drama department after school. I'd told my mum that I wouldn't be back till late. The suggestion she give me my phone back was considered, till she turned it on and a slew of horrible texts came through that she wouldn't even show me. I knew they were horrible only because her eyes narrowed and she mouthed 'little bitches'. I was glad I hadn't seen, but was also desperate to see.

It was a table-read rehearsal, which meant we all sat round on plastic chairs – there was no table – and we read the script through in full minus the songs. We'd changed out of our school uniform into comfier clothes. I was wearing black leggings and a hoodie from the Mulberry Island Theatre Society, which was white with maroon writing and had Norah printed on the front and a screen print of the *Singing in the Rain* poster on the back because that was the last production I'd done with them. I'd only been chorus because the society was all ages, and there were a lot of amazing old actors and musicians living on the island. The productions were like professional events, the cast so stellar it always sold out. I should have had that fact ready as a comeback for Coco when she was making out I would let the show down. We'd get write-ups in the paper and quite often made it to local TV news. My mum and Jackie would always do the costumes.

In *Singing in the Rain* my dad had played Cosmo, the comic lead. It was a part made for him: all acrobatics, silly walks and a show-stealing solo. Everyone thought he was just a natural joker, but I'd been privy to his endless rehearsals at home on the boat. 'Always like a duck, Norah,' he'd say, 'calm and unruffled on the outside,' and I'd say, 'But paddling like the devil underneath.' He would make it look effortless.

'Nice jumper,' Coco sneered as she pulled up a chair.

Coco, of course, was not wearing an old hoodie. Coco was wearing a cashmere cream sweater, the cuffs hanging like silk cocoons down over her hands, her leggings were some expensive luxe sports brand, her make-up flawless. Ezra appeared next to her. He had on faded blue jeans, the hems threadbare, black flipflops and a black T-shirt. I tried not to stare. Freddie wore grey sweatpants and a marl-grey T-shirt, black hair tied back in a knot, legs stretched out in front of him. Emmeline slipped into the seat next to mine with a shy sort of smile and a 'Hi.' It felt like we were circling a tentative friendship since she'd been to my mum's Portobello stall.

But then Coco called, 'There's a seat here, Em,' and pointed to a vacant chair next to Verity, who was stretched out in a black velour tracksuit examining her nails.

Emmeline moved to sit by Verity. She was dressed similarly to Coco, in pale pink cashmere and soft grey lounge pants. I couldn't believe she would move just because Coco said to. I wondered if I would do the same were I under Coco's rule. Tabitha came in late, dressed in a skirt, tights and a peach blouse and slid into the spare seat next to me.

Mr Benson, of course, was wearing his fleece. 'We'll read from the top. Get a feel for your characters, experiment. You can do no wrong tonight.'

We skipped over the opening song which would be me and Ezra, forlorn that we couldn't be together after a summer romance. Then there was me arriving at the school unexpectedly after a change of plan, then Rizzo teasingly introducing me to Ezra's character, Danny, who is torn between keeping his cool in front of his crew and being excited to see me. The read-through didn't start brilliantly. I got embarrassed and kept fumbling my lines. Still sulking about not getting the lead, Coco muttered her bits. Ezra kept scruffing up his hair as he read, I think for something to do.

At one point Mr Benson held up his hand and said, 'We're playing it British, so you can cut the dreadful American accents.'

Coco made a face. 'Mine's pretty good.'

Freddie said, 'Yeah! Me too,' like he'd been insulted.

Mr Benson took off his glasses and rubbed his eyes. 'Some are better than others,' he said diplomatically. 'Now carry on, let's get some flow.'

Coco muttered, 'Mine's fine.'

Assistant Director Daniel took Mr Benson's weariness as a cue. Clapping his hands together, he said, 'From the top, people.' He was a very serious apprentice, dressing the part in a waistcoat over an olive-green T-shirt and a flat cap.

Ezra looked confused. 'Do you mean top of the page?'

Daniel nodded like he was an imbecile.

Freddie sniggered. Ezra elbowed him. Coco crossed her legs and preened as she watched, her expression suggesting there would be none of this muddle if she were the lead.

Ezra went again. It was a different scene, one without me. I watched his mouth move and his eyes twinkle as he relaxed into character, bantering with Freddie's character, Kenickie. I thought about the trophy cabinet where he'd been holding the cup, grinning next to Rollo. I wondered what had happened to change things.

'And good, skip the song,' Mr Benson shouted as he turned the page, trying to keep up the momentum.

Ezra sat back, draping his arm along the back of Coco's chair, smiling, high on his performance. She took the movement as a cue to rest her cheek momentarily on his hand, then sit up and retie her hair, as if knowing she couldn't push for too much.

I suddenly realised I was going to have to kiss him. At some point in the future, our lips would touch. I'd thought about it before, when I got the part, when I went to sleep at night, but never when looking directly at the lips in question. They were perfect lips, the type you'd draw on a picture, a neat cupid's bow, top lip same thickness as bottom. I wondered if Coco had kissed them. Of course she had. I wondered if I would put my hands to his cheeks, where the bones were sharp like razors. If my thumbs would graze the tiny creases by his eyes when he smiled.

I had kissed two other boys before. James Robertson and Michael Wharton. Both lived on the island. Both I'd known since I was little. James was skinnier and shorter than me, and we'd kissed at one of the summer barbecues for something interesting to do. It hadn't meant anything. His lips had been hard and cold and skinny. We hadn't kissed again. Michael I'd been out with for a month at the beginning of summer. We'd held hands as we walked home and my mum had cooked us spaghetti bolognaise and my dad had taught him how to play the card game Gin Rummy. The odd kiss had been like a practical solution to the fact we got on pretty well. For him, because he had three really young chaotic siblings, he'd loved being round mine. I think he would have preferred to be my brother than my boyfriend. It had been nice, though. I'd bought him a birthday present. Then my dad was arrested and my world turned upside down. Michael's dad had invested a good chunk of his savings. He didn't come round after that and, when I saw him in the street, it was apparent he was more heartbroken by my dad letting him down than by not being able to see me any more.

I shouldn't want to kiss Ezra, but there was something enticing about it – especially considering I would never in my life appear on his radar as someone worth kissing. Yet, in the guise of someone else, we would kiss. It was like sampling something I couldn't afford, made doubly sweet by the fact I couldn't have it. I would taste what his lips tasted of. I would feel what they felt like.

I blushed.

'Pick it up, Norah. Pay attention,' Daniel called, pulling no punches in his new role.

My cheeks were flaming. Coco's eyes narrowed like she knew exactly what I'd been thinking.

But then I focused on the script, and I didn't know anything else because I was gone. I was someone else. I had escaped reality and stepped into something new. That was what I did this for: the immersion, the swallowed-up-ness. No jostling for position, no wishing for friendships, no worries, no fears, no hopes. This was me, alive.

'Nice,' said Mr Benson when my bit was done. 'Coco, this is you. You need to be quicker on the uptake than that.'

I left the read-through on a high. I felt like as long as I had this little pocket of happiness and escape in my life, then I could cope with everything else.

It didn't matter that Coco, Verity and Freddie strolled out together, shouting to Daniel that they'd see him at Sorrentos. Daniel was too busy with Mr Benson for me to hang around and wait on the off-chance he might invite me to tag along. Ditto Emmeline, who was in deep discussion about something with Ezra.

It didn't matter that there was no one home when I got back to the cold, messy boat, dirty washing-up still in the sink.

It didn't matter that when my parents came home and thought I was asleep, I heard my dad pacing, saying, 'I can't believe Old Percy has to sell his boat, Lois. And, Christ, did you know Marty Brown had a heart attack from stress? Why didn't we know that?'

Marty Brown. Becky's dad. Oh my god. I lay in bed, remembering the hate-texts she'd sent, thinking about poor Old Percy's beautiful Mississippi steamboat up for sale, the island crumbling, my pillow wet with silent tears I was trying to wipe away with the duvet.

It didn't matter.

Except sometimes it was hard to keep reminding myself of that fact.

The stall at the weekend was terrible. My mum, pale and monosyllabic, bristling when Big Dave went through the court case point by point.

'Bill's coming off a bit better than the other two, but those lawyers are good. They tie them in knots, don't they? You need to tell Bill not to look so flustered.' Dave had been in the public gallery. He spoke like he'd got all the answers. 'You can see him start to look shifty when someone's on the stand saying something he doesn't like. Tell him to look a bit more relaxed. He looks guilty half the time, that's the problem. He's got too much expression on his face. You got all that money now; you need to buy him a face coach.'

Jackie shooed him away, but I saw her later, chatting with Big Dave and Jim from the burger van, secretly agreeing with them, making signals with her face and hands like an American football coach during a game. Me? I would have had my fingers in my ears if I could, going la la la. Instead I straightened the clothes on the menswear rail, repeating my lines under my breath.

And then there followed another stilted Sunday, eating dry cake at my grandparents' house. My grandmother didn't flee in tears this time, so there was no hint of the camaraderie between me and my grandfather that we'd had on the last visit. Instead I was asked how often I went to church, and had to face my grandmother's shocked disappointment at my answer.

Ludo lay on the carpet farting occasionally. The smell was horrific, but no one commented. My grandmother just did a prim cough and asked if I'd like more tea, as if the dreadful smell would disappear if we ignored it. Much like our own swirling mass of discontent.

At school, during the day, I was still lonely. My acquaintance with Daniel and Emmeline hadn't quite reached the level where I could tag along. If I saw them in the lunch hall, then sometimes I'd sit with them if they weren't with Coco and her lot, but they didn't wait for me when the bell went or anything like that. In lessons they sat next to each other, and I sat at whatever available desk there was. Except for English when I had started to sit next to Tabitha. I breathed a sigh of relief every time I saw that on my timetable. At break, quite often I sat on my own pretending to learn lines that I already knew by heart while looking at everyone else huddled in groups chatting or playing rugby, polo and hockey out on the fields.

So the following week, when we'd had a really funny rehearsal – run by Daniel, all jazz hands, singing each other's songs, girls doing the boys' bits and vice versa, lots of laughs, even Coco smiling, me wearing my mum's best pale pink silk long-sleeve and grey leggings (not making my hoodie mistake again) – and at the end Freddie held the door and said, 'Norah, you coming?' I practically whooped with delight.

Of course I didn't. I was now a demure-silk-top-wearing kind of person who spent all their energy trying to play it effortlessly cool. Instead I said, 'Yeah, OK,' with a nonchalant shrug like I could take it or leave it.

I had told my mum I would be home straight from rehearsal. They had a big meeting with solicitors and lawyers. She'd asked if I could be on hand to make teas and coffees because she needed all her energies to concentrate on details that were becoming more and more complicated by the day.

But Freddie would only hold the door for a bit. Tabitha would only pause and wait for me for so long. This was the only time Daniel would scurry up next to me and whisper, 'Let's go, go, go before Mr Benson comes back. Save me. Now, now, leave!' So I went with them, ignoring the fact my mum would be waiting. I wouldn't be long. She could make the first round of teas.

Ezra was up ahead, dressed in black tracksuit pants and a green T-shirt. He glanced back. 'That was alright tonight,' he said when he saw me. 'You were good.'

The compliment made my whole face smile. I fell into step with him. 'You weren't too bad yourself.'

He laughed. 'I wasn't the best. Not my day.'

I shrugged. 'I thought you were good.'

'Thanks,' he said, like he actually appreciated it.

We came through the double doors into the cool evening air. I liked the way walking with Ezra and Freddie, Daniel and Tabitha made me feel accepted, included – visible.

Coco was on the pavement outside with Verity. She rolled her eyes when she saw me but turned away like she couldn't be bothered to complain. Rollo appeared at the side entrance with his lacrosse stick. I wondered if there was a sport he didn't play.

Stepping into Sorrentos was like everything I thought it would be – crammed, loud, smelling of tomato sauce and pizza dough, packed full of life and energy and exuberant hellos. Emmeline was already there, reading her book and drinking a vanilla milkshake. There were only two other chairs at her table. Daniel sat down next to her and Tabitha opposite. All the others slid into the booth opposite, their seats seemingly assigned.

I hesitated, not knowing where to sit. Everything on the verge of being ruined when Tabitha slid over and said, 'Darls, you can share my seat. My arse is huge but not that huge, I promise.'

I felt a rush of gratitude for Tabitha as I perched on the edge of her seat. But my eye was drawn to Coco et al crammed into the booth opposite, home to the leaders of the pack. Rollo took up the whole corner, legs and arms spread wide. Freddie sat right up on the back of the booth, his feet either side of

Verity, talking over her head. Ezra was on the edge, Coco opposite, filming the set-up on her phone and then finishing by saying something to the camera. She replayed it, scowled and did it again. This time Freddie stuck out his tongue and Ezra covered his face. On our table Daniel was huffing about artistic differences with Mr Benson. Tabitha was telling me a story but I wasn't listening. When the harassed waiter came over I ordered the infamous grilled cheese along with everyone else, except Verity who ordered a cucumber salad and Coco who purred, 'You know how I like it, Mario,' when it came to her turn.

I looked out of the window at the pavement, the red-brick mansions opposite, the people stalking past on their phones. I was on the inside looking out. Exactly where I'd wanted to be.

In the reflection I could see Daniel talking to Ezra about how he could play a scene differently and Ezra leaning over, closer to our table than his as he listened.

'Norah, what do you think?' Daniel asked. 'I think we need a rehearsal just the two of you, tomorrow,' Daniel said, pulling out his iPad to check his availability. 'I've got a forty-five-minute window after school.'

Ezra nodded. He didn't need to check.

'Norah?' Daniel asked.

'I'm free.'

'We have Maths in the morning. You'll have to try and not get detention,' Daniel added.

Ezra glanced up. 'You get a lot of detention?' he said, surprised.

'I'm not Mr Watts's favourite person,' I replied with a shrug.

He laughed.

Never before had detention felt so glamorous.

Coco looked up at the sound of Ezra's laugh. 'What are you talking about?'

'Just an extra rehearsal,' Ezra said, casually dismissive.

'When? Should I come?' she said, already looking at her calendar.

'You're OK, Coco,' Daniel said, cheeks going a little red. 'It's just Norah and Ezra.'

'Oh right.' She put her phone away. 'Fine. I have polo this week anyway.' She gave a toss of her hair and nearly knocked the waiter with her elbow as he appeared with a giant tray of sandwiches.

'Ah, excuse me!' the waiter said, stumbling back. A bottle of San Pellegrino – Coco's – wobbled and smashed to the floor.

I laughed, purely out of nerves. My hand immediately up to my mouth to stop myself but Coco had heard. Her eyes moved my way like a wolf picking up a scent. Everyone else was grabbing their orders as another waiter came to mop up the spill. But Coco just stayed looking at me.

I swallowed, betraying my fear.

Then someone else hurried over with another San Pellegrino and proffered it with a profuse apology and Coco was back, all big toothy smile and quips about how dangerous her huge and perfect hair could be.

In my pocket I felt my pager vibrate with a message I knew was from my mum.

'Last one?' the waiter called, holding up a spare sandwich.

'That's mine,' I said, and he reached over and placed it down on the table.

Coco started to tell a story, and everyone turned her way to listen as she held court.

My pager buzzed again and again.

I took a bite of my long-anticipated grilled cheese, but it didn't taste anywhere near as good as it should have done.

CHAPTER THIRTEEN

'Where have you been?' my mum hissed, the front door thrown open as soon as I hauled my bike up on to the front of the boat. 'For goodness' sake! I thought you were dead. I've been calling hospitals. You selfish, selfish little girl. As if I didn't have enough . . .' She paused. Put the heel of her hand to her forehead. I waited. Heart thudding. 'Just get inside.'

I locked my bike to the railing, bottom lip trembling. She'd never spoken to me like that before. Like I was a problem. On the island I bowled home whenever. But then again, there were only about three places I might have been.

Inside, the boat was full of people in suits. There were papers all over the table, my dad had his tie undone and askew, shaking his head as a man next to him with thin wire glasses asked him a series of questions.

I tried to scurry past, invisible.

My mum had already resumed her seat. Her slightly greasy hair was scraped back, her face with a glow of sweat like all her make-up had rubbed off during a stressful day.

'Norah, everyone needs tea and coffee,' she said without looking up, her jaw rigid.

I put the kettle on.

All the next day I was nervous about the evening's rehearsal. Hyper-aware it would be just me and Ezra. I syphoned a grey fine-knit woollen jumper from a pile of clothes my mum was mending for the stall at the weekend. Her invisible stitching was second-to-none, and she managed to make anything look good as new. My intention was to hand-wash it when I got back and replace it as soon as it was dry. It looked good, especially with my hair, which was increasingly shiny since I'd wrapped it in a mixture of whisked egg and olive oil after reading up tips in an old *Vogue* beauty book of my mum's.

I needed to look good. I needed to feel good. The pretence was that we were going to work on our chemistry, our bond – but I had this feeling that this was to get the kissing out of the way.

Daniel had booked the smallest of the rehearsal rooms. It was like a white pod with two chairs, black carpet and a giant yucca plant in the corner. One wall was a window with a view out over the playing fields. There were hockey and rugby practice games over on the far pitches and polo in the distance. I imagined I could see Coco's hair flying.

The space was claustrophobically intimate.

Ezra was sitting with his forearms on his knees, his hair

freshly washed after games. He smelt of shower gel and clean clothes. He was wearing jeans and a red sweatshirt that had been washed so much it had turned raspberry. I knew he did Taekwondo now rather than hockey. I did netball. On the island I'd been one of the best. Here I'd be lucky to scrape into the C team.

'We're going to start with something different. Mr Benson's idea. You're just going to chat in character,' said Daniel, leaning up against the big picture window.

I saw Ezra cringe at the idea. Never had I wanted to be outside more.

'What should we say?' he asked.

'Don't ask me,' said Daniel, a little smug on his power. 'I'm not here. Off you go.'

Ezra ran his hand through his hair.

I took a deep breath. *I'm not me.*

My wool top was too hot. I pulled at the neck.

Then in the silence Ezra said, 'Come here often?'

I laughed.

'It's my school,' I said.

'No kidding. Mine too. Like it?'

'It's OK.'

'Better than where you were before?'

'Different,' I said.

'Norah, you're very rigid. Try and relax a bit,' Daniel interjected.

Suddenly I was back to being Norah in this tiny room in my too hot-jumper.

I was rigid about the whole thing. I couldn't help it. All I could think about was the fact we might have to kiss.

'You start this time, Norah,' Daniel said. 'Maybe flirt a little.'

'OK,' I said. But my brain short-circuited at the suggestion and went completely blank.

Ezra was sitting watching, hands clasped, slight smirk on his lips.

I cleared my throat. 'I don't think Sandy would flirt.'

Daniel groaned. 'Well, she'd do something. Jesus, Norah, it's just warming up.'

'OK,' I said.

All I seemed to be saying was OK. I moved closer to Ezra. I could feel myself getting more awkward. He looked up at me, brow raised in anticipation. I started to say, 'Hello –' but as soon as I said it, I giggled.

Ezra grinned down at the floor.

Daniel sighed. 'Come on, Norah.'

'Sorry,' I said. 'Sorry.'

Daniel narrowed his eyes. 'Is it because of the kissing?'

'No!' I said, embarrassed, cheeks flaming from the itchy wool top.

Ezra stood up, his hands on his hips, damp hair slicked back. 'Do you want to just get it over with?' he asked, completely unfazed.

I made a face. I have no idea what it looked like. It was meant to convey nonchalance but it definitely didn't. The nerves were making my hands shake.

'Good idea,' said Daniel, very serious. 'Break the tension.'

'No,' I said and took an involuntary step back.

Both boys looked at me.

Daniel sucked in his top lip. 'So what are we going to do?'

I stayed where I was, eyes fixed on the carpet, furious that I'd stepped back. Why couldn't I just get on with it? My heart was thudding. I really wanted to take my jumper off.

It was Ezra who spoke in the end. 'It's this room,' he said. 'It's too –' He gestured with his hand. 'Too bare.'

'Bare?' Daniel looked puzzled.

'This is not the environment that two people are going to kiss. Especially not with you watching, Dan,' Ezra said with a grin.

'I hate to break it to you, but a whole lot more people are going to be watching soon.'

'I know. But first time, it's weird.' Ezra pointed between himself and me.

I knew he didn't find it weird. He was doing this for me. I took a deep breath, starting to relax.

'We need to get to know each other,' he went on.

I nodded. Just happy for the reprieve.

'What are you doing Saturday?'

'Nothing in the afternoon,' I said.

'OK,' Ezra said. 'I'll meet you Saturday. Battersea Park?'

Daniel was checking on his calendar. 'I'm busy Saturday afternoon.'

'Not you, Dan,' Ezra said. 'Just me and Norah. That work for you, Norah?'

I swallowed.

'Yes,' I said, before I had a chance to think about it.

I must have looked as terrified as I felt because when Ezra picked up his bag, he bashed me on the shoulder and said, 'Don't worry. It won't be that bad.'

CHAPTER FOURTEEN

Saturday at the stall I could barely concentrate. I kept looking at my watch, wishing the morning away while also hoping time might slow. The day was bright, sunshine streaming under the bridge in wide beams, but still cold. I had my hat pulled low and my scarf up round my nose with the aim of keeping my head down and getting on with it.

Rehearsals were starting to take up all my spare time and I was glad. I was home to have breakfast, but more often than not made sandwiches to take for dinner or reheated something when I got back before going to my room. My parents were barely there, always some meeting somewhere or muttering around the boat in hushed tones. If I asked questions, I got quick harassed answers, as if there wasn't enough time in the day to fill me in. Twice my grandfather appeared and he and my dad took a walk. My mum sat at the table and mended clothes for the stall, hemming dresses and darning holes. She hadn't noticed the wool top I'd slipped back into the pile, now smelling sweet of rose hand-wash. She looked thin and tired. Her smile hadn't returned since the night I came in late. Radio

4 prattled on in the background as usual. 'It's just background noise,' she used to say, asking me and Jess – who came home with me for dinner every time her mum was on nights – about school, lessons, what we'd had for lunch, the new gossip. Now no one talked. The radio filled the silence as I ate my dinner.

It felt like we had never lived any other way. Fractured and fragmented. The court case bigger than all our lives. Like a spider's web, we were caught in limbo.

As Jackie and my mum stood warming their hands round takeaway coffees – I had declined – I busied myself at the back with the accessories, straightening out diamanté earrings and big chunky Bakelite necklaces.

'So how does the new evidence affect things?' Jackie's voice was low and hard to determine above the clatter of the market.

My hand stilled on a sparkly orange brooch.

My mum blew out a breath. 'I don't know. Bill's with his dad and the lawyer now. I don't know, Jackie.'

Jackie sighed. 'What a disaster.'

'Don't say that,' my mum snapped.

I stayed completely still. I'm not sure I breathed.

Jackie put her arm round my mum's shoulders.

My mum moved out of the embrace, spilling her coffee. As the liquid tipped down her coat she swore – then just dropped the cup, let it go completely, coffee sloshing out everywhere, staining the sleeves of the rack of men's shirts next to her. Then she started to cry. Not little tears but huge great wracking sobs.

I stood rooted to the ground.

Jackie pulled my mum back and pressed her face into the padding of her giant pink marshmallow coat. I could see my mum's shoulders shaking, her hands over her eyes. Jackie was whispering like she was soothing a baby.

I had never seen my mum cry like that. My dad, he cried a lot – at movies, songs, when the big ginger island cat killed a nest of baby robins, even *X Factor* auditions. But my mum, hardly ever. Or at least, never in front of me. It felt like it had all gone too far. It wasn't meant to snowball like this.

Big Dave looked over from his army surplus stall. He made a face at me to ask if my mum was OK. Weirdly I pretended I hadn't seen, just walked away to tidy the jumpers like I couldn't admit she was breaking down.

She stopped almost as soon as she started. Jackie led her to one of the fold-out chairs, guiding her like an invalid. My mum laughed and batted her away, then, once she was sitting, took out a handkerchief and blew her nose. 'I'm fine,' she said. 'Gosh, I don't know what came over me. Oh, look at all this coffee,' she said, taking in the spill.

'Norah and I will clear it up,' said Jackie.

My mum nodded but didn't look over at me. She just wiped her eyes and got her breathing back under control.

I felt like the ground beneath me was disintegrating. There was nothing to hold me in place.

My hand adjusted a grey jumper with white stars knitted into the sleeves. It was new on the stall – Jackie had bought the stock from a liquidation sale of a chain of boutiques. It was cashmere, soft as the fur of the baby rabbits we'd once rescued from a flood on the island, and had a two-hundred-pound price tag.

When no one was looking, I slipped it off the hanger and shoved it into my puffer jacket.

CHAPTER FIFTEEN

Ezra was waiting by the main Battersea Park gates, chucking a tennis ball against a tree trunk with his black sweatshirt sleeves pushed right up. The ball thwacked bang on centre of the wide oak, over and over.

The day had got warmer. I was hot from nerves and the cycle over, so I paused on my bike, and watched him for a second or two while getting my breath back and psyching myself up. I checked my reflection in a car wing mirror. I'd popped into Boots on the way to put on some expensive make-up from the tester tubes and pots, plus a slick of some glossy hair serum. I'd spritzed on some Chanel just because it was there, but now I couldn't work out if it was a bit too much.

I realised as I stood up from scrunching my hair in the wing mirror reflection that he'd seen me and immediately blushed. He watched with a grin as I walked my bike in through the main gates.

'Nice hair,' he said as I came closer. I wished my face back to its normal colour. 'Thanks,' I mumbled.

He lobbed the tennis ball out in the distance, across the grass. I frowned.

'It was just some dog's,' he said.

I made a face and he laughed, wiping his hands on his jeans. 'It's fine,' he said.

'Just dog slobber,' I replied.

He grinned, grabbing his bike from where it lay on the grass. I felt exponentially pleased with myself for making him smile.

'So what d'you want to do?' he asked, loping along, glancing around as if something fun might crop up.

'I don't mind,' I said.

We walked in awkward silence for a bit. I was wearing the star-print cashmere top I'd stolen from the stall. It felt lovely, all soft and expensive. I hoped it made me look the same.

He was in a black sweatshirt and jeans, normcore casual but all of it as pricey as it was unpretentious.

The sun was low over the trees, sparkling light like confetti on the ground.

'Nice bike,' he said, nodding towards my shabby Peugeot racer, which was white with orange and blue stripes along with the odd fleck of rust.

'It's really old,' I said, pausing. It was just my bike. 'It washed up on the shore near where we used to live, My dad fixed it up.'

'No way.' The corner of his mouth tilted up.

I suddenly saw my bike in a different light. 'Yeah, I love it.'

'It's a classic,' he said. And somehow, in contrast, it made his bike look almost too brand new. Gleaming. It was at least a couple of grand's worth, the type people used for triathlon.

'So, really, what do you want to do?' he asked again.

'I *really* don't know.' It was surreal enough being with him in the park. My brain couldn't come up with a plan of action as well.

He smiled and shook his head, like the two of us were useless. We stopped walking and looked around. There weren't many people out. It was sunny but cold. The trees were all the colours of autumn, the pavement littered with amber leaves. I tried to think of something really exciting that we could do, but came up blank. The sun went behind a cloud. I shivered, pulling my hands into my cuffs, wondering what he would be doing if he was with his friends right now. I became suddenly aware that we were meeting because of the play rather than anything else. I didn't want to feel like a burden. I wracked my brains, but couldn't come up with anything more crazy than, 'Do you want to go for a cycle?'

He seemed genuinely pleased with the simplicity of it. 'Yeah,' he said, eyes crinkling with approval.

He got on his bike. I got on mine, but realised I had a twig stuck in the wheel so had to get off again. One of the branches had stuck in the spoke, making it tricky to pull out. It meant he went ahead, standing up on his pedals, looking back over his shoulder to see where I was. When he saw I hadn't even started moving he turned the bike in a circle almost on the

167

spot. 'What are you doing?' he called.

'Nothing,' I said, pedalling to catch up.

He zigzagged across the empty path. Arms crossed, no hands as he cycled. It felt like he was showing off and that made me smile inside.

We weaved our way round some pedestrians and a golden retriever.

'Down here,' he shouted, nodding towards a side path.

'We're not allowed to cycle down there,' I said, pointing to the sign with the crossed-out bicycle.

He looked over his shoulder. 'What do you think's going to happen?'

I caught up, taking in his profile, his shaggy hair, eyebrows like the flick of a black pen, the perfect cupid's bow of his lips. 'Someone might tell us off?' I said without much conviction.

He snorted a laugh, then dipped down on to the shingle path canopied with trees, shaking his head as if my concern was beneath him.

Someone did tell us off. A man in a flat cap with two yappy dogs who snapped at Ezra's feet.

'Serves you right,' I remarked as we popped back out on to the bike track, vindication giving me confidence.

We cycled side by side for a bit, silently smiling.

It made a nice change to be outside. Too much of my life at the moment was spent in the dark melancholy of the boat, or the windowless theatre where it was difficult to know if it was night or day.

The boating lake was on our left, the water glass-flat, like a mirror for the swans and the trees.

Ezra stopped and gestured towards the café on the edge of the lake.

'Do you want a drink?' he said.

I braked next to him. 'I don't have any money,' I said.

He laughed good-naturedly, raking his hair back with his hand. 'I was offering.' He leaned his bike against one of the picnic tables. Then, glancing at the window of the café where a sign read 'Cash only', he got some change out of his pocket and said with a rueful smile, 'Actually I'm not sure I've got enough.'

'I'm fine, honestly,' I said, climbing on to the picnic table with my feet on the bench.

Ezra jogged over to the café. I watched him until he disappeared inside, absorbing his casual confidence, pretending to be looking at some kids scaring the pigeons beside me. He seemed so different to the boys on the island, more grown-up somehow. Perhaps it was an inherent self-belief that came with wealth. I turned away, looking towards the lake where people were trying to navigate rowing boats around the pond.

After a couple of minutes, Ezra came back to the table with one can and two straws. Handing me the Coke, he said, eyes twinkling, 'Mine's the green straw.'

I laughed, caught slightly off guard by the sweetness of the gesture. 'Thanks,' I said. The metal of the can was cold, my fingers wet from condensation.

He sat on the table next to me. 'Don't backwash in it.'

'You can't backwash with a straw,' I pointed out.

He smiled, glancing across at me for a second, then back at the rowers. I could feel my cheeks pink at the attention.

We watched a couple failing miserably with their rowing boat, the whole thing toppling precariously as they beached on the far edge. The attendant in charge bellowed instructions from the bank. We passed the Coke between us, wincing and laughing at the flailing couple in the boat, bonded by the humour of someone else's disaster. Eventually the couple were rescued by the sighing attendant and their boat towed back.

Ezra handed me the almost empty Coke can.

'I don't want it, thanks,' I said, waving it away. 'Not after the whole backwash chat.'

He grinned. 'Me neither, actually.' And he chucked it into the nearby bin with perfect aim. Then he stretched his shoulders and leaned back, hands resting behind him on the picnic table. 'What do you want to do now?'

I looked at my watch. We'd been together nearly an hour.

'You got stuff to do?' he asked.

I shook my head, glancing across at him, still finding it hard to believe we were out together. This close I could see every mark on his skin, the slow fade of his tan, the faint smattering of freckles on his cheekbones. 'I thought you might.'

He shrugged. 'I don't have anything else to do.'

We sat side by side again in silence. I could hear him breathing. I stared ahead at the lake. I loved being on the water and the tangy smell, the sound of the rippling waves. Watching all the people rowing so badly was making me jealous. I found myself summoning up the courage to say, 'Do you want to take a boat out?'

Ezra weighed the idea up in his head.

I waited, almost holding my breath.

'Yeah, alright,' he said, and pushed himself off the picnic table.

I grinned down at the ground where pigeons pecked at the crumbs. His arm brushed against mine as we walked. For a moment I almost forgot to take the next step. The idea of me and him boating together on a Saturday afternoon was suddenly unreal. Like most of my life at the moment.

'You kids know how to row?' the boatman asked, sizing us up.

'I've done it at school,' Ezra said. 'I lived on an island,' I said, as if that explained things.

'Couple of hotshots,' the boatman said, pulling the rope of one of the wooden skiffs so it was level with the jetty and we could jump on board.

Ezra got in first. He held out his hand for me. I could get in by myself but I took it anyway, just to see what it felt like. His hand was cool, calloused from the hockey, his fingers long. My thumb touched the edge of his frayed cuff.

The boat wobbled as Ezra took the oars. 'Shall I start?'

'OK,' I said, leaning back against the stern. It was getting chilly, so I wrapped my arms round myself and pulled my hands into the sleeves of my jumper.

'Are you cold?' he asked, paddling us out into the middle of the pond. We were face to face, close in the little boat.

'A bit,' I said. 'But I'm alright.'

He stopped rowing for a second. 'Do you want my jumper?' he asked, tucking the oars under one arm to steady us, ready to take his sweatshirt off.

'No! Then you'd be cold.' The idea was absurd.

He seemed momentarily thrown by the logic, unused to having his chivalry denied. I wondered if Coco would have taken the jumper.

'I'll row for a bit,' I said, reaching to take the oars. 'It'll help me warm up.'

'Aye aye, captain.' Our hands brushed as he passed the oars over, then sat back against the bow.

There were two other boats out on the lake already but they were sticking near the shore. I paddled us right out and then round an island draped with weeping willow, where swans sat under the dappled canopy and the ground was covered in bird poo. The other side of the lake was all huge leafy rhododendron bushes, exactly like the ones on Mulberry Island that popped with red flowers every spring.

Ezra watched me, his dark eyes hooded. 'So you lived on an island?' he asked.

'Yeah.' I was starting to get a bit out of breath, overly conscious of his gaze. 'But not at the moment.'

'Where do you live now?' He sat up and beckoned for the oars.

'Over there.' I nodded in the direction of Battersea Reach. 'We live on a houseboat. We won't be here long, though. I'm hoping we'll be back home before Christmas.'

He nodded, taking the oars from me. I had to pause to catch my breath, unsure suddenly whether it was because I was tired, or because that was the first time those words had sounded like a lie.

Ezra kept on rowing further round the big willow tree island, getting so close as one point that we bumped the bank and the boat got half beached. I looked back, realising we were hidden from view by the draping curtain of the weeping willow.

'Wow,' I said, my attention caught by the willow leaves fluorescent with the sun behind them and the light flickering on the ground. It was magical.

'Pretty good, isn't it?' Ezra sat smiling, a little smug at my reaction.

'Have you been here before?' I asked. It was clear that he had.

He shrugged, all nonchalant. 'A couple of times.'

'With Coco?' I don't know why I said it. I think because it seemed like such a potentially romantic spot. Maybe I was jealous. It just came out, and I immediately wanted to suck it back in again.

Ezra gave a surprised laugh. 'Why do you think I would come here with Coco?'

I was blushing. 'I don't know. I thought the two of you went out.'

Ezra shook his head but didn't answer. A smile played on his lips.

I looked down at my hands, embarrassed that I'd brought up their relationship. That it meant I'd fished around at school for facts about him.

After a pause, he sat forward, elbows resting on his knees, dark hair flopping half over his eyes. 'I used to come with my brother. He really likes birds. He'd climb out on to the island and feed the swans.'

I eyed the huge white birds, a bit dubious as to whether I'd go close enough to feed one. 'That's sweet,' I said.

'Yeah, it was.' He didn't offer anything more, just lay back on the boat so his head rested on the lip of the bow. I watched him for a second then did the same, my head at the opposite end of the boat, my legs up next to his.

'We'd better not fall in,' I said.

'We won't.'

I stared up at the sunlight flickering through the willow, trying to stay relaxed despite our proximity. I could feel his knee touching mine. I listened to the water lap gently on the shore. 'Is your brother older or younger than you?' I asked.

There was a pause. I glanced over to see if he'd heard. His eyes were open, staring up at the sky, I saw the sharp line of his nose, his teeth biting on his lower lip. He was clearly thinking.

'Younger,' he said.

I imagined a younger version of Ezra, breaking hearts in the year below. 'Does he go to Chelsea High?'

Ezra sat up and the boat wobbled. 'You don't know?'

I sat up too, uncertain what was going on. 'Know what?'

'Seriously?'

'Seriously.' I was aware suddenly that our calm intimacy was broken. 'I don't know what you're talking about.'

His face was a silhouette, the willow leaves luminous behind him. 'He fell off a cliff in the summer. On the beach. He's ten.'

My eyes widened.

I could sense him checking my reaction, almost to gauge if I was lying. 'You really don't know this?' he asked, still uncertain, dark eyes assessing.

I wasn't sure how to convince him I was telling the truth. I didn't want this all to be over. 'Ezra, how would I know? No one tells me anything. I know nobody. No one talks to me at this bloody school,' I said.

He was still frowning, but I saw his shoulders relax as he decided to believe me.

I didn't move. Neither did he.

'Is he OK?' I asked, tentative.

'Not really,' he said with a bitter laugh as he dipped his hand in the water and flicked it, making ripples on the surface. 'He broke nearly every bone in his body.'

'Oh my god. How did it happen?' I asked, unsure if I was prying.

He brought his feet up to rest on the bench dividing us. 'We were on holiday. My family and Rollo's – we go every year. We'd climbed up – Rollo and me – and Josh, my brother, followed. I didn't see him. I didn't know he'd followed us. I thought he was down the beach with my parents.'

I watched him – the furrow of his brow, the tight line of his mouth. This close, his eyes looked a hundred different shades from amber to deep rich chocolate.

'The rocks were really loose,' he went on, rubbing his hand over his face. 'It was OK for me and Rollo but . . . well, you know. Josh wasn't as strong. I just remember seeing him at the bottom, broken.'

What must it have been like at the top of the cliff, looking down? I wondered if he had seen his brother fall. I thought about the scramble down the rocks when he'd have been praying it wasn't as bad as it looked.

As Ezra pushed his hands back through his hair, I saw his watch on his wrist. The face was cracked. I knew immediately that he'd been wearing it the day his brother fell.

'And how is he now?' I asked.

'He's in and out of hospital all the time. The list of injuries just went on and on. He broke both his legs, his arm, his foot, three ribs, and crushed a vertebra. That could have paralysed him. And his brain swelled. That was the scariest thing. No one even knew whether he would wake up.' Ezra took a deep breath. I wondered how many people he'd talked to about this. It didn't seem like many. 'It's worse because he's so little. It's a real cliché to say that I'd swap with him in a second, but I would.'

My panic about the trial suddenly seemed so small, so selfish and silly, when here was a guy wishing for his little brother's life back.

'God, it's awful. I just can't imagine . . .'

I didn't know what else to say so we sat there, the light shimmering between us.

Ezra blew out a resigned breath, then smiled at me like he was exhausted. I smiled back in sympathy. He lay back down in the boat. I did too. I could feel the cold shivering through my body, but I wouldn't have swapped the moment for the world.

We stared up at the bright blue sky through the leaves.

'You got any siblings?' he asked.

'No,' I said. Our willow tree canopy rustled like raindrops. 'But you didn't really need them on the island. We were all like family.'

'How do you feel now you've left?'

'A bit lost,' I said.

'I know what you mean,' he said.

It was easy to talk looking up at the sky. I stretched my hand up to see if I could brush the willow leaves but they were too high. I rested it behind my head instead.

I asked him about his parents and he said that it was all the same at home as it always had been except it was hollow. And time was slow. Evenings never-ending. His mum never looked him in the eye.

He talked about the dreams when he woke up because all he saw was his brother at the bottom of the cliff and the mornings when he forgot what had happened and the shock of the memory. He sat up on his elbows. 'Sometimes I want to turn back time so much that I can't believe it's not possible.'

The boat dipped as Ezra shifted his position. My fingers brushed against something behind me. I froze at the unexpected touch. Then suddenly something was biting me. A huge beak. A giant swan.

'Oh my god!' I shot up, yanking my hand away.

The swan hissed. I panicked. The boat lurched and tipped as Ezra sat bolt upright too.

'Shoo!' I shouted as the swan hissed again.

'Don't move!' Ezra shouted, the boat yawing precariously.

Another swan had joined the first and now there were two of them, hissing and getting really close. I tried to right the tipping of the boat. So did Ezra. And suddenly we were falling and the boat was rolling in slow motion and then the freezing water hit.

Every muscle in my body contracted as we splashed head first into the lake. I coughed and spluttered in the murky water with ice in my veins. Ezra was on his knees, wiping the water from his face. The swans retreated at the noise and chaos. I stood up, hands clenched with the cold, pushing my hair back from my face.

He looked up at me and laughed. I shook my head, my foot stuck in pond mulch, unable to believe this was happening. He reached to pull me out, stopping the boat from floating off with his other hand. My woollen jumper had stretched almost down to my thighs and was soaked. I swept my hair from my face and wiped lake water from my eyes. He was still holding my hand.

And then suddenly I wasn't thinking about being freezing cold because his face was really close to mine and he was looking down at me and I was looking up at him and I swallowed and I didn't feel at all like when we had meant to kiss in the rehearsal room. I felt like every nerve ending in my body was on fire. Like if we didn't kiss each other now, I would be left with that feeling when a train stops and lurches you forward and you're on tenterhooks for it to lurch you back to normality.

'Do you think this would be a good time to practise our kiss?' he said, all crooked grin and dancing eyes.

I half smiled with agreement.

Really slowly he dipped his head. We were millimetres apart. I didn't care that I was in a lake and my teeth were chattering. I stood on tiptoes and our freezing lips touched. Heat and ice. I reached my hand up and touched his wet, cold face, threaded my fingers into his hair so that we were even closer, our chattering teeth clashing. When I opened my eyes I could see his eyelashes fanned against his cheeks. The light from the willow flickering like stardust.

'Alright, you two. Easy now. Let's get this boat back to shore.' The voice of the boatman came out loud and clear through a megaphone over the noise of the rescue-boat engine.

We pulled apart in an instant. I bit my lip, cherry red with embarrassment and nervously giggling. Ezra's fingers were still laced through mine. He squeezed them for a second, then let go so he could turn the boat the right way up. My body started shaking as the cold kicked in.

The boatman shook his head. 'Always the same with teenagers. Come here for a snog and ruin my boats.'

We climbed into the rescue boat and towed our little rowing boat to shore. There was a line of people watching with interest as we arrived back at the cabin. We had been that afternoon's excitement.

The boatman made us tea and wrapped us in foil blankets. We sat huddled in his little cabin, squished together in front of a heater. I was clutching the memory of our secret kiss. Every now and then we glanced at each other as the boatman told endless rescue stories. We sipped our sugary tea, our sides pressed tight together.

CHAPTER SIXTEEN

Ezra and I left the boatman's shed when we'd stopped shivering enough to cycle. The sun was low through the trees, casting shadows like broomsticks on the grass. We cycled still wrapped in our silver blankets, the foil catching the wind and billowing behind us like superhero capes.

'Do you want to go home?' Ezra asked as we reached the entrance to the park.

'Not particularly,' I said, not wanting the afternoon to end. My teeth chattered as I spoke. 'But I think I have to. I'm too cold to stay out.' Ezra seemed to weigh something up, then said, 'Follow me.'

We cycled fast over Chelsea Bridge, the wind like ice in my face. I couldn't feel my fingers – the tips had turned white – but my heart thrummed with excitement.

Ezra kept checking behind him that I was still there, still moving. I pedalled harder to get level with him.

I could see the turrets of the Chelsea High building on my left as we cycled up towards Sloane Square station, past beautifully coiffed shoppers and expensively adorned theatre-goers. We looked completely out of place, soaked through in our silver capes. Ezra took a right into Belgravia, a land of beautiful white mansions with Corinthian-columned porches. Everything still and quiet and perfect. We tarnished the picture as we cycled past windows with hand-crafted rocking horses on display and giant pieces of art, grand urns spilling with extravagant bouquets and little dogs perched on velvet cushions.

I didn't think I could get colder than I was, but my whole body was shivering again when Ezra pulled to a sudden stop.

'Why are we stopping?' I asked, barely able to talk.

'This is my house.' He gestured to the black front door of the huge white mansion. Two topiaried trees stood either side of the columned porch, observed by a security camera. Above us, the windows stretched up almost as far as I could see.

I laughed in shock. I never thought these places were people's family homes. I don't know who I thought *did* live in them, but certainly not anyone I would ever meet.

We locked up our bikes, then Ezra climbed the steps to the front door, getting his key out of his pocket.

'Is anyone home?' I asked, trying to make myself look more presentable, retying my soaking hair.

He shook his head. 'My dad's in New York. My mum's at the hospital. My sister's at uni.'

He opened the door and gestured for me to go in first. It was like stepping inside another world. The marble floor dazzled under the low lights, the air smelt of fresh flowers, the staircase swept up like a fairy tale. It wasn't gaudy or over the top, but full of understated affluence.

A woman appeared from the kitchen, shaking her head when she saw the state of Ezra. She was probably in her sixties, a little plump, buxom, with greying blonde hair that was cut neat at the jaw. She had spectacles on her head like an Alice band and a red apron over a cream shirt and blue trousers. 'You're soaking wet!' she said with a tut.

Ezra grinned at her. 'Annie, this is Norah,' he said. 'Norah, this is Annie.'

By 'no one being home', I realised he didn't include the staff.

'Hi,' I said and held up a hand, self-conscious that I was dripping wet and shivering.

'A pleasure to meet you, my dear.' Annie looked me up and down with interest. She clearly knew I was new to the scene. 'I don't even want to know what happened to the two of you,' she said. 'Go upstairs. There are fresh towels in all the bathroom cabinets, Norah. Get warm, get dry and I'll make some tea. There's a vanilla sponge down here that's just come out of the oven.'

It was all said with such comforting efficiency. I wished she lived in my house. It felt like she would make everyone happy and smiling again with a wave of her wooden spoon.

Ezra took the stairs two at a time. The staircase was wide, carpeted in thick cream. I followed more slowly, my eyes absorbing it all with quiet disbelief. The wallpaper in the hall was cream with thin gold stripes that matched the marble floor and shimmered in the light of the gold sconces. My entire boat could have moored in the ground-floor hallway. Before going upstairs, I took my wet shoes and socks off, not wanting to mark the pristine carpet.

'Just leave them by the door,' I heard Annie say, and realised she was still watching.

My bare feet sank into the soft carpet as I gazed up at the giant crystal chandelier that hung at the top of the stairs. It was antique, Venetian probably – Jackie was always selling cheap rip-offs of them in her shop. She would have gone nuts for this one.

Ezra bypassed the first floor, but I peered round the corner for a quick nose. Through one half-open door I could see a dining room – a huge table and another chandelier, this one more modern, rectangular, stretching almost the length of the table. At the opposite end of that floor was another giant room, decked out in rich dark reds and blues, with the kind of furniture I'd only ever seen in a stately home.

Upstairs Ezra was standing in the doorway of one of the bedrooms, waiting for me to catch up. 'This is my sister's room. Go through her stuff, find something you like. She has pretty good taste.'

I nodded, still dumbstruck. 'I can't believe you live here.'

He looked around as if seeing it for the first time. 'It's just my house,' he said with a shrug.

'You're never coming to mine,' I said, then immediately felt myself go pink at the suggestion he would ever want to.

From the smile on his face as I walked past him into his sister's room, I realised my blushes amused him greatly.

'Her bathroom's over there,' he said, gesturing to a door in the corner of the bedroom, then added, 'My room's over there.' He pointed across the landing.

The other door on this floor had a big green 'J' on the door and loads of stickers. I presumed that was his little brother's.

I glanced up the next set of stairs. His parents' room, presumably. It was hard to determine the exact number of floors.

'Shout if you need anything,' he said, crossing to his own room.

My coldness was overriding my bewildered amazement. I walked further into his sister's bedroom, shutting the door behind me. To say that she had pretty good taste was an understatement. The room was gorgeous. It was all pale grey walls with squishy white bedding and fluffy angora cushions. In one corner, houseplants tumbled from woven baskets over a slim wooden desk. There was a string of white bulbs draped over the curtain poles, and on the wall behind the bed someone had painted a mountain range in different hues of pink so it receded into the distance. Two Picasso pencil prints hung on the wall adjacent to the bed. I paused to look at them on my way to the bathroom, wondering suddenly if they were real. My finger traced the signature underneath the glass.

I shook my head, unable to comprehend the wealth.

The bathroom was all white pillar-box tiles and more plants. The giant mirror above the sink showed the full force of my bedraggled appearance. I cringed, pushing my wet hair away from my pale, frozen face.

My eye caught a picture on the shelf, propped up among the expensive bottles of bubble bath and shampoo. I leaned closer to see a whole bunch of Chelsea High students, the photo like the one on my grandparents' piano, all of them grinning and whooping for the last day of term. Their shirts were scrawled over in marker pen with notes of goodbye. The Rollo-esque sportsman of their year stood proud at the back. Their Coco posed next to him. Their Verity pouted, her red-hair tied high in a knot above her head. All of them had the same caramel tans. The girl in the front row, grinning ear to ear, looking all healthy and head-girly, smile as wide as her face and the spitting image of Ezra, had to be the girl whose room I was standing in. Another picture – an intricately decorated calligraphy – told me her name was Leah. It was hard not to imagine her life was as perfect as it was in that photograph. But of course it couldn't be. Perhaps since the accident she too, like Ezra, was now a little lost. Nothing was as perfect as it seemed.

The shower was like torrential rain and the water was

boiling. It was the exact opposite of the terrible shower over the bath on the boat. The shampoo smelt delicately of the tiny wild strawberries that grew in our patch of river-bank garden and tasted of the first days of summer. The towels were brand-new fluffy. I used the tiniest blob of her tub of moisturiser, then, emboldened, tried a weeny sweep of her Chanel blush, a flick of her mascara and a lick of her pale pink Charlotte Tilbury gloss.

Back in the bedroom, my hand stilled on the door of her wardrobe. I felt like I was breaking and entering, rifling through her possessions. Equally I was daunted about what I might find, what could I take. These were her clothes.

The wardrobe didn't disappoint. There were rows and rows of flirty boho dresses, exquisite black-tie numbers by an eye-watering list of designers, twenty pairs of jeans – I had one – and little T-shirts in every colour of the rainbow. There was a whole section just for sportswear – her school hockey kit, her hockey tour sweatshirt with *Captain Leah* embroidered on the front.

In the end I picked out a pair of black skinny jeans and black T-shirt. I was just pulling on a dark grey polo neck, the fabric thin, gauzy and expensive, when Ezra knocked on the door.

'You ready?' he asked, poking his head round the door. He laughed. 'You look like my sister.'

I shrugged a smile. Course I would, these being her clothes.

He had on a grey hoodie and black tracksuit bottoms, feet bare.

As I took one last look around the room, catching a glimpse of myself in the smoky wardrobe mirror – eyes big from the mascara, cheeks rosy, beautifully cut clothes – I thought how easy it was to slip into this world. To get comfortable in it. To get used to the reflection that money could buy.

Downstairs, the kitchen smelt of fresh vanilla and baked cake. Annie was standing behind a white marble-topped counter in the centre of the cream country kitchen. Copper pots and bunches of herbs hung from the ceiling. There was an Aga in the corner and a giant wooden table by the window with an equally giant dog asleep underneath it.

Ezra sat down on the table bench. Immediately the dog sat up, panting with delight that he was there, head resting on his leg as Ezra gave it a scratch. 'This is AT-AT,' he said.

I looked at the dog all tall, grey and leggy and laughed. 'Like in *Star Wars*?'

'Exactly,' Ezra said, pleased I'd got the reference as he ruffled the dog's drooling face.

Annie came to stand beside me, resting her hand on my shoulder, warm and comforting, 'What can I get you, Norah? Tea, hot chocolate?'

Ezra cut in. 'I'll have a hot chocolate. You never make hot chocolate.'

'Well, we have guests,' said Annie. 'And it's a special

occasion. You don't bring anyone back here any more,' she added, her tone like a reprimand. For the first time, I saw him blush and those razor sharp cheekbones start to pink. He shook his head at her, despairing.

Annie beamed. 'So what'll it be, Norah?'

'I'll have a hot chocolate too. Thanks,' I said with a grin, sliding on to the bench next to Ezra so I could pet the dog.

'Don't listen to anything she says,' Ezra said, nodding towards Annie, trying to cover his back.

I looked to where Annie was warming milk on the stove, trying to suppress a smile. Then I focused on scratching AT-AT's back, a slight flutter inside from what had been said: that Ezra had chosen to bring me back here.

The dog immediately changed allegiance and came to rest his head on my thigh.

'Thanks a lot, AT,' Ezra said, hands held wide in disbelief.

I laughed, giving Ezra a playful nudge, stroking the dog, feeling more relaxed than I had all day. The presence of Annie and the warm comfort of the kitchen softened Ezra, made him more normal. Took away the pedestal.

Annie bustled about some more, then brought over two hot chocolates topped with marshmallows in thick white mugs, and two slices of vanilla sponge. 'There you go, enjoy.' When we thanked her she stepped back, wiping her hands on her apron and added, 'Right, I have work to do, so I'll leave you to it.'

She said this with a grin in her voice, like she had no work to do whatsoever. I felt my face colour. Ezra rolled his eyes. Annie smiled wide, then trotted out of the kitchen.

Ezra and I sat in silence for a bit, stroking the dog and spooning up gooey marshmallow.

I glanced across at him, his hair wet from the shower, his face relaxed and content.

I said, 'How come you don't bring anyone round here any more?'

He looked at me, one dark brow raised. 'I told you not to listen to her.'

'How can I not listen to her?' I asked, blowing on my steaming hot chocolate.

He picked up the slice of cake and took a massive bite. Then leaned back against the wall. 'I just don't want to, I suppose,' he said, through a mouth full of vanilla sponge. The dog jumped up so he was stretched out over Ezra's knees, far too big, like a giant blanket. Ezra swallowed his mouthful of cake. 'It just doesn't feel the same any more.'

I broke off a piece of cake. It was warm and buttery on my tongue, like the ones my mum used to bake.

The last of the sunlight was streaming through the window making AT-AT close his eyes. 'Why not?'

'It's just changed. It's a different place.' He glanced round the kitchen. 'Too much has happened to bring people here to have fun –' He paused. 'I don't mean you, now. But you know?'

I nodded. 'I think I know what you mean.'

He made a face. 'It's like there are talks about whether my brother will ever walk again over dinner, about having a lift installed for his wheelchair. I have to see it as a road in my head that will end, a journey. He will get better, he will walk again, he will run around. I'm really bad at explaining this.' He sighed and scratched his head, restless, the lumbering dog still lying across him. 'I just don't want things to go on as normal with that playing out in the background. Does that make sense?'

It did, completely. 'I understand what it's like to have your life on hold,' I said.

Ezra scratched the snoozing dog on the head. 'What do you think it'd be like if you went back to your island now?' he asked. 'I don't know a lot about your dad's case, but there seem to be a lot of people out of pocket. Do you think you could go back to normal?'

'Yes,' I said without hesitation. I took a gulp of my hot chocolate. It was too hot, scalding my tongue.

He looked surprised that I could be so adamant. 'Really?'

I nodded. 'I have to believe it.'

Ezra thought for a second, hands rubbing the dog behind one ear. 'When Josh fell I don't have any idea how I got down that cliff.' He swallowed. 'No memory. I maybe skidded down, maybe I jumped. I honestly don't know.' He glanced at me, then back down to the dog. 'I remember hearing my mum

192

scream. I remember having this tunnel vision down to Josh lying there looking all wrong, blood everywhere. But I do have this crystal-clear memory of Rollo saying, "It wasn't our fault."'

Ezra rubbed his eye, as if to rid himself of the image. 'He said it twice. And afterwards, when I was sitting in the hospital, that was all I could think of. And I thought who cares? Who cares? There's a ten-year-old boy down there, and all Rollo can think about is saving his own skin.' He shook his head, his hair falling over his eyes. 'I hear it every time I look at him.'

I didn't say anything. I could imagine the scene so clearly, Rollo denying responsibility as fast as he could.

Ezra bent his head and whispered something to the dog, a distraction to break the moment.

I picked up my hot chocolate. Thought about the fact I was no longer allowed my phone. Even if all this blew over, could any of us really forgive each other? Could I really gloss over what people – my friends – had written in the heat of the moment? Could they forgive us for leaving? For running away to save our own skins and leaving them with nothing? Would anyone ever forget? They had to. I had grown up with the people of Mulberry Island. They were my memories, we were theirs. They couldn't blank us out of their history. We had all shared too many things, good and bad – births and deaths, parties and marriages. I had sheltered from thunderstorms in their houses, fed their cats, babysat their children, borrowed their pumps when our boat flooded, been taught by them, eaten picnics with them, danced with them, cried with them, sang with them. Surely that was worth more than one mistake.

'Do you still want to be friends with Rollo?' I asked. 'Would you go back if he said he was sorry?'

Ezra shook his head.

'But don't you think it was just panic? Emotion? I'm not defending him, I –'

Ezra scoffed. 'Yes you are.'

I held up a hand. 'Let me finish. I just . . . I feel like you should talk to him. Give him a chance to rectify his mistake –'

'It wasn't panic, Norah,' Ezra cut in. 'If there's one thing I know about Rollo, it's that he only thinks about himself.'

I wanted to say that was the anger talking. To remind him that they had been friends once. I remembered the picture of him and Rollo grinning like best buddies in the trophy cabinet at school.

Ezra broke off a piece of cake and fed it to AT-AT. Then had some for himself. I drank some more hot chocolate. Outside a car horn beeped. The dog flinched, then settled.

'When my mum came out of the hospital room she said, "I love you but right now I can't look at you." I think she would deny that she said it if you asked her now, but she said it.' Ezra frowned, the sharp lines of his eyebrows drawn together. 'I suppose when I look at Rollo I'm angry that he doesn't have that. I'm angry by how free he is.'

I wondered if that anger was how the people on the island thought about us. 'But you're still friends with them all,' I said, confused. 'At school.'

Ezra half laughed, unapologetic. 'We grew up together, all of us. It's hard to change.'

What he said felt so familiar. But where I was looking for answers – solutions that wrapped everything up nicely and let me and my family move on with the past forgotten, and forgiven, behind us – it felt like Ezra was on the other side, holding a mirror back at my dreams.

The dog got up and turned round so his head was on the bench next to me. I reached over to stroke him, my hand brushing against Ezra's.

He looked at me through thick fringed lashes and said slowly, 'So with the play . . .'

'Yeah?' I replied, keeping my attention on the dog.

'Do you think you're going to be OK with the kissing now?'

Just look at the dog, I told myself. 'I think so.'

Ezra nodded. Thought for a second. I wondered if he could hear my heart like a drum beat. 'Do you think –' He paused. I could feel him watching me. 'Do you think we should maybe do it again, just to make sure?'

'Maybe,' I said, holding in a smile and feeling my skin prickle with excitement. I gave the dog a final little pat, pretending I was considering the question some more, then sat up straight so my eyes met Ezra's, which were dark with mischief. 'Maybe just to make sure.'

I thought how Jess would be so proud of me, how cool I was playing it. I could imagine a silent high-five.

It was so quiet suddenly I could hear the clock ticking in the hallway. Ezra leaned across and his mouth touched mine ever so gently. More hesitant this time. His hand went round the back of my neck and pulled me closer. He smelt of shampoo and soap. I wondered if I smelt of wild strawberries. My heart thrummed like hummingbird wings.

Then suddenly the door opened and Annie darted into the room. 'Only be a sec, sorry!' She looked almost as embarrassed as us as she grabbed some rubber gloves and fled.

I grinned down at the table. 'I should go.'

'OK.' Ezra smirked as he pushed back his hair. 'I'll cycle with you.'

CHAPTER SEVENTEEN

The tension was broken. The kissing had bonded us. Ezra and I were starting to mesh, as all good lead actors should. We didn't kiss again unless it was on stage, but a small window had opened where we were equals and almost friends. I liked being liked by him.

Over the next few weeks we did more and more rehearsals with just me, Ezra and Daniel – a little unit. I could pre-empt their banter. I knew how to make Ezra laugh, we high-fived when scenes went well, we shared a water bottle when one of us forgot, we sat patiently when one of us was struggling. I got used to having his smell on me, I got used to the feel of his hand in mine, I looked forward more and more to rehearsals. I stopped being nervous. I gave back his sister's clothes, but I never returned the cashmere jumper I'd stolen from my mum's stall. I'd managed to salvage it from its river dip and wore it more and more. I even took another, less expensive but more plain, like Ezra's sister's polo neck. I was perfecting a subtle monochrome wardrobe – a far cry from the bright reds and yellows I'd wear on the island.

I got used to Ezra jogging in sweaty and late from Taekwondo, to the point that I would tell him he had to go and shower because otherwise the whole room stank. And it wasn't all confined to the rehearsal room. Around school he'd say hi if he saw me in the corridor. We'd chat in our corner at registration. One day there was a Coke on my desk and when I looked at him he said, 'I owed you your own.' I didn't drink it, just slipped it in my bag. It sits on the sill of the huge window in my bedroom, alongside a sprig of dried mulberry bush and a plastic Funshine Care Bear that Jess fished out of the river and gave to me.

Coco was away a lot with more and more promos. Or perhaps it was the same one, because she regularly appeared with her unicorn hair. I noticed a couple of girls in the year below copying the look, strutting around school with their identikit pastel rainbows. It was good when Coco was away because the dynamic in the lunch hall changed. Rollo would lounge with his rugby pals and Verity sat with some girls from the year above, so I would sit with Daniel, Tabitha and Emmeline. Coco was clearly the glue that drew them all together. A couple of times Ezra came and sat at our table instead of one of his endless other options, making Daniel raise a questioning brow in my direction. I tried to brush it off as if it were nothing but I couldn't help my quiet delight that he was there.

Sundays changed as well. My grandmother had clearly sought some advice about bonding with teenagers and we started going on excursions. The first was grouse shooting. My grandfather's role was to beat the undergrowth with a stick to scare the fat little birds up into the sky so they could then come tumbling down again when the guys with the shotguns and the flat caps took aim. Ludo the dog made a slow attempt to collect the dead birds but more often than not was beaten to it by a younger black Lab. My grandmother served the tea from a silver urn, dressed in a floor-length Barbour and sturdy green wellingtons. I didn't even think birds should be kept in cages, let alone shot for sport, so I sat wincing in the Range Rover, the autumn drizzle obscuring the view. We didn't go shooting again.

When I arrived the following weekend they were standing in the hallway, both of them with their coats and hats on. My grandmother had her handbag halfway up her arm like the Queen. Harold had his driving gloves on, waiting.

'We thought you might like to tell us where you would like to go today, Norah,' my grandmother said, punctuating the question with a little cough, nervous, like the territory was unfamiliar and she was a little scared about where it might lead.

I thought about things that I might like to do: films I wanted to see, shops I wanted to go to. Ideally they could just sit me in front of a computer with unlimited access for a couple of hours where I'd freak myself out with details about the trial and probably end up in a deep-dive wormhole of Coco's Instagram.

Then I looked at them, both so hesitant, both, I realised, trying so hard. Waiting in their best coats, their outdoor shoes, my grandfather with his paisley silk scarf, my grandmother with her pink lipstick and floury rouge.

'There's an exhibition . . .' I said, thinking of the still life at the Royal Academy that Mrs Pearce had urged us all to visit as we drew our rotting fruit in last week's class.

Their eyes lit up at the idea, clearly relieved that I hadn't suggested street dancing or whatever else had been conjured up by their innermost fears.

So Harold had driven us in the Bentley to the Royal Academy, where my grandfather of course was a member and we had tea beforehand in a quiet little private members' room where everyone seemed to know them. I sat, awkward, as they introduced me to everyone with such pride as their granddaughter. I would smile, take a mouthful of cake, or shake a plump hand while trying not to spill my Coke.

The exhibition itself I loved. Giant black canvases of pomegranates and skulls, curls of orange peel and fish on platters, all elevated to the status of kings. I could have stood and stared all day, my mind quiet. The original Sanchez Cotan was there – the melon, cabbage, apple and cucumber hanging iridescent against a black background – and I was so excited to see it I actually gasped.

'This is the one we're –' I started.

I saw my grandparents' expectant faces as I spoke, possibly for the first time with them with no forethought, no reserve. I thought about shaking my head and brushing the moment away, maintaining our polite status quo. But it felt suddenly so exhausting. Whatever had gone on with them and my parents was a history that didn't include me. It surely had to be up to me to make my own judgment. Otherwise I was no better than someone like Mr Watts, basing his opinion of me purely on his past with my dad. Or even my friends on the island, who had written me off alongside my dad, all of us bundled up together in one tatty parcel and sent flying.

'This is the one we're drawing in Art,' I said. 'All the fruit's going off, though. There are flies and the whole room stinks.'

My grandmother made a face.

My grandfather smiled. 'Sounds delightful.'

I smiled back.

We walked on round the room, the three of us together. I took my coat off, held it draped over my arm. My grandfather took it from me even when I insisted I was fine, and carried it for me. My grandmother paused and started to explain the symbolism of one of the pictures, glancing at me to check that I wanted to hear it. I listened. At the next picture I paused, waiting to see if she had anything to say about that one. Found myself wanting her to speak. She was more interesting than I'd thought someone in a tweed skirt and pearls could be.

When at the end they suggested a late lunch at the Wolseley across the road, I agreed rather than automatically turned them down. I felt suddenly like my life was that first Improv class: seeing where saying yes got me. Over the best steak frites I'd ever eaten, under yet another chandelier, I learned that my grandmother had studied Art in Paris. Had been quite acclaimed in her time, before she had my dad. That they had met when my grandfather bought one of her paintings, then another, then another until he could pluck up the courage to ask her on a date. They laughed when they talked about it. I think it was the first time I had seen their genuine smiles.

I wondered if, when they went home that afternoon, they said the same about me.

CHAPTER EIGHTEEN

The afternoons started getting darker, the autumn leaves a slushy carpet, the air crisp with the promise of winter. At the stall on a Saturday I wore another layer of thermals. We rehearsed all the time.

A post-rehearsal gathering at Sorrentos had become the norm. Mr Benson even came a couple of times. It made me laugh to think of the significance it once held, now I was on the inside practically every night. I didn't dare think about what life might be like when the play was over.

I always came home to a boat that was dark and empty. When I saw my parents, my mum's face was pinched, my dad either stressed or vacant. I'd stopped coming out of my room when I heard them open the front door. I dreamt of days when we'd stroll the river bank, breath in clouds, and they'd listen with indulgent smiles as I wittered on about school or friends or last night's dream.

The evening after our first full run-through, practically the whole cast went to Sorrentos. There was a buzz in the air because it had gone really well. Even Coco seemed pleased, hugging Rollo tight when she saw him waiting for us in the café. With her stripy hair in a thick plait down her back, she wore skin-tight blue jeans and a white jumper with *Coco* knitted three times down the front in blue. Rollo sat with his arm round her waist, almost unable to believe his luck. I could grudgingly admit that Coco had been really good. Mr Benson had cast her really well as Rizzo. Incredibly, she even managed to pull off a solo where the words suggested she had a heart under the bitchy veneer.

We had our set places now in Sorrentos. Verity took her seat opposite Coco and Rollo with Freddie. Me, Tabitha, Emmeline and Daniel sat on the adjacent table. Ezra sat next to Coco, which was across the aisle from me. Daniel was opposite. He wanted to go through some notes he'd made as we ran through.

'Oh, not now, Dan,' Coco sighed, twirling the end of her plait. 'This is meant to be relaxing. Emmeline, tell us about the party.'

Daniel sat back in a huff.

I looked over at Emmeline. I didn't know anything about a party. I immediately shrank back against the seat, aware that this discussion could easily not include me.

Emmeline tossed back her curtain of shimmering hair. 'OK, so the end-of-term party this year is at mine and Freddie's. Theme is *The Beautiful and Damned*. No costume, no entry.' Ezra rolled his eyes.

Then Emmeline started handing out invitations. Big gold

envelopes with names beautifully printed on the front: *Coco Summers*, *Daniel Rhys-Morgan*. I watched them land in people's places and passed into outstretched hands. And then suddenly there was mine, on the table in front of me: *Norah Whittaker*. I could feel my face colour with pleasure at the sight of it, red bubbles popping like candy under the surface of my skin.

'I'm going to get my dress from your mum's stall,' said Tabitha, sliding her knife under the envelope to slice it open all properly. I just tore into mine.

'Oh, me too,' said Emmeline. 'There was a really beautiful long green one that I saw last time. Is it still there, Norah?'

I had no idea but I nodded all the same.

Verity looked up from tapping something into her phone with the tips of her pointy nails and shuddered. 'I don't wear second-hand. I just don't see the appeal.' Coco grinned.

I wasn't listening. The invitation was thick and navy-edged with diagonal gold lines embossed deep into the card. *Frederick and Emmeline Chang invite you . . .*

There was going to be a lobster barbeque. Indoor swimming. Guest DJs.

It took everything I had not to press it to my chest.

They were all chatting around me about possible outfits.

'I might paint one half of my white tux red,' said Rollo.

Freddie snorted. 'That'll look good.'

'Shut up.'

Sitting amidst the banter with the invite clutched tight in my hands, I felt like I was outside my body, looking down. I could see my hair shining in the overhead lights, the egg-white mix starting to pay off. My black polo neck and a pair of skin-tight vintage French trousers with a gold stripe down the side I'd taken from the stall the week before. I could see the black ballet shoes with the tiny red hearts on the toe, also from the stall, and a simple pearl teardrop necklace my grandmother had given me when we'd left the Wolseley. I felt chic and sleek and confident. I fitted in next to Emmeline in her oversized pale grey jumper, slate leggings and black-leather biker jacket; Verity in her little green woollen dress and zebra-print boots.

No one would pick me out from this crowd. I was a part of it, and that gave me an excited bubble of what I could only call happiness.

Because I was so lost in this daydream, I didn't hear the banging. Or rather, I heard it but didn't register it – until Coco drawled, 'Norah, isn't that crazed woman at the window your mother?'

My head shot round, eyes wide. There indeed was my mother – stone-washed dungarees, black and white striped jumper, yellow hair, red lipstick, huge pink coat – one hand slapping the glass, the other holding up a fistful of star-print cashmere. Eyes furious.

Everyone – the whole cast, the whole *restaurant* – was watching. I could sense the smirks from Coco's table. I couldn't even look at Ezra. Daniel looked bemused.

Verity leaned forward, all cool and languid. 'I think she wants you, Norah.'

As if that weren't plainly obvious.

It wasn't just my cheeks popping with colour. My whole body was alight as I stuffed my invite into my bag and stood up. 'I'd better go,' I said, trying to make light of it. From the look of spitting rage on my mum's face, there was no light to be had.

'See you tomorrow,' Tabitha called.

I nodded, trying to breathe as normal, weaving my way out of Sorrentos without catching anyone's eye.

Outside was a blast of cold air.

My mum was furious, waiting for me, hauling me by my arm out of the vicinity of the place.

I gave one quick glance back and I saw them all watching. The pity in Ezra's eyes was the last thing I wanted to see. Then Coco bashed him on the arm to get his attention and, just like that, the group merged, Tabitha sliding across into my seat to hear whatever Coco was saying – and I was forgotten.

I shrugged my mum off my arm. 'Do you know what you just did? How embarrassing that was?'

My mum was breathing really hard. Her mouth pursed and her eyes narrowed as she looked me up and down. 'What are you wearing?'

'Nothing,' I said, looking away at the brickwork.

She held up the star-print cashmere. 'I thought *this* was bad enough.' She looked both angry and crestfallen. 'I can't believe you've been stealing from us, Norah. Just the jumper's worth about two hundred quid. And what is *that*?' She pointed to my teardrop pearl necklace. 'Did you take that from someone? From Peggy? Is that from Peggy's stall?'

'No,' I said sulkily.

'Where's it from then?'

'Nowhere.'

She put her hands on her hips. 'Where's it from?' she said, voice like ice.

'Granny,' I said, staring her straight in the eye, knowing the shortened familiarity would really hit her.

'Granny?' she repeated, letting the name roll slowly off her tongue. 'Take it off.'

'No.'

She swallowed. 'Take it *off*.'

'No way. Why should I? You've just humiliated me in front of all my friends –'

'They're not your friends, Norah. Those girls from the stall? Coco Summers? They're not your friends, believe me.'

'And how would you know?' I could hear my heart thumping in my ears. 'I don't know why you're even here. That was the most embarrassing thing you've ever done. And for what? Some jumpers? I was *borrowing* them.' I spat the words out like she was beneath me.

'Borrowing, Norah? I'd call it stealing.'

'Is that why you're here?'

The door of Sorrentos swung open and Verity's head poked out. When she saw us, she grinned and disappeared back inside, clearly giving a status update. They'd all be laughing now.

My mum took a deep breath in through her nose. 'I'm here because I was worried about you. You weren't home. You weren't answering your pager. It's late.'

'Yeah, well, it's late most nights when I get home and you aren't there,' I said, arms crossed, tone sulky.

'Because in case it had escaped your notice, your father's freedom is at stake. This is our lives, Norah. It's not just about you. It's about us. And the last thing I expected was that you'd be stealing from me on the sly.'

I kicked the wall.

The door to Sorrentos opened again and Coco came out, phone pressed to her ear. She guffawed loudly at something, leaning up against the window, toying with her hair.

I pulled my mum further into the shadows, dragging her by the coat sleeve into a fire escape.

Coco hung up the phone with a loud, '*Ciao, ciao*, darling,' and then skipped back inside.

'Is that what you're doing it for?' my mum asked.

'I don't know what you mean.'

Her face softened. She knew. She could see it in my face. I

knew she could.

'This . . .' she said, waving her hand up and down my outfit, from the plain little shoes to the classic black jumper. 'I've been here, Norah. I know what it's like. If they're the kind of people who will only be friends with you if you're dressed like them, they're not the people you want to be friends with.'

I huffed at the floor.

It had started to drizzle, the streetlights catching the haze of water in the dusk. We moved further into the fire-exit doorway.

'Seriously, Norah. You've just got to be yourself.'

'You think?' I scoffed. 'Ever think how hard it is to fit in somewhere where everyone thinks your dad's a criminal? You're telling me you wouldn't do everything you could? Seriously? My *self*, Mum, doesn't exist any more. It's all gone. And now I have this.' I pointed to the café. 'Do you know how hard I've worked to get this? Yes, I nicked a few jumpers, and I'm sorry. But you can't just turn up like that and ruin it for me.' I could feel the tears welling in my eyes. 'I'm a laughing stock.'

It was my mum's turn to look down at the floor. The rain was getting heavier. Puddles appeared on the pavement as cars splashed down the road.

Behind us were two tatty chairs and a milk crate with an ashtray on the top. Obviously this was where people who worked in the building came for a smoke. My mum sat down on the most broken of the two seats.

I stayed where I was.

She looked out at the traffic. I looked at her thick blonde fringe and her chalky red lips, at the moles on her cheeks and the soft downy hairs on her skin. I could smell her. She smelt of when I was really little, of hugs and sprays of perfume before she went out, all boho beautiful, for a dinner.

'I'm sorry,' she said.

I swallowed.

She picked at her fingernail. 'It's been really hard, and I know I've been looking the other way.' Then she stared up at me with big eyes. 'I'm sorry I just embarrassed you. I was so worried coming over here, and then I think it was a shock, that's all. Seeing you in there with the likes of Coco Summers. All shiny.' She waved her hand at my outfit. 'You didn't look like you and that frightened me. I wanted my little girl back. And seeing you in that necklace . . .' She exhaled, clearly envisioning my grandmother presenting it to me. 'I can't even begin with the idea of those two back on the scene.'

'They're OK,' I said.

She snorted. 'Maybe they've mellowed,' she said, as if she didn't believe it for a minute. 'You're mine, Norah, and I don't want them giving you bloody pearls. You don't like pearls, do you?'

I shrugged. 'This one's OK.'

'I'll get you a new necklace.'

'I don't want a new necklace.'

She put her head in her hands. 'No, I don't suppose you do.' She looked out at the traffic again, chin rested on steepled fingers. 'I think I just thought you'd be alright. You're so strong and capable that I thought you'd be alright while we just dealt with this bloody trial. I can see that was stupid.'

I sucked in my top lip, annoyed with myself for letting her down. 'I am alright.'

She huffed. Then held up the jumpers. 'Don't steal from me,' she said.

I shook my head and sat on the chair next to her.

'I know it's a tough school to find your place in but –' she reached over and tucked my hair behind my ear – 'you're so pretty and so lovely. I don't want you thinking you have to conform.' She gestured towards the café. 'You're ten times any of those people.'

'That's what all mums say to their kids.'

'Because it's true,' she said. She sat back, legs crossed, coat wrapped round her. 'If no one conformed, there'd be a whole load more interesting people.'

I toyed with the long cuffs of my jumper.

'Norah, it's not about being worth something to everyone.' My mum touched my arm briefly. 'You don't mould yourself. You find the people that fit you as you are.'

I kicked my feet against the chair legs. 'Why didn't you tell me that you'd gone to Chelsea High? About this life?'

'Because it didn't feel relevant,' she said, looking out at the rain. 'I suppose because it didn't fit me. The people didn't fit me. And I found somewhere that I felt much more comfortable. It wasn't so much not telling you; it was more that it wasn't any semblance of who I was now.'

She put her arm round me, softly gave my shoulder a squeeze, then let go. 'I'm sorry,' she said.

'That's OK,' I replied.

She ran her hand along the chain round my neck, lifting the pearl then letting it drop with a laugh. 'It's awful,' she said.

I grinned.

She stood up. 'Come on, let's go home,' she said, smoothing down her coat.

'I have to get my bike,' I said, pointing up the road.

We walked side by side in the dark rain. I didn't even glance at Sorrentos. As I unlocked my bike, my mum offered to push it, lightening my load, but I kept it. We walked all the way home in a strangely comfortable silence. It didn't feel like we were quite back to normal, more like we were equals of some sort – fallible equals.

Maybe that was what normal was now.

CHAPTER NINETEEN

The next morning, I got up early. My dad was sitting in his dressing gown on the sofa, watching cartoons on a channel we hadn't clicked on since I was a kid, the type with adverts for glitter shoes and Transformers. The rain had stopped, and the sun was peeking out through grey clouds. The river was flat and empty, just seagulls soaring in circles. He was eating dry Rice Krispies because the milk had run out.

I poured myself a bowl and sat next to him. He looked up, almost surprised to see me. Neither of us said anything. We just curled up like we used to, in our pyjamas and dressing gowns, the cereal crackling on our tongues.

My mum appeared, dressed and ready for a day in court. Maybe she'd heeded her own advice from yesterday, because instead of the usual plain courtroom clothes, she had on a red and white vertical-striped shirt tucked into high-waisted wide blue trousers. Her lipstick was as red as her shirt.

My dad smiled when he saw her. 'You look nice.'

She nodded at the compliment, then glanced at her watch. I waited for her to say something about being late. Instead, to my surprise, she came over and sat down next to my dad, wrapping her arm round his shoulders as he ate his cereal, tucking her legs up underneath her. She kissed his cheek and I heard her whisper the words, 'Stop worrying, it'll all be over soon.' I saw my dad's spoon hover momentarily over the bowl.

Then my mum stretched her arm so that her hand could stroke my hair and hold the ends of the strands between her fingers. 'We'll be back to normal before you know it,' she said.

And we both smiled, me and my dad. If she had said it, then it must be true. My mum never lied to make someone feel better, never hesitated to point out the truth.

I felt a flutter of relief. We all did. The whole mood lifted in an instant. We were back. Our unit.

My dad turned the TV off and almost jumped up to get dressed. When he came back, he was wearing one of his old ties – a comedy cat with a toothy grin. 'Too much?'

My mum tipped her head. 'Maybe.'

He disappeared and came back with one covered in orange and blue triangles. Not quite the comedy cat, but at least not boring grey.

I waved them off as they slipped into the big black saloon. I couldn't quite work out why I was smiling. It was like I'd been told I was allowed to believe something, but my mind couldn't quite grasp it. Like trying to clutch soap. Every time I thought I had it, it would pop away, bouncing out of reach.

For school that day, I was back with my standard damp shampooed hair pulled up into a high ponytail. No egg whites and painstakingly glossy blow-dry. The rehearsal clothes in my bag were black leggings and a striped blue and white T-shirt. It was the best I had after my mum had taken all the other stuff. She'd made me call Jackie to apologise when we got home, which had been excruciating.

I kept my head down all morning, arriving late and keeping myself busy in the corner of every lesson. At lunch break I walked a lap of the playing fields, past the pool and the tennis courts, through the beautiful manicured garden where Mr Watts was on lunchtime duty, searching out problems, a steaming cup of coffee in his hand. I edged away without him seeing me, bypassing the polo field where Coco, Emmeline and Verity were practising, ponytails flying under their helmets. I skirted along the edge of the hockey pitch and ended up sitting with my back against the wall at the furthest end of the school, underneath huge plane trees that were bare now the weather had turned.

'Are you hiding?' a familiar voice said.

Ezra's skin was pale from the cold but his cheeks were slightly pink. He looked tired but exhilarated. He was wearing an old grey hockey jumper for a team that wasn't Chelsea High, the cuffs frayed with a rip along the bottom, black faded tracksuit bottoms and green Converse. His hair was a bit greasy. There was mud on his cheek and dark smudges under his eyes.

I laughed, because it was perfectly clear that I was.

I noticed he had a hockey stick. He leaned it against the wall as he sat, pushing his hair back, his face damp with sweat.

'You OK?' he asked.

I nodded, because I was. While I was still embarrassed about my mum at Sorrentos, the balance of my life had tipped again, and I felt safer than I had in ages at home. I looked forward suddenly to the end of the day when I could be back on the boat. When I would make spaghetti and have it ready for when they came home.

'That's good.'

He unscrewed a bottle of water and gulped it down.

I watched him – the long lashes, the erratic smattering of freckles, the muscles lithe and sinewy like a fox, the slanting brown eyes. The wind blew, rustling the little hedgehog balls hanging from the plane trees. I'd forgotten my jacket, so I pulled my hands into the sleeves of my maroon school cardigan and buried my face in my scarf.

When he saw that I was shivering, he put his arm round me and rubbed my arm to warm me up. The gesture was automatic. But after it was done, I think we were both suddenly aware that he had his arm round me, that I was tucked in snug. I could smell the mud from the hockey and the sweat. I shifted away and he moved his arm. We stayed side by side. In a couple of weeks the play would be done. I wondered if we'd ever sit like this again. It felt like limbo for both of us. Real but unreal. Like an end was coming.

'Were you playing?' I asked, nodding towards the hockey stick.

'Sort of,' he said. 'Just helping Coach out for a bit with the U13s. He asked, and . . .' He shrugged. 'I felt bad saying no.'

'Why would you say no?'

'Because I don't do it any more.'

'Why not?'

I saw him think for a second, then smile. 'I don't want to tell you because you'll think it's stupid.'

'I will think it's stupid, or everyone will think it's stupid?'

He tipped his head. 'You specifically, I think.'

'Why?'

'I dunno.' He looked down. 'You're different to everyone else.'

'I am?'

He glanced up with a lazy half-smile. 'You maybe have more integrity.'

'I don't think my old friends would agree,' I said. 'Come on. You can't say all that and then not tell me.'

He scrunched up his face, putting his hand over his eyes. 'No.'

'Go on!'

He took his hand away and looked back out at the hockey pitch, not meeting my eyes. 'Because when my brother was in the hospital and they didn't know if he was going to survive, I swore that if he could just make it then I'd never play hockey again.'

'Like a bargaining chip?' I asked.

He nodded. I didn't say anything, just nodded back.

After a second he nudged my knee with his hand. 'Well?'

'Well, what?'

'Say what you want to say.'

'I don't have anything to say.'

He scoffed.

'OK,' I said, twisting to face him. It was so cold suddenly in the wind that I had to pull my knees right up and wrap my arms round them. 'I think you're right.'

He looked surprised.

'I do think it's stupid.'

He laughed. 'You know that was a serious confession? I've never told anyone,' he said.

'I completely understand. But I just don't believe that life is like that.' I thought for a second. 'It's not tit for tat. Stuff just happens. Like what I was saying just then about my friends at home? Some of them turned against me. Their families had lost everything; it was understandable. Hate my dad, hate me. But we *all* got conned. We were *all* victims. And now I'm at the will of a judge and jury. You can't control these things. Sometimes life's fair and sometimes it's not.' I sat back against the wall. 'And if there *is* some part of the universe making these life-or-death decisions, you really think they care if you don't play hockey any more?'

Ezra laughed. 'I suppose it's about sacrifice.'

'Rubbish,' I scoffed. 'Go do some good, go and help kids in your spare time. Coach the U13s. Do that *and* play hockey. Then you become *more* rather than less. Surely that makes more sense?'

I saw him listening, eyes staring out to the bright lush hockey pitch.

'Maybe,' he said after a second. He looked at me. 'What are you going to do?'

'What do you mean?'

'About your friends? About going home to your island?'

'Oh.' I shrugged. 'Pray that when Dad's proved innocent, they forgive us.'

I looked back at the game, but I could see him looking unconvinced out of the corner of my eye.

CHAPTER TWENTY

I walked back across the grass on my own, Ezra had been pounced on by all the adoring U13s keen to show him stuff post-practice. I'd waited for a bit, but realised he was really enjoying himself as they hung off his every word so I figured I'd leave him to it.

I was so cold. I buried my face in my scarf. Over in the far corner I could see the polo team charging round the warm-up track, flashes of colour as they raced, ponies sweating. It was meant to be a games afternoon, but anyone in the play was allowed to bunk it for rehearsals as the performance date loomed.

As I walked across the grass to the Drama block I said my lines out loud, my breath like smoke in front of me. I crossed my arms over my chest, remembering how warm it had been bunched up close next to Ezra.

The sudden sound of cantering hooves and yelling pulled me up short. Ponies weren't allowed past the stables that separated the track from the school. I turned just in time to see Coco and Verity bearing down on me, full tilt. I screamed.

Coco pulled sharp at her pony's reins and laughed. 'Calm

down, Norah. Christ, what a baby.' Verity pulled up, eyes wild with excitement. She made a clicking noise and her pony started to prance slowly round and round us in circles. 'Everything alright with Mummy last night, Norah?' she asked. She ran her tongue underneath her top teeth as she waited for a reply.

My heart was still thundering from the shock. People were staring. The ponies were out of place here near the car park and the Drama block.

'What do you want?' I asked.

'You didn't answer Verity,' Coco said, unbuckling her helmet and flicking her unicorn hair. 'That's not very nice. She was only being polite, asking you a question.'

I sighed, turned towards Verity. 'It was fine, thank you,' I said, wanting this to be over.

'Getting cosy with Ezra, I see,' Verity said, looking over at Ezra with the U13s. 'That won't last long. He'll come to his senses soon. Old Ez has always been a sucker for a lost cause.'

I huffed a laugh. 'Whatever.'

Verity grinned. She drew her pony to a stop, exactly in line with Coco's. 'Oh, Norah, I really pity you.'

I shielded my eyes from the low rays of sun. 'Is that it?' I asked.

Coco jumped effortlessly down from her pony. 'Not quite,' she said.

Verity dismounted as well, taking the reins of both ponies

so Coco could get something out of her pocket.

Her rose-gold phone with the bunny-ear case.

'Do you want to see something?' Coco asked.

'Not really,' I said.

Coco scrolled. 'Are you sure?' she said.

She pressed play and I heard a man's voice. 'Tell me, Mr Whittaker, in light of this new evidence, is there anything you'd like to tell the court? Anything that perhaps maybe you might have forgotten? Anything you may accidentally have mistaken to recall?' The voice drawled with arrogant glee.

I didn't want to see but I couldn't help it. I had to watch. I had to put one foot in front of the other till I was so close to Coco I could see the individual coloured strands of her hair, smell the coconut sunshine, see the manicure as it shaded the screen and the skin like honeycomb. They were sniggering.

I stared.

The camera work was shaky. It looked like someone in the gallery had taken it. I didn't know much about court and cameras, but this filming didn't look legal.

My dad was slumped in the box, his mouth quivering like he wasn't quite sure what to do. I saw him glance at someone. My mum? His lawyer? Even from a distance, I could see the plea for help in his eyes.

He looked weak and grey.

I felt my eyes well up. I was biting my fingernail without realising it.

'Answer the question, Mr Whittaker!' the lawyer snapped.

And then suddenly my dad put his head in his hands and sobbed, breaking down completely in the witness box.

I covered my mouth with my hand.

Beside me Coco smirked.

'Did you or did you not know that you were obtaining money through false and misleading information and actions, Mr Whittaker?'

'No,' I whispered.

The lawyer pressed on. 'Did you or did you not know that you were wilfully defrauding not just people, but your closest friends? Mr Whittaker, it's a simple question.'

My father's shoulders were shaking.

I thought of when he would laugh so much his shoulders would shake. Watching Charlie Chaplin and Laurel and Hardy on the TV. Telling a joke in the bar. An impromptu dance at a barbecue lit by candlelight with shadowy hollyhocks tall on the riverbank, music played by a couple of the guys with guitars. I thought of when he'd twirl me round and round as a kid in the meadow, mulberry blossom swirling like confetti. I thought of us jumping the rope swing over the river and it snapping because he was too heavy and me laughing and laughing and laughing. I thought of him being there when I came home from school and when I woke up in the morning and when we went cycling on weekends and pulled crackers at Christmas. I thought of all those things that I loved more than anything. They suddenly seemed so far away.

'Yes,' my dad said through shaky breaths and I gasped. He looked up at the lawyer, plaintive. 'Yes, I knew.'

'Speak up, Mr Whittaker.'

But I didn't wait to hear it again. I smacked Coco's hand so the phone went flying into the air and she said, 'What the hell?' and then I ran as fast as I could away from her and Verity and the sound of the phone smashing on the concrete and Coco yelling, 'You'll pay for that!'

I ran and I ran across the grass, inside, down corridors, till I was almost at the main doors and all I could think was that I had to get out. I had to leave. I had to get home.

But as I was about to pull open the door, a hand shot out and grabbed my arm.

'Get off me,' I shouted, twisting out of the grasp.

'Not so fast, Miss Whittaker.'

I recognised the whistle on the W, and stopped struggling. I would never escape Mr Watts's vice-like grip.

I stopped where I was, trying to catch my breath, furiously wiping away tears with my sleeve.

'Now,' he said, relaxing his hold slightly and straightening his cape. 'I presume you are aware that it is against school policy for a child to leave the premises during school hours.'

I just stared angrily at the floor.

'Answer me!'

'Yes,' I said, without looking up.

'So where were you going?'

'Nowhere,' I mumbled.

'It didn't look like nowhere. It looked like you had somewhere very important to be, Miss Whittaker.'

I shook my head.

I could feel his scrutiny. His coffee breath. Then he straightened his tie and changed tack. 'You may not be aware that under special circumstances, arrangements can be made for a pupil to leave the school grounds. Were you aware of that, Miss Whittaker?'

I met his greedy, prying eye. 'No, Sir, I wasn't.'

'We might be able to arrange something, if you wanted to discuss your reasons for escaping.' He could sense the gossip. Smell the downfall of my father.

I couldn't allow Mr Watts the satisfaction. I owed it to my dad, that last shred of decency. But I couldn't process what he had done. All those lives he had ruined. He had taken their money knowing they wouldn't get it back. I wanted to protect him from others, protect him from their dirty grasping claws as he fell.

'It's fine, Sir, thank you,' I said, straightening up. 'I made a mistake. Took a wrong turning. I thought this was the way to the drama department.'

He snorted a disbelieving laugh. 'No, Miss Whittaker, this is not the drama department. Allow me to escort you to the drama department.'

We walked side by side back down the corridor. I glared straight ahead. Adrenaline kept me moving, kept one step in front of the other.

We passed Ezra coming in from the pitch. 'Norah?' he said, looking confused. I ignored him and kept my eyes fixed in front, Mr Watts storming along next to me.

'You should be in class too, Mr Montgomery,' Mr Watts commanded. 'Bell's gone.'

And then we were outside and walking across the courtyard and he was yanking open the drama-department door and everyone was there, waiting in the huge concrete theatre space.

Coco lounging on a chair, smirking, waiting.

'Here we are, Ms Whittaker. The drama department,' Mr Watts said, as if I were the stupidest person he'd ever met.

'Thank you, *Sir*,' I said.

'Watch it!' he said, controlled and hard. 'You have more of your disgraceful father in you than I realised.'

I was about to spit something back again, but the words stuck. I saw our island. Old Percy having to sell his lovely Mississippi boat, Becky's dad having a heart attack, Jess's mum crying at their kitchen table. My father charming each and every one of them. I turned my back on Mr Watts and took my seat. There probably hadn't been time for them all to have seen the clip, but in my head Coco had shared it free and easy.

Mr Watts would get his hands on it soon enough too.

Mr Benson clapped his hands. 'Settle down, everyone, let's begin.'

I whispered my lines under my breath and felt myself slowly disappearing.

It felt like the safest place to be.

CHAPTER TWENTY-ONE

I sleepwalked through the rehearsal. Daniel kept pulling me up. 'Nearly there, Norah, but it's just not quite right . . . I'm not feeling it, Norah . . .' And finally, 'OK, take a break. Norah, it's like you're standing on the outside looking down at yourself playing this part.'

I was sweaty and exhausted and frustrated with myself.

Coco pranced on to the stage for the next scene with Emmeline and some others. She was a good actress but a bit embarrassing, overplaying it with big gestures and cheesy smiles. She got told off a lot by Daniel to pare it back, but she just ignored him.

The lighting guys were in today, messing around with the spotlights. Different parts of the stage kept lighting up unexpectedly. They were a good distraction. I found it hard to look at Coco, giggling and happy on stage, as I waited in the wings for her song to finish.

When it was my turn to go on, the lighting guys called for a pause so they could adjust one of the spotlights. I saw Coco get her phone out of her pocket and tap Emmeline on the shoulder to watch something on the screen. I knew exactly what it was, felt a sick fury rise up. My dad's life was nothing more than a momentary thrill of gossip to them. Coco glanced up with a smirk to meet my eye just as one of the lighting guys shouted, 'OK, good to go!' and Daniel called out, 'Norah, you're on.'

I was singing 'Hopelessly Devoted'. The same song as my audition. The one where I had wowed the crowd. But today they were just words coming blandly out of my mouth.

'No!' Daniel shouted midway through. 'No! Do it again.'

The lights from the rig flashed red and blue on the stage.

'Norah.' He beckoned for me with his finger.

I crouched down so I was level with the edge of the stage, aware of all eyes on me. I was tired. My body and brain exhausted.

'What's going on?' Daniel asked. 'Do you need to stop?'

'I'm fine.' I couldn't stop. I needed to do this now. What else would I do?

'Well, you don't look fine.' He took off his glasses and rubbed his eyes. It was a habit learned from Mr Benson. 'The thing is, Norah, you just look . . .' He searched for a word. 'Numb. Absent. This scene is about betrayal and hurt and sadness. This is where you have to connect.' He stared at me, eyes willing. Then he put his glasses back on and walked away to confer with Mr Benson.

I walked back to centre stage. Daniel's words circled inside

230

me – hate jostling with betrayal and sadness. The music started. I felt numb because I *was* numb.

I thought of my dad knowing that it was all over, that he was going to jail. He wouldn't be able to step out into the sunlight whenever he wanted. He had lied. He had ruined all those lives. He had been holding this secret hugely, painfully inside him. I saw him in his dressing gown on the sofa with his cereal, blankly watching those cartoons and the adverts for sparkly shoes. What had been in his head? Had he been screaming, 'Tell them! Tell them the truth!' I wondered if he had been sitting there with my mum and me curled round him, humouring our false hope, thinking how much he would miss us.

I started to sing. Could hear the thinness of my voice, the waver, the off-key high-notes. Every bad habit that would make Mrs Butterworth my junior-school singing teacher tap a triangle to highlight the fault.

Then suddenly the main spotlight burst on, flooding me in bright white light. For a second I could see nothing else. Just me and the light. Just me and my mum at home. A huge empty space where this lively, exuberant person should have been. A person that I adored who would never be the same again, who had done this to himself, to us – and yet a person that I loved, who loved me and who would soon be gone.

I was suddenly so angry. If I hadn't been singing, I would have screamed. My fists clenched. My eyes welled up. I begged myself not to cry, not here, not with them. But tears rolled down my cheeks all the same, and I couldn't brush them away. I was angry, I was humiliated, I was betrayed. I was sad. I was singing.

I was singing not outside myself but right there in that spotlight, staring straight into the bright whiteness. My voice doubling, tripling, filling the space, the gaps under the seats, the spider's webs in the rafters, getting bigger and bigger. My heart filling my chest, my fingers tingling, my streaming eyes fixed on the luminous white.

And then I was finished.

The light switched off.

The whole place stood silent and still in the greyness.

No one spoke.

No one moved.

Mr Benson was smiling.

Daniel had his mouth open in surprise.

I blinked. Had I even sung?

Then Daniel clapped and then everyone clapped and I swallowed and hung my head, wiped my cheeks and walked quickly off the stage. I found a seat at the front and sat down, half devastated, half high above the clouds.

'Mesmerising,' Mr Benson said.

'Thank you.'

He tilted his head. 'No, thank *you*.' And just as I was sitting, hand up to my mouth, savouring the rush of it all – the knowledge that I had not been numb, that I had cracked it, that I had lived it – the double doors at the back of the room banged open.

'This is a rehearsal!' Daniel shouted without turning round.

Ezra, Freddie and Verity were on stage.

But the people entering would not be stopped. I was surprised to see the headmaster stalking down the aisle towards Mr Benson. With him was a broad man in an expensive-looking suit: old-fashioned handsome, silver-haired, lined face, powerful.

Now Coco was trotting down the steps of the stage to join them. 'Hi, Daddy,' she gushed. It was clearly no surprise to her that he was there.

'Hello, princess.' The silver-haired man acknowledged her with a barely perceptible smile, but rested his hand affectionately on her shoulder. Everyone was coming out on stage to see what was going on. Coco winked at her friends. Ezra frowned.

As I watched Coco's father and the head with Mr Benson, the tingle coursing through my body from the song disappeared. Now the adrenaline made me shake. Something, instinct perhaps, was urging me to be on guard.

Coco and her father looked prepared, in cahoots, as the head ushered the conversation away to the side of the room. Mr Benson shook his head as if what was being said were preposterous. He almost seemed to be laughing. Coco's father wasn't laughing. Neither was Coco, nor the headmaster as he gestured for Coco to say her piece.

The others started to get on with things: chatting, checking their phones. But something kept me watching. Some feeling of dread in the pit of my stomach told me this had everything to do with me. I could sense it, like animals in the wild.

'I won't allow this!' Mr Benson shouted.

Everyone turned. Coco's father stayed very calm, as did the head. Coco lowered her chin, all doe-eyed and demure. They talked, low and hushed, while Mr Benson stood with his arms crossed, glaring at the stage.

The headmaster steered Mr Benson to the side and put his hand on his shoulder, seemingly in a gesture of compassion. But by the look on Mr Benson's face it was more a show of forceful hierarchy. Whatever he said clearly didn't require an answer. Now the headmaster and Coco's father were walking away. Coco sashayed back up the stage. I breathed out, feeling foolish suddenly for getting so paranoid. My heart started to resume its normal beat.

But then I realised the headmaster and Coco's father weren't leaving. They were, in fact, walking towards where I was sitting. They had just taken a circuitous route.

I'd never been in a room with the head before, except during assembly when he was like a toy figure on a distant stage. Now I could see how tall he was, towering above me as he approached, his leathery olive forehead creased with a frown.

Coco was twirling her hair round her finger, staring straight at me. Waiting for me to look at her.

My stomach hollowed.

I realised that for five minutes I'd forgotten about my dad. Forgotten the day.

And suddenly the headmaster was standing in front of me saying, 'Norah, could we have a word outside?'

I knew it.

I knew what was about to happen. I could feel what I had being peeled away. My hope, my achievement. My escape.

Mine. It was *mine*. I wanted to hold it tight somehow. Realised I was trying to do just that as I hugged my arms round my body.

Mr Benson looked so angry I thought he might cry. Then he shook his head.

I followed the headmaster and Coco's father into the stark corridor. Posters for past productions were framed along one white wall. The windows looked out on to the car park and the playing fields. I saw the spot where Coco had shown me the video of my dad admitting his guilt. I saw Mr Watts getting something out of his car. He paused when he saw me. His expression no longer had the hint of grasping for gossip. Instead he just looked amused. He had won.

The headmaster cleared his throat. 'Norah,' he said, talking to me like we'd met before, 'I'm going to have to ask you to be very grown-up about something.' I looked at his teeth, all so straight and white. 'I know you are a very mature young lady and you have been through a great deal lately.'

I couldn't cope with the insincerity of his smile, or the disinterest of Coco's father beside him. I was nothing to them. I looked at the floor, at the lines in the bare concrete. He knew nothing about me.

I only wished I had still been numb.

'We have noted events concerning your father today, and believe it's in all our interests to keep attention on you to a minimum. For your own good. It's very difficult being in the public eye.' The headmaster cleared his throat. 'My team, our governors and, of course, those people who contribute a great deal financially to the school –' at this Coco's father raised his chin – 'do our best to ensure that Chelsea High becomes the subject of no undue negative attention. We balance any incidents against the risk to the school's heritage and reputation. Now in this case, as we know the very generous and influential Summers family, especially young Coco, are kind enough to bring so many of their press contacts to the school performances . . .'

I barely listened from that point.

I heard only: 'We will be making a few adjustments to the cast,' and, 'Coco will be taking over the lead role.'

I wanted to rant and kick at the injustice. I wanted to push

Coco's father so hard that he fell.

I glanced at the stage doors. Longing for the cast to walk out at the injustice. Desperate to see Mr Benson leading Ezra and Daniel, Emmeline and Tabitha in protest.

But of course they didn't. I didn't do anything either. I was exhausted. I had sung my song, I had had my moment. I was done with them all. My family had fallen apart, and now these people had taken the only thing from me that they could.

Why waste my time on this?

Because I loved it.

But I would give them nothing. They had taken enough.

So I said, 'That's fine, Sir,' and I picked up my bag and I walked the long corridor to the door. And I didn't look back.

Coco had done what she set out to do.

If I hadn't hated her quite so much, I would almost have admired her.

CHAPTER
TWENTY-TWO

As I was unlocking my bike I heard Ezra call my name. 'Norah!'

I was struggling with the stupid chain, trying to get away before I saw anyone.

'God, Norah, I'm sorry,' he said when he reached me. 'It's a shit thing to have happened.'

Finally, the lock opened and I could shake the chain loose. 'Yeah,' I said, not wanting him to see my face, the frustrated tears in my eyes. 'It's fine, whatever.' I wrapped the chain round my bike, unable to stop one tear from escaping. I swiped it away, annoyed.

Ezra half stretched out a hand. 'It's just a play. It'll be over next week.'

I was unable to believe he could just brush the whole thing aside like that. 'Are you serious?' He was all languid and easy, eyes almost smiling. 'You think I should just forget about it? I've worked so hard, and they just get to take it away because Coco wants the part?'

He made a face. 'It wasn't all because of Coco.'

238

I scoffed, wiping away any remnant of the tears with my cuff. 'Rubbish. You all know it, and none of you did anything.'

He frowned. The idea of doing something had clearly never occurred to him. 'What could we have done?'

'Anything,' I muttered. 'Something. Complained, stood up for what was right. All of you just sit back and allow her to win.'

'Don't pin this on me. It was your –' He stopped himself just in time.

'I'm not pinning it on you,' I said. 'I know damn well whose fault it is. But I didn't deserve to lose my part in the play over it. That was just Coco using the whole thing to her advantage, and all of you just let it happen.' I heard my voice waver. I couldn't work out if I was being fair or not, but I needed to say it. 'She's a rich bully who's allowed to get her way. And you let her. Every time.' I got on my bike, stumbling a little because I was so angry. 'You're spineless, all of you.'

'Oh, come on, Norah –'

'You are,' I said. 'Not one of you stood up and said that what just happened was wrong. You're all so rich and privileged. You've never had to make a real decision in your lives. It might just be a stupid play to you, but she took something that was mine and you did nothing. I thought you were my friend.' I started to pedal away. Called over my shoulder, 'One day, Ezra, you're going to have to get off the fence and do something. Take some responsibility.'

'What's that supposed to mean?'

'You know what it means.' I stopped, looked back, pushed my hair back from my eyes. The wind whipped cold at my face.

He stood, hands in his pockets, dark eyes accusing, 'Clearly I don't. You want me to quit the play?'

'It's too late for that. It would just ruin it for everyone. I wanted you to do something. One of you to *do something*. You're not hers. Stand up. Stop running away.' I was so angry that words were tumbling out of my mouth. I could hear my blood rushing in my ears. 'Talk to Rollo.'

'What's Rollo got to do with this?'

'Nothing, but I've wanted to say it for ages,' I said. The look in his eyes dared me to carry on. 'Tell him what you think of him. Apologise to your mum. Apologise to your brother. Take some blame and then it'll be done. Stop lurking in the shadows.'

He looked horrified, recoiling physically from the words.

I shook my head and cycled away.

I couldn't really believe what I'd just said. Wheeling my way through the back streets, I realised that while I'd been shouting at Ezra, I could have been shouting at my dad. Or at myself. Wishing it was as easy to face up to mistakes as it was to make them.

CHAPTER
TWENTY-THREE

I went straight home, cycling as fast as I could for most of the way and then slowing, almost to a stop, afraid of what I might find. Would they even let him home? I wondered how I would look at him. I wondered how he would look at me. I thought of Ezra once saying how sometimes he wanted to turn back time so badly he couldn't believe it wasn't possible. I wanted that too. I wanted to be cycling along the leafy towpath, freewheeling down the rickety footbridge and weaving in and out of the mulberry trees till I could throw my bike unlocked to the ground by our overgrown patch of garden.

Instead I slunk, shivering, past the sleek, cold barges, their owners abroad or squirrelled away behind closed shutters. I was ten metres from our boat when I knew that there was no one home. No glow of light from a single window. I kept walking all the same, just to check that they weren't sitting, heads hung, in the dark. But when I unlocked the door there was no one.

I sat for a bit on my own. Staring out at the black swirling water, the monsters in the eddies clawing for us.

I went into my parents' room and rifled through the drawers in search of my phone. I was desperate to talk to Jess. But it wasn't there. My mum had either hidden it somewhere better or taken it with her. I remembered her that morning saying it would all be over soon. Had she known? Had she guessed?

I could smell them, here in their bedroom in the dusky light. Her perfume, his aftershave. I could see my dad's pyjama bottoms just poking out from under his pillow. Were they allowed their own pyjamas in jail, or did they wear regulation grey ones? Would he be allowed to take his shoes, his dressing gown? Or would they stay in the wardrobe, on the back of the door, waiting years for him to come home? Would we throw away what he couldn't take, or leave it all untouched? Would we dust it? Would my mum sleep in the middle of the bed or still on her side? Would he take his pillow? He takes it on holiday with him; he'd have to take it – he couldn't sleep without it. My mind was spiralling, thoughts colliding in their frenzy.

I had to leave.

I got back on my bike and pedalled furiously up the gangplank, up the jetty ramp and out on to the pavement, eyes searching till I found what I was looking for. A red telephone box.

I threw my bike up against it, rummaging in my pockets for change.

Inside it smelt of stale urine and the glass was covered in graffiti and scratches. The phone hung off its wire but thankfully there was a dial tone. I pressed the numbers for Jess's mobile and waited, head tipped back against the dirty glass panels, feeling like all my emotions were waiting in my throat, clamouring to get out as soon as she picked up.

'Hello?'

'Jess, it's Norah,' I said, voice shaky. 'Oh god, have you heard?'

'Yes, I've heard.'

'Why did he do it?' I groaned in a stream of fearful consciousness, burying my face in my hand. 'Why did he lie? I don't know how I'm going to cope if he goes to jail. I don't know how to look at people on the island. What am I going to say to them? We're never going to be able to come home.' There was no response on the other end of the line, and I worried suddenly that the payphone was broken. Then I heard Jess say, very calmly, 'You know *I* live on the island?'

I swallowed. 'Yes,' I said, a little hesitant.

'OK, good. Just checking,' she said. 'Because you ring, Norah, but you never ask about me. You never see how I am, how I'm coping. You know my parents invested all their savings in that company because they believed in you and your dad. It was going to pay for me to go to university.'

I stared down at the dirty concrete floor of the phonebox. 'I'm sorry,' I whispered.

I imagined her shaking her head, loose strands of her ponytail falling in front of her eyes. 'I don't want to hear that you're sorry. I want you to think about *me*. I work in Asda now after school to help pay the mortgage. My mum does more and more night shifts. My dad cries. I don't care about your dad, Norah. I care about *my* dad. I'm not like the others; I'm not turning against you. I just want you to have thought about me. I want you to realise that I've lost everything and I don't have rich grandparents to back me up.'

I could hear the hitch in her voice. The threat of tears so rare from Jess. I felt awful. Silly and selfish and small. I was everything I had accused Ezra of being.

'Norah, your dad will go to jail because he deserves to,' she said. 'Forgive me for not sympathising.'

There was nothing I could say. Jess and I had known each other since we were born. We had never argued in our lives. She had been more than a sister to me. We had slept in the same bed, read each other's diaries, attempted to cut each other's hair with disastrous results, gossiped about the minutiae of life, sat in comfortable silence for hours on holidays. We could talk without talking. We were one. But in that moment, we cracked apart.

She hung up without saying goodbye. Suddenly I was back on my bike again, weaving through traffic, past gleaming sports cars and polished Rolls-Royces, tiny dogs yanking tight on their leads and yapping at my wheels as I cut up on to the pavement and down again, through hot amber lights and beeping horns, swerving pedestrians trying to cross the road and avoiding doormen beckoning sleek limousines to hotel kerbs. I pedalled as fast as I could until I was there, until Harrods loomed in front of me and I jogged up the steps of the tall white mews house, my bike by my side.

The door opened as I was still knocking.

CHAPTER TWENTY-FOUR

'Ms Norah,' said Harold, the butler, with a smile. 'An unexpected pleasure.'

I was mute. I couldn't even admit that I was there, let alone smile back and be welcomed with such warmth.

He took my bike without hesitation, depositing it in a room to his right. His attire was no less casual than it had been any other time I'd visited. I don't know what I expected. I supposed that he relaxed in jeans and a shirt when there was no scheduled appointment. Perhaps they *had* been expecting me.

'Are my grandparents here?' It felt odd to say it out loud.

'Your grandfather is in the garden. Would you allow me to show you through?'

It was just starting to get dark, the light fading to the dusk of a winter's afternoon. It was cold, but I had grabbed the bomber jacket I wear at the stall as I left the boat. It felt shabby in such plush surroundings but still I wrapped it tight round me.

Harold left me on the patio and went off in search of my grandfather. I stood looking at the garden. It was hard to believe something so beautiful existed amidst the urban sprawl of the city. A little oasis. The plants and trees were bare, seedheads poking up like aliens, but there was still the lushness of the evergreens, the prickle of holly and the spikes and cones of the fir trees.

'Norah!' My grandfather was strolling towards me, pulling his gardening gloves off. He was wearing a padded green gilet over his thick cream shirt, burgundy cords and wellingtons, the dog ambling slowly behind him, blindly trying to keep up. 'How lovely to see you; come in out of this cold.' He beckoned me ahead of him, to be first into the warmth.

I was about to head into the living room but he stopped me. 'Wait there,' he said, leaning against the wall to steady himself as he pulled off his boots. He looked old as he shuffled his feet into his slippers. 'We'll go through here.' He gestured towards another door. 'It's warmer; there's a fire already lit.'

He led the way, standing in the doorway so I could pass and pointing towards a big leather chair on one side of a huge old desk. 'This is my study,' he said, as he saw me looking around. 'I tend to stick with one room when I'm on my own.'

I wondered where my grandmother was. Had she gone away to escape the scandal? Or was she in the courtroom, facing it head on?

The study was much cosier than the living room. The wallpaper was dark red, printed with green and gold flying ducks. The fire roared in a little wood burner as the dog flopped himself down on a ratty old tartan blanket. There were a few stacks of papers on the leather-topped desk, the surface peeling and scratched. Books and paintings lined the walls, lit softly by the warm glow of sidelights.

Harold came in, threw a couple more logs on the fire and drew the woollen tartan curtains. The dog snored happily. I watched my grandfather take out a pipe and fill it with tobacco.

'Harold, can we have some tea?' he asked, tapping the pipe on the desk a couple of times.

'Very good, Sir.' Harold's eyes widened a touch. My grandfather look puzzled for a second, then coughed and added, 'Unless you'd like something else, Norah? We have some Coca-Cola that your grandmother thought you might like?'

'Tea's fine, thank you.'

Harold did a quarter bow and left the room.

I shuffled back in my huge chair, finally feeling warm enough to take my jacket off.

My grandfather was feigning concentration on lighting his pipe but I could feel him observing me.

Finally, after a couple of puffs, he said, 'I assume this is about your father.'

I bit my lip and nodded. The smell of tobacco and wood smoke filled the room. The dog yawned. My grandfather leaned back, pipe in hand, tapping it occasionally on the desk.

I realised why I had come. His presence slowed life down. His deliberation before speaking calmed the atmosphere, like everyone could wait and take a breath. Even the world, it felt, took a pause in turning.

Harold came in with the tea. No special tray with sugar, cups and saucers and a pot this time. Instead he carried two big steaming mugs of perfectly brewed tea and a plate of chocolate Hobnobs.

'Thank you, Harold. These are my favourite,' my grandfather said, picking up a chocolate biscuit and dunking it in his tea – half, I think, to show me that that was acceptable behaviour here in the study. 'Help yourself.'

I smiled weakly. 'I love a Hobnob.'

'All good Whittakers are fond of a Hobnob.'

I snapped mine in half and dunked, watching the tea slide off the chocolate. I wanted to ask if he'd been in the courtroom, what had made my dad finally break down. I wanted to know if my grandfather had suspected. I wanted to know what happened now, where my parents were, whether I'd see my dad again. But most of all, and I could barely admit this to myself, I wanted to ask if it was still OK for me to love him.

I could feel my grandfather watching me.

I nibbled the melting chocolate from the corner of my Hobnob.

He leaned forward in his chair. The wood creaked. 'You can ask me anything you like, Norah,' he said.

I stared at my biscuit. 'Do you think my dad is a good person?' I asked, unable to meet his eye, fearful of the answer.

My grandfather took a bite of his biscuit. 'Your father has always been a wild one,' he said, reclining again. 'Even as a small boy. Never satisfied. Always thinking that he was missing something. Something that he thought everyone else knew about, I think.' I watched the pipe in the ashtray, forgotten. He took a sip of his tea.

I cradled my cup in my hands, the warmth spreading up my arms. I found it hard to hear what he was saying; I wanted to hurry him to the point, braced for impact. The dog inched closer to the fire, happily scorching his skin.

My grandfather went on. 'One outcome of that, Norah, is that it's very easy to be led. To follow. Like the Pied Piper. You know that story, the man with his pipe and the rats and the children all following? Yes. Yes.' He nodded, pleased that I'd had some education on this point. 'And your father has always been easily led.'

I had never thought about my dad that way: the led rather than the leader. It was confusing.

My grandfather ran his hand over his mouth, thinking. 'I cannot tell you the number of times I have bailed him out of things. Rescued him. Pulled him out of scrapes. But there's only so many times one can try, Norah. Or –' he put his hand to his chest – 'I *believe* there are only so many times. My wife would disagree. But there you go.'

He picked up the pipe again, relighting the tobacco with big puffs. I knew then that my grandmother was with my dad now.

'Don't you take on this problem, Norah,' he said. 'This isn't for you. This is your father's. Yes?'

I sipped my tea. I could feel it catch over the worried knot in my throat. 'It's all of ours,' I said.

He sucked in his breath. 'No,' he said, more brusquely than I think he'd intended.

He pushed the biscuit plate towards me, taking one for himself at the same time. 'Hard to resist, eh?'

I smiled. The tension dissipated.

'Why did you stop talking to each other?' I asked.

He sighed. 'Because I made a decision a very long time ago not to help your father out of one of his scrapes, and he never forgave me.' He bit the Hobnob, chewed. 'Long before any of this business. When he was, gosh – twenty-five, twenty-six? He was cast in what was supposedly a big feature film, but at the crucial point the studio funding collapsed. Of course it did!' My grandfather rolled his eyes. 'Your father appeared on the doorstep begging me to invest, having been gallivanting around for years with no steady job. I said no.'

I gasped. That had been my dad's Laurel and Hardy big break. His moment to hit the big time, his big regret. 'Why did you say no?'

'Well, you've heard of the Pied Piper, so I presume you've heard of the boy who cried wolf?'

I nodded.

He tapped his pipe. 'There had been a string of similar things, Norah. I had lost a lot of money, and a lot of faith. A person can only do so much before they tire when their goodwill is constantly abused. I'm afraid I didn't trust him. I didn't believe that, had I invested, he would have changed.' He rubbed his eyes, as if telling the story wearied him. 'I'd already paid for him to go to theatre school, and he had dropped out. What would he have done when the director told him he had to work harder? When things weren't going quite to plan? When one of his friends sniffed out a better deal somewhere else? He leaves things, Norah, when they are tough.'

He put the pipe down in the ashtray. 'Maybe I'm being unfair. Maybe if I'd invested then, he wouldn't have been so quick to jump on to this hare-brained scheme and we'd all be in a very different place.' He sighed and shook his head. 'What you have to remember is that you don't just get one shot. Your father fixates on missed opportunity. But there's no such thing. Not with hard work and dedication. A man – or woman, for that matter – cannot rely on talent alone. He never wanted to do the work. I have no idea why. And, believe me, I've thought about it a lot. The best I can come up with is that he's afraid of being seen to try and then failing. But who knows?'

I didn't like hearing about my dad like this. I didn't want this clarity. The focus was too sharp. It left no room for romanticism.

I could feel him watching me. 'You can't fix everything, Norah. You learn that in the end. You have to let people deal with their own mistakes. Otherwise they never grow up.' His chair creaked as he sat back, elbows resting on the leather. 'Your mother knows it. She knows she's encouraged him.'

'My mother?'

He got up and went to get a photograph from the bookshelf. 'Bill has always been her Achilles heel. She let him drift along with his dreams. It's not good, to live outside of reality.'

He handed me the silver-framed photograph.

'There's Bill.' He pointed to where my dad was grinning at the back. 'And there's your mother.'

I looked at the girl perched on the railing. The big thick blonde fringe over her eyes, the shirt half unbuttoned, a look in her eyes of self-assured certainty.

'It's not her fault, I suppose,' he went on. 'Can't help who you fall in love with.' His face softened. 'You don't have to stop loving him, Norah, to understand him. As you get older, you learn that sometimes even good people can make very bad mistakes. We are none of us perfect.'

I felt like I wanted to cry. Instead, I nibbled a bit of Hobnob. Then, when I felt like I could speak without tears, I said, 'So why did you bail him out this time? Why did you pay for our mooring and the lawyers?'

He looked at me with big watery eyes. 'Because we heard about you, Norah. We heard about you.'

CHAPTER
TWENTY-FIVE

My pager bleeped as I sat on the rug in front of the fire, stroking the snoring dog. It was my mum.

My grandfather called her back. They had a hushed discussion which I barely even tried to eavesdrop. I was so tired I could have curled up with Ludo the Labrador and slept next to him, the flames warming my tummy.

'They're still with the lawyer. She thinks they'll be some time,' he said as he hung up the phone. 'We've agreed you'll stay here the night.'

I thought about how, when my dad first dropped me off at the steps to their house, the prospect of staying the night would have had us both in stitches. Now I was almost relieved.

'Write a list for Harold and he can buy you anything you need,' said my grandfather, searching for a pen on his desk.

'Oh, I don't need anything,' I said, amused at the idea of him popping next door to Harrods to fetch me a clean shirt for the morning. 'Just a toothbrush.'

My grandfather paused, surprised by the simplicity of my request. He popped the pen back in the pot. 'Very well. We'd better go and see about rustling you up something for supper.'

He stood by the door, holding it open so I could pass, then rested his hand on my shoulder to direct me down the hall. It was a gesture my dad sometimes made. I realised how similar they looked. I don't think I'd allowed my eyes to make the connection before, but now I could see his features morphing, resetting comfortingly into those of my father. He was concentrating really hard, trying to make sure my stay was a success. I knew he'd have it in the neck from my grandmother if anything went wrong.

I'd have to stop calling her 'my grandmother' soon. Granny, maybe, or Gran? It seemed more certain, with the turn of events in the trial, that they would become permanent fixtures in my life. Before I had assumed I would just shake them off like a dog. But I was tied now to these people. And I didn't mind the tether. There was wonderment in being wanted.

I slept in the spare bedroom in the eaves. I passed others on my way up the stairs, all chintzy and floral, and wondered why I wasn't in one of them. But when I got to this one, I noticed the freshness of the yellow paint, the newness of the white bedspread and the bright scatter cushions embroidered with birds and butterflies. On the wall was a framed poster for the Still Life exhibition we'd been to at the Royal Academy, bright yellow and orange tulips in a blue and white vase. The cream carpet felt like I was the first person to walk on it – thick and squishy beneath my feet. The cream towels folded on the bed looked fluffy and new. By the door to the tiny en suite, there was an old chest of drawers, and on it a few books for someone my age – a Jane Austen and a Rosamond Lehmann – and a couple of ceramic boxes, not really my taste but clearly selected from the house as the most avant garde they had to offer. Above it hung a gold-rimmed mirror. I realised suddenly that this room had been decorated for me. For the hope that perhaps, one day, sometime in the future I might know them well enough to stay. I bit my lip. Glanced at Harold, who had shown me to the door.

'Your room, Norah,' he said.

He handed me a Harrods bag. 'We want you to be comfortable,' he said when I frowned at how full it was. 'I didn't pick any of it, so no need to worry. I handed control to a lovely sales girl in the ladies' department.'

Then he left, pausing to rearrange the dried flowers on the window sill on his way.

I sank down into the thick feather covers on the bed and looked gingerly into the bag. What had they bought me? I pulled out a pair of the softest brushed cotton pyjamas, pale blue with white stars. Slippers with fur linings and a light grey dressing gown made out of – I shook my head in disbelief as I looked at the label – cashmere. There was designer underwear in boxes, new socks, a hairbrush, shampoo, soap, a toothbrush. I kept rifling through. There was everything and more than I would ever need. And while I knew it was over the top and unnecessary in its extravagance, I slipped on the pyjamas all the same and wrapped myself in the cashmere and padded to the bathroom that smelt of lemons and fabric softener, brushed my teeth with my brand-new brush and snuggled down into the warm fluffy bed. Alone but not alone. Afraid but strangely comforted in the calm, peaceful bubble of a house where it felt like, for one night, no harm could reach me.

I dreamt that I still had the part of Sandy in the play, standing in the spotlight next to Ezra, with my dad clapping and cheering from the audience. Even Jess was there, giving a standing ovation. Everything the way it was supposed to be. For a split second when I woke up, I remembered what it was like to be happy.

I left for school earlier than normal. My grandfather – 'You can call me Granddad if you like' – tried to persuade me to let Harold drive me in the Bentley but I shook my head, trying not to laugh at the idea of it. Overnight I become the girl pulling up on the yellow zigzags in the shiny great car . . . No, it wasn't for me. I thanked him anyway. As I left I felt the urge to turn round and give him a hug, but I didn't. I gave him a wave instead.

'You'll be alright, Norah,' he said. Then he smiled, wrinkled eyes crinkling, the hint of my dad in them. 'You will be alright.'

I couldn't believe how desperate I had been to hear it. I clung to the sentence like a limpet, clutching it to me as I cycled away.

CHAPTER TWENTY-SIX

I didn't go to school. There was less than a week till the end of term, and I had no intention of setting foot in the place. They could have their play and their parties. I wasn't interested.

Instead I cycled away past Harrods, along the Brompton Road to the Victoria and Albert Museum where I swung left – the route embedded from trips to museums as a kid – and hopped off my bike at South Kensington tube. I'd put my leggings on instead of tights, so I tucked the skirt of my school uniform up into my baseball jacket as subtly as I could, locked my bike to a railing and went into the Underground.

The District Line tube was cold as we chugged out of London towards the suburbs. At Richmond I took a bus. It wasn't a long journey but I was nervous, so every stop felt like a hundred. My fingers thrummed against my knee. If I'd been sitting next to myself, I'd have be annoyed by the movement, but I couldn't stop.

On the bus, I passed the time thinking about Coco. About her smug pleasure at taking my part. How she must have sat at dinner last night across the table from her parents, chinking glasses with her father at their success. Maybe she'd even shown the court-room clip to her mother. Although Coco's mother was probably just like Coco – only interested in herself.

From the bus stop it was a twenty-minute walk to the island. Across the park, the bare trees watching, the mulch of leaves and grass damp with early-morning dew under my feet. It was the same but different, the scene I had left stolen by the seasons. The last time I was here, the leaves were a lush green canopy over the river, the cowslips were out, and the fat red mulberries were so dark they were almost black. Now everything felt barren.

I pulled my scarf up when I reached the bridge and walked with my head down. It was cold and so early that there weren't many people about, only rowers finishing their dawn outings and tired fishermen who'd been out all night. Even so, I couldn't face any awkward hellos or deliberate ignores.

I saw the For Sale sign by Old Percy's Mississippi steamboat. Hurried past the Mulberry pub, trying to ignore the million desperate signs in the window for cheap drinks and the patched-up roof. I didn't pause to wave through the cracked café window that no one had replaced. The grass around the mulberry bushes was long, unkempt. Phyllis's display of gnomes had gone green with mould.

I wondered if it was always like this in winter, or whether it was all because of us.

Seasons changed and grass was probably often uncut, but now everything was a symbol. Everywhere I looked I saw decay.

Droplets of rain fell like fingers flicking at my skin. I pulled my baseball jacket tighter, glancing at my watch, checking that I still had time.

Jess was on the junior GB team and going to go all the way to the Olympics. That was the aim. I'd never stopped to think what an achievement it was, her sporting success. All my life I'd just found it a supreme hassle. Every plan we'd made always centred around her training sessions. But now I felt like a stranger to this place. Nothing seemed normal. Jess the athlete, her morning workout something to be revered. I felt like an outsider, exuding the city. I felt like my mouth wouldn't even know how to say hello.

She was standing on the concrete out the back of the canoe club, washing down her boat in a pair of hideous multi-coloured leggings, the ones we'd always laughed about looking like fluorescent vomit, and a bright blue anorak. Her hair was pulled up right on top of her head and damp with rain and sweat. Her cheeks were pink.

She'd seen me. I knew she had. Nothing gets past Jess. Maybe she was expecting me. Maybe she'd been waiting.

I stayed where I was, hands in my pockets, biting my lip, watching.

Jess turned off the tap and dried her hands on a manky

towel that I couldn't believe was so familiar – orange and purple, frayed at the edges, always slung over the plastic brown chair with one leg shorter than the others. If you were sitting on it, as I always was, waiting for Jess to finish, you were constantly fighting the pull of the floor.

She disappeared inside and came back out wearing her navy-blue tracksuit bottoms with a red stripe up the side. I knew everything about her. I knew the bounce in her walk, the wonky set of her mouth, the chipped front tooth, the weird spoon shape of her nails. And yet she was a stranger walking towards me, and I was a stranger waiting here in the shrubbery.

My teeth were chattering. I wondered if she was going to shout at me. Or tell me to go away. Or worse, just blank me.

But she did none of the above. She stopped a foot or so away from me, tilted her head to one side and said, 'Hello.'

And I looked down at the muddy gloop of leaves on the floor, swallowed and said, 'I'm really sorry.'

I'd meant to say hello back. But the words were already in my throat, and wouldn't be bypassed.

Jess sort of laughed. Then she too looked at the gloop on the ground, pushed it a bit with the toe of her trainer, and said, 'There's no one upstairs. Do you want a cup of horrible tea?'

I nodded. Rain pitter-pattered on my face. 'Yes please.'

'Come on then.'

I followed her into the canoe club. The smell, the black-and-white pictures, the grubby carpet, the muddy floor, the dirty teaspoons, the chipped mugs all exactly as they had been before I left.

CHAPTER
TWENTY-SEVEN

We sat side by side in two easy chairs overlooking the river like two grannies in a retirement home, hands clasped round our cups – hers with a picture of an Irish terrier on it, mine with stick people canoeing badly.

'So how's the posh school?' she asked.

'Posh,' I said. 'They're called Rollo and Coco and all have really glossy hair.'

She snorted a laugh into her tea.

I smiled.

We stared at the rain as it started to hammer down on to the river. The ducks slid by as if nothing was happening, calm and unruffled on the outside, paddling like the devil underneath. That was me now, desperately scrabbling to find a new normal while sipping casually from my canoe-club mug.

But now wasn't the time to be calm and unruffled. I remembered what I'd shouted at Ezra: *Take some blame and then it'll be done.* I put my cup down. 'I'm sorry that he knew,' I said. 'That my dad knew what he was doing when he took the money off people. I'm sorry for what happened to your family.'

She nodded, eyes looking out at the river.

I looked right at her. 'I'm sorry I believed him,' I said. And I was definitely not calm and unruffled – I was welling up and sniffing and wiping my nose with my sleeve. 'I'm really sorry I believed him.'

'Oh, Norah,' Jess sighed, putting her cup down and fishing around for a tissue. She was the type of person who always had a tissue. 'Don't cry. He's your dad; of course you believed him. I just . . . I wanted you to see it from our point of view. Just for a second.'

'I know. I know and I'm sorry I was so selfish.'

She watched me for a bit as I tried to gasp my breath back and wipe my face with the Kleenex. Then, when I was as far from calm and unruffled as it's possible to be, she stretched over in her seat and gave me a hug.

I pressed my face into her anorak and could smell the river water. I could feel the pressure of her hands on my back and her cheek against my head. I could feel the familiarity of her, her niceness. And suddenly I felt like I could breathe, like I could gulp in this river-scented air. This person. This place. This home.

I pulled away from the hug and sat up straight, blowing my nose and wiping away the tears. Taking a deep breath, I pushed my hair back from my face. 'I'm sorry.'

'You don't have to apologise any more, OK?' she said.

I nodded, sniffing.

'It was just . . . it was so frustrating that you never acknowledged it,' she said. 'That he might have been a part of it. Even if he hadn't known what he was doing, you couldn't see he still had to carry some blame for not having the nous to check it out. For being fooled, and letting us all be fooled alongside him. I understand that this hasn't been great for you, Norah, but it has been *so* bad here.'

I felt myself welling up again in empathy. I felt so awful.

She swiped at her eyes and went on, 'And what makes it worse is, I like your dad. I do. Or I did. But he ruined our lives, and you were there defending him all the time.'

I had the same battle inside. I liked my dad too. I loved him. But I hated what he had done. What had my grandfather said – *sometimes even good people can make very bad mistakes*. I picked up my mug and stared at the stewed tea.

'That's what made it hard.' She pulled her legs up underneath her. 'I just wanted you to see what he'd done.'

I inhaled, my breath shaky. 'I've seen. I've seen it. I promise.'

She nodded. 'I know.'

'I think he's definitely going to go to jail,' I said.

She picked up her mug. 'He knew what he was doing, Norah,' she said, her voice both blunt and kind.

I looked back out at the river and so did she, rivulets of

rain wriggling down the glass. I had sat in this spot so many times, idling and carefree. A whole other life. Completely unreachable.

Then next to me, Jess shifted in her seat so she was facing my way. 'So go on. Tell me about this glossy-haired school . . .'

And I turned so I could see her shrugged half-smile, felt my heart soar at the lifeline she had thrown. I could have hurled myself into her arms and never let go. Instead I took a sip of my tea and told her all about Chelsea High. And she rolled her eyes and she laughed and she gasped and she shook her head at the ridiculousness.

And as I talked, my reflection in the window started to change. I started to see myself. I saw who other people saw. I saw the blue eyes and the long brown hair with the fringe that wouldn't stay where I wanted it to and the jacket and the chipped nail polish holding my cup.

I felt like I was seeing it for the first time. Seeing a reality I had taken for granted. Before, I had blindly followed. But now I was out in front.

Jess walked with me back across the island to the bridge. We paused at the patch of grass that used to be my garden. Our mooring was already filled by another barge. Our bench gone. Our weeds shorn.

I would never live here again. I knew that now.

Perhaps I'd had to come back to understand. It had been as much about the people as the place, and we would never be welcome. It felt alien now to live so comfortably surrounded by those I loved, all in one place.

'I'm glad you came,' Jess said, holding up a big canoe-club umbrella over us.

'Me too.' I glanced dubiously out over the bridge at the rain.

'Do you want to keep the umbrella?' she asked.

'No, it's OK.' I shook my head. 'Do you think we'll be friends again?' I asked, trying to sound casual as I focused on the downpour.

All I wanted was for her to say yes. It would all be easier if she did. Even things at school wouldn't seem so mammoth if I had someone to laugh about them with on the phone.

'I don't know,' she said. I felt my heart sink. Then she added, 'I hope so. It'd be a waste otherwise, wouldn't it?'

I smiled. 'Yes it would.'

'Maybe it could be a new us,' she said.

I nodded. 'A new us.' Then after an awkward tentative hug, I ran out into the rain.

'Wait,' she shouted.

I stopped on the bridge, rain sheeting down. 'What?'

'The glossy hair – it's just silicone,' she called. 'Silicone coating the hair. It's gross really, if you think about it.'

I laughed.

She shrugged and smiled.

I ran for the bus.

CHAPTER
TWENTY-EIGHT

I waited all day for them to come home.

I scrubbed the boat from top to bottom, hoovered, cleaned, washed up, dried up. I even dusted. I don't think anyone had ever dusted on our boat. I worked in tandem with the cleaner on the sleek barge next door. And then I waited.

And finally the lock turned and the door opened.

My mum walked in first: steady, calm like she was holding herself together to stay strong for the patient. Her face softened when she saw me and her shoulders dropped. I hugged her tight. She smelt of hospitals – the sterile environment of the court – and coffee, and mints. I felt her hand squeeze the fabric of my jumper for a second. I felt her smell my hair. I felt that I had given her, for a moment, what Jess and my grandfather had given me – a tether. A grounding. The feeling that you weren't at any minute going to float off the surface of the world.

Behind her I saw my dad.

Stooped and tired and old.

His skin was grey. The bags under his eyes black. He didn't

look up. I realised he couldn't. And when he finally did, it was just a quick glance. 'Hey, Norah,' he said, exhausted.

I forced myself not to cry.

A few months ago, I would have hurled myself wailing at him, but he didn't need that burden on top of everything. 'Dad?' I said. 'Why don't you sit down over there and I'll make you a cup of tea.'

He looked disorientated, rubbing his tired eyes.

'Mum, why don't you have a bath? I'll make dinner.'

'I don't need a bath,' she said, faffing in the kitchen for something to do.

'Have a bath,' I said, more forceful.

She stopped what she was doing. I watched her look over at my dad, who had plonked himself down on the sofa.

'Maybe just a quick shower,' she said. 'Bill, do you need anything?' She was stalling. As if they'd been so tied together during the trial they didn't know how to be on their own any longer.

'I'm fine.' He waved a hand.

My mum went into the bathroom. I made the tea. My dad undid his tie and top button, took his shoes off, put his feet up on the table and sat with his head back, eyes shut, staring into the black of his eyelids.

I carried the tea over to the table.

At this point I could still brush it all under the carpet, curl up next to him and never ask. That was how our relationship worked. We ignored the difficult in favour of the fantasy.

I sat down next to him. 'Here's your tea.'

'Thanks.'

He'd opened his eyes now, but was still staring up at the ceiling. I studied the stubble on his cheeks, the wrinkles round his eyes, the grey hairs round his temples, like I was seeing him, for the first time, as a real person.

'Why did you do it?' I asked.

He immediately sat up straight. He opened his mouth to speak but didn't say anything. I wondered if he was deciding whether or not to lie. He went to speak again, but again he didn't.

Then finally he leaned forward, hands clasped together on his knees, and he said, 'Because I wanted to be a success.'

I could feel myself blinking. I could hear my heart beating.

'Because I wanted to make those films. I wanted to make it work. And I thought it would.' He bit his lip and I realised where I got the habit from. 'And then I couldn't make it stop. And once you're in, how do you get out? All those people had lost all that money and I just kept telling myself if we just made the films, then maybe it would be a success, maybe somehow we'd make enough if we just kept ploughing on . . .' He shook his head. 'It was too terrifying to believe it was real.'

'Are you scared?' I asked.

'No.' He laughed.

'You don't have to lie,' I said.

He looked at me, surprised.

I felt older.

He tapped his fingers to his mouth. 'Yes,' he said at last. 'I suppose I am.'

I nodded. 'Me too.'

He reached out his arm and I leaned into him. 'You smell,' I said, laughing.

'You try being in court,' he said.

I tried to hold the moment in time. Pause it so it would last forever.

After a few minutes he said, 'How's the play going?'

'I lost my part.'

'What!' I could feel his outrage as his arm tightened round me.

'Yeah. But it doesn't matter.'

'Of course it matters!'

'It did matter,' I said. 'It doesn't matter now.'

He didn't ask why I'd lost it. Perhaps in fear of the answer. 'You're much stronger than me,' he said into my hair.

I felt a sudden jolt of terror, imagining how he would fare in jail. Who he would be when he came out. How he would change. But I said, 'No I'm not.'

'You'll be a star one day, Norah. I can feel it in my bones.'

I snuggled into the weight of his arm round my shoulders, wondering when it would be taken away and when I'd get it back. 'So will you,' I said. 'They'll make a film about this. You can be in it. You can write it.'

'What, in jail?' he said.

'Yes. There you'll have a project. Something to focus on.'

He shifted position. 'That's not a bad idea actually,' he said.

And we sat for the next half an hour or so discussing who we would cast in our movie. Then my mum came out of the shower and decided to order a takeaway.

We ate Chinese and we laughed and we watched a bit of TV. All of us more normal than we'd been for months. All of us aware how soon it would end.

CHAPTER TWENTY-NINE

On the day of the first performance of *Grease* at Chelsea High, my dad was sentenced to four years in jail. I went to the court, sandwiched between my grandparents in the gallery.

As we waited for the judge, I thought about the play, everyone getting ready at school, and I felt my heart tug a little. If none of this had happened, what it would be like to feel the heat of the spotlight and that adrenaline-fizzing moment when the whole chorus comes together in a unison far greater than its parts? I wanted to be losing myself in someone else's line, to be zipping up my costume and waiting nervously in the wings and smelling the make-up and the sweat and the hairspray and feeling the giggling elation of the applause. I wanted to forget reality for just a precious few moments.

I didn't dare look around at the angry faces I knew so well sitting in the other seats. When at one point curiosity got the better of me, I found a glance of sympathy from Mrs Jackson rather than the venom I expected. I knew she wouldn't look at my dad the same way. It brought with it the feeling of both relief and shame. It was like my grandfather had said. My dad's mistakes did not have to be mine, but to separate myself felt traitorous.

The judge accused him of 'acting out a charade and abusing the trust of those who believed in him on a colossal scale'.

My dad hung his head, cheeks pink, shamed.

I tried really hard to keep the statement confined to the trial. Occasionally it seeped out, like an octopus in a box, the tentacles of his deception infecting my memories, but I pressed down hard on the lid and snapped it shut. I loved him more than I could blame him. I didn't want to hold him accountable. But as I stole a glance at Old Percy, stooped shoulders, tears streaming from cloudy cataract eyes, I knew he hadn't destroyed my life as he had destroyed theirs. He'd simply changed it.

It was all confusing and messy and horrible. I felt my shoulders shudder. When my grandmother touched my arm and said, 'Shall we go?' I had never been more relieved to be ushered out under a sweep of her camel-coloured wrap.

That afternoon I took the tube and bus ride back to the island, and I met with Jess on the concrete steps far up the riverbank, and I cried and she cried. And we wrapped our arms round each other's shoulders and she laid her head on mine.

'We'll be OK, Norah.'

'I hope so.'

Over the next few days, people with normal lives got excited about the end of term and Christmas. I listened to my mum, endlessly on hold on the phone, trying to arrange our first prison visit. She had tried to convince me to go to school, but I flat out refused. The last thing I needed to see was Coco and Ezra and everyone buoyed up about the play. My mum didn't have the energy to fight me.

Red tape and a shortage of staff had denied us the standard protocol prison visit in my dad's first seven days of incarceration. It was all agonisingly slow. To us it was the whole world – to them he was just another inmate. A number.

My dad had problems with his phone card and getting our phone number approved so he only managed to call late one evening when I was in the bath. My mum spoke to him. When I asked, she said that he didn't sound like himself. He'd said that everything was fine. His cellmate was fine. The food was fine. The guards were fine. The exercise was fine.

I closed my eyes and remembered the hug he had given me the morning he was sentenced. I could see it now only in snippets of memory – the tightness with which he held me, as if he might crush my bones, the feel of his hand to the back of my head, the welling up of his eyes. He'd held my face and said, 'I'm so proud of you.'

Saturday was the day of Emmeline and Freddie's party, the event that I had been so joyous about getting an invite to and which now felt like a distant memory. We were at the stall.

I realised I'd been left on my own for ages unpacking, so I went in search of my mum and Jackie. I found them huddled in the back of the van, my mum silently weeping into Jackie's old faux-fur coat, Jackie clutching her tight saying, 'You'll get through this, Lois. You're strong; you will.'

The mirror image of how I had been with Jess almost broke my heart. But there was something in knowing these people were around us, dispensing hope, buoying us up and sending us back out there.

CHAPTER THIRTY

The play of course was deemed a hit. At the stall, I borrowed Big Dave's phone to read *Tatler* online, which said, 'IT girl and Instagram sensation Coco Summers dazzled in the role of Sandy.' There was a photo of her in a floaty white nightie singing 'Hopelessly Devoted'. In contrast, I was standing in the icy wind tunnel of Portobello Market, the earflaps of my fur-lined hat pressed tight to my face by my huge wool scarf, wearing two pairs of thermal underwear, a floor-length belted cream puffer jacket of my mum's and moon boots, looking like a Moomin. But I found that I didn't care. There were more important things in life.

When I handed the phone back Big Dave – who had discovered a new true crime podcast and was never without one earphone glued to the unfolding saga – sighed at the screen and said, 'Jesus, Norah, *Tatler*? I'll be getting adverts for all sorts of posh crap now!'

My affection for Big Dave had trebled that morning when he'd come in handy with a mate in the prison service, who was sorting out all our kerfuffle with visitation. We were hoping to see my dad first thing Boxing Day morning.

'A nice Christmas present,' Big Dave had said, all shy-affection to my mum as we were unpacking.

I saw my mum and Jackie exchange one of their looks. The type I hadn't seen for months that said, 'This guy's a total moron but what would we do without him?' The type that used to be the norm before the trial and all the sobbing.

I scrunched my hands tight in delight at the change.

Then I thought of my dad in his cell or wherever he was, and I felt guilty for feeling any kind of happiness.

Jackie was watching me.

'He'll pay his dues and then he's done. That's it,' she said. 'He's still alive. He's still your dad. He's just banged up.' She ruffled my hat and gave my shoulders a squeeze. 'Blimey, Norah, how many clothes have you got on?'

'I'm cold,' I said, stamping my ice-block feet. 'Even the parrot's unhappy.'

We all looked at the poor African Grey. As if not humiliated enough living in a cage on a market stall, he was now sporting a purple knitted jacket and matching cap that he continually tried to flick to the floor, but Barbara had tied it on tight.

'I'm going to set him free one day,' Jackie said.

I was no longer concentrating on the parrot. Out of the corner of my eye, I could see Daniel and Tabitha heading our way.

'Hide me!' I said, tugging on Jackie's sleeve.

'Why?' she asked, looking perplexed.

'Just *hide me*.'

'Not until you tell us what's going on,' said my mum, hands on her hips. She looked quite menacing in a big black floor-length coat, a furry red Cossack hat and red boots.

Daniel was getting closer. Tabitha had paused to look at Barbara's stall, her hands wrapped round a Starbucks cup, a grey bobble hat on her head.

'Oh god, OK,' I said. And reeled off a very reduced version of the entire losing-my-part-in-*Grease* fiasco.

My mum's eyes got bigger and sadder as I talked. 'I can't believe you didn't tell us.'

'It doesn't matter,' I said, hopping from one foot to the other, desperate to leave.

'It clearly does,' said Jackie. They were getting closer still. Daniel had been been distracted by the parrot, pausing to guffaw as it muttered something. I watched Tabitha pick up a brooch from Barbara's stall and examine it as Daniel tried to get the bird to say more.

'I knew that Coco was a little bitch,' my mother went on, incensed. 'Her mother was just the same at school.'

'OK, OK, can I go now?'

Over on Barbara's stall the parrot had stopped playing ball and couldn't be goaded to say more.

My mum shook her head. 'I'm not letting you hide from them. You need to stand up tall. Show them how strong you are.'

'What? No!' I pleaded.

'It's them that should be ashamed,' said my mum in her loudest voice as Tabitha and Daniel arrived at the stall.

'Hi, Norah,' said Tabitha shyly, clearly having heard what my mum just said.

'Hi,' I said, barely meeting her eye before going over to straighten out the coats.

'Can I help you?' asked Jackie, nose turned up, voice lacking any emotion.

'Can we just have a look around?' asked Daniel.

'You can do what you like,' said my mum with complete disinterest.

Tabitha and Daniel browsed in awkward silence. It was excruciating.

My mum watched, one hand on her hip. 'Is it for anything in particular?'

Tabitha did a little cough. 'We have a Beautiful and Damned party tonight,' she said.

My mum started flicking quite violently through the dresses to find something for Tabitha.

At that point, Daniel sidled up to me and said, 'Hey.'

I focused on smoothing down the jacket sleeves and straightening the suit trousers on the hangers. 'Hi.'

Daniel started to browse the rail, following me as I worked. After a moment he said, 'The play was rubbish.'

I glanced back. 'Really?'

'Yeah,' he said, hands flicking through the suits. 'Really bad. The spark went completely.'

I feigned interest in the buttons of a cream safari suit. 'It did?'

Daniel's hands stilled on the rail. 'Norah, no one wanted it to happen.'

'So why did no one say anything?' I said, voice rising in frustration.

'I don't know. Because that's the way it's always been.' He rubbed his forehead as if trying to think of what to say. 'If Mr Benson couldn't do anything, what could we do?'

'If there was no cast, there wouldn't have been any play,' I said.

Daniel's mouth twisted. 'Yeah,' he said. 'Yeah, you're right.'

It didn't feel great to be right. I moved away to the shirt rail.

On the other side of the stall, my mum snapped at Tabitha, 'Do you want to be Beautiful or Damned?'

'Beautiful, please,' Tabitha stammered.

My mum plucked from the rail a peach satin Pride and Prejudice style empire-line dress with poppies embroidered round the hem and dangly lace over the upper arms which she thrust at Tabitha. 'There you go. Beautiful,' she said, and ushered her into the rickety changing cubicle of three sheets held together with string and clothes pegs.

Daniel was still next to me, working his way through the men's wear. 'It's been weird without you at school,' he said.

I shook my head. 'No it hasn't.'

'It really has. I'd got used to having you around.' He gave me a little nudge on the arm but I tried to ignore him.

'I saw you smile just then,' he said.

'No you didn't,' I said, adjusting a gold and white swirl-print shirt that actually was vintage Versace.

From the army surplus stall, Big Dave cut in, 'She did smile. I saw it.'

'Butt out, Dave!' Jackie snapped to my defence.

'Time out.' Daniel held up a hand. 'I have to have that shirt,' he said, grabbing the swirly Versace from my hand. 'It's a miracle of clothing.'

Jackie was a sucker for someone with outlandish taste. 'It is fabulous,' she said, changing immediate allegiance to Daniel as he slipped the shirt on.

I gave her a look that suggested she was fraternising with the enemy.

'I love it,' said Daniel, admiring himself as he turned from side to side in the mirror. 'What do you think, Norah?'

I gave him a cursory glance. 'It's disgusting,' I said. But I was really just thinking about how he'd said he missed me at school. I'd missed him too. And Tabitha. They made me laugh.

Daniel grinned. 'You love it, really. Admit it.'

'I really don't,' I said, but it was getting harder to keep a straight face with Daniel posing gleefully in the garish shirt.

'You do, you do!' he laughed, pointing. I had cracked under the pressure and my traitorous mouth wouldn't stay serious.

Tabitha appeared out of the changing room looking like a Pre-Raphaelite princess in the gauzy poppy dress. Even my mum softened at the sight of her. 'Very nice,' she conceded.

As Jackie wrapped their purchases, Daniel and Tabitha stood in front of me, all of us huddled into our coats.

'So are you coming to the party tonight?' Tabitha asked, tentative.

I shook my head. 'No.'

Jackie appeared with their bags, the outfits all beautifully wrapped inside. 'You should go to that party, Norah, you know.'

'No way,' I said, wanting the subject changed.

'You really should,' my mum cut in.

'Don't you start!' I said, laughing, incredulous.

Tabitha was nodding like an eager puppy. 'Do come, Norah.'

I shook my head. 'The last people I need to see are Coco and everyone.'

'Just stick with us. We're your friends,' said Tabitha.

I smiled down at the floor when she said it. The words so sweet, so unexpected. 'Thanks,' I said. 'That's lovely of you to say.'

Tabitha said, 'So you'll come?'

'Maybe.'

Tabitha clapped her hands, but Daniel narrowed his eyes. He was right not to believe me. There was no way I was going to that party. I definitely didn't want to see Coco. But I also couldn't face seeing Ezra after everything we'd said to each other last time.

When they had gone, I slumped down in one of the fold-out chairs, exhausted by the whole scene.

Jackie handed me a cup of stewed tea and a Kit Kat. 'They're nice.'

'They're some of the good ones,' I said.

My mum sat down next to me. 'I don't think your dad ever missed a party in his life.'

I rolled my eyes to show she was barmy if she thought that logic was going to work.

'You'll regret it if you let Coco win again.' She blew on her tea, steam rising from the mug like billowing smoke. 'Never regret the things you haven't done. That's what Dad always says, isn't it?'

Big Dave's voice chipped in, his head poking through some army surplus bags to our stall. 'Except I might point out, Lois, that logic got him in the slammer.'

My mum closed her eyes, meditatively, as if he might pass.

Jackie tried to stifle a laugh. My mum opened her eyes and threw her a warning look. I felt my mouth twitch. Big Dave was watching with big excited eyes, like he might have just unwittingly cracked a great joke. Jackie couldn't hold it in any longer. She really started laughing. As I found my grin growing, my mum finally relented, shaking her head with a reluctant half-smile. 'We shouldn't be laughing.'

'Oh, for Christ's sake, Lois,' Jackie gasped between snorts. 'If you can't bloody laugh, what can you do?'

My mum looked up at us from underneath her furry hat, huge blue eyes half obscured by her fringe. 'I'm so annoyed with him,' she said.

'As are we all,' Jackie replied, her arms crossed.

My mum nodded. 'And I miss him.'

'Yes,' said Jackie, sitting down in the chair next to mine.

Big Dave was about to say something.

'Be quiet, Dave!' my mum shouted.

Dave was so shocked that he tripped back over his basket of army surplus hats, which made Jackie start laughing again. She waved her hand and spluttered, 'Sorry, I can't help it.'

This time my mum did laugh, properly, the two of them in hysterics as Dave scrabbled around on the floor, hoiking up his builder's-bum jeans and trying to gather up his hats. They giggled like schoolgirls. Tears streamed down Jackie's face.

When they finally pulled themselves together, my mum wiping away her mascara with one of the vintage handkerchiefs, Jackie put her arm round my shoulder and said, 'So what are you going to wear to this party?'

'I'm still not going,' I said.

'Yes you are,' she said. 'Because I have decided I'm taking your mother out tonight to get rip-roaring drunk, and you can't be left on that boat alone moping. We need to know that you are safe and sound at a party.'

'I don't think that's the way it works, Jackie. I think you're meant to try and ban me from going to parties, rather than force me to them.'

My mum replaced Jackie's arm round my shoulders with her own and said, 'Norah, you're going to go to the party not because we say so, but for you. You've had a tough term, you've been super brave and you need to finish it properly. You need to face it. Otherwise I think you'll regret it.'

I looked up at her as best I could with my mammoth scarf and hat and met her eyes under her huge hat and wide fuzzy scarf. She looked at me like when I was a really little kid, and added, 'And we'll make sure you've got the best goddamned outfit there is.'

Jackie whooped and jumped up to start flicking through the rails faster than gunfire.

'OK?' my mum said to me.

I nodded. 'OK.'

She kissed the tip of my nose, and we sat side by side, her clutching me tight to her side as Jackie compiled the *crème de la crème* of their stock.

CHAPTER THIRTY-ONE

I was damned.

But tonight I was beautiful.

I wore the white Chanel suit that Jackie had discovered at the end of the summer. It was immaculate, never been worn. The jacket was hip-length, tailored at the waist but not so much that it nipped in; it just gave the perfect silhouette. The trousers were narrow cigarette pants, slicing off at the ankle with a little slit in each hem. I wore it with just a black vest underneath that you couldn't see. Jackie had rummaged around in the van and produced the most amazing pair of black vintage stilettos. They weren't a brand or anything special but they had the pointiest toes and heels killer enough to give me a strut. My mum did my hair, curled it in big waves then pinned back one side letting the other side flick down over my eye. My brows were dark, my lips were pale, my eyes were smoky. Round my neck was a yellow diamond that blinked like a cat's eye. It was fake but it still looked priceless.

My mum gave me the money for a black cab to the giant

Chelsea mansion where the lights were bright and the music thumping.

I don't know what I expected, what it would be like when I saw Coco and Ezra, but my mum was right. I had to go.

The door opened and a butler in a haunting plain white mask directed me into the lavish house while a photographer called on me to pose as I entered. The house was as grand as Ezra's, but the opposite aesthetic. This was all giant colourful Warhols that were probably originals, stark white walls and a glass staircase that made it look like you could walk on air. Everywhere I looked there were photographers. There were faces I vaguely recognised and others I'd never seen in my life. I snaked through the corridor, adrenaline thumping through me in time with music. In the distance I could see decks and a DJ in the main living room that seemed to have been cleared of furniture, just a sputnik chandelier bursting from the ceiling – another one that Jackie would die for. Ahead was the kitchen with what looked like an entire waiting staff prepping food and drinks. To the right was a giant conservatory, and next to that I could just catch a glimpse of sparkling blue swimming-pool water. All around me were costumes that took my breath away: a boy as a fallen angel, his torso painted silver, his feather wings ravaged; a mermaid with a long green tail, shimmering all over; the devil with his trident, eyes blazing red.

I squeezed past girls in nineteen-twenties numbers, purple satin and sequinned silver, feather boas and kiss curls. There were guys in tuxes with top hats and canes and others in shredded rugby kit. As I rounded the corner into another network of corridors, Freddie appeared on the staircase, jumping the banister in a giant feather headdress and just his turquoise swimming trunks.

'Norah! You made it!' he yelled, as if nothing had ever happened. To Freddie, it probably hadn't. 'Have you seen Ezra?'

I shook my head.

'I don't understand where he is,' Freddie said, arms wide. Then he raced up the stairs, laughing at something that was happening on the landing.

I felt someone at my side, edging me round to talk to them. It was Tabitha, in the pale pink dress with the poppies my mum had found her, curls piled high on her head.

'Norah, you look amazing,' she said.

'Thanks,' I said, relieved to see her. I'd just caught sight of Coco and Verity draped on the conservatory sofas. Coco had poured herself into a gold sequined jumpsuit, her hair slicked back in a centre parting, tied in a low ponytail, her eyes huge and black like a tiger. Verity, sitting tall and sipping from a glass through a straw, wore a baby pink bikini top, the back a network of ribbons that tied round her waist in a little bow, a tiny pink skirt and a pair of thigh-high white boots with sharp spiked heels.

Rollo was sitting on the edge of a fancy coffee table in wide cream trousers with a blue pinstripe, a blue golfing tank top and a pale cream shirt, the sleeves rolled right up to his biceps. He had a flat cap on his head and brown and white brogues on his feet.

I felt my heart rate rise when I saw them all laughing and languid.

Tabitha was talking. 'I'm so glad you're here. You're the only person who doesn't make me feel like I'm completely invisible.'

I looked back at her in surprise. 'Really? I thought only I felt like that.'

She guffawed. 'You're not invisible. You're the strong one.'

I laughed. Preposterous. 'I think you've mistaken me for someone else.'

Emmeline appeared, dark and sultry in the black velvet dress. She'd done her make-up to echo the bruise she'd got at the beginning of term. 'What do you think?' she asked, pointing to her eyes.

I nodded. 'Amazing.'

She smiled. It was the first exchange we'd had in a while. 'I'm glad you came. I was worried you might not.'

'I didn't want to miss it,' I lied, wishing I could have spent the evening just talking to Tabitha, and Daniel, wherever he was.

'I think it'll be fun,' Emmeline said, glancing round. 'Well, as soon as the photographers leave, which is in an hour.

Hopefully they'll take my parents with them.' She grinned, then quickly pouted as a camera flashed and smoothed her glossy hair into place.

'Emmeline!' It was Coco shouting.

We all turned.

'Come over here,' Verity called, beckoning her over.

'I'd better go,' Emmeline said.

I frowned. 'Why?' Emmeline looked confused. 'Because . . .' She pointed to where Coco and Verity were staring impatiently.

'But you were talking to us,' I said, feeling suddenly every inch the strong one Tabitha deemed me to be. There was a confidence in having nothing to lose.

Emmeline still seemed perplexed.

I waved my hand. 'Don't worry about it,' I said. 'Go.'

'I don't get you, Norah,' Emmeline said, eyebrows drawn together. 'I've tried to be your friend. I was nice to you when you first arrived and I thought we got on OK. I've been nothing but friendly to you.'

I pushed my fringe away from my eyes. At the very beginning, I'd have done anything to be at this party. I'd have forgiven them all anything just for an invite. But now my world had contracted even more than on the day our boat had sailed down the Thames. My layers of protection had hardened, taking my tolerance with it.

'You've been OK to me,' I agreed. 'But only within the limits of what she'll allow.' I angled my head in Coco's

291

direction. 'And I'd much rather be lonely than have friends like that.'

Tabitha's expression validated her claim that I was the strong one. Emmeline's face looked like thunder.

'Emmeline!' Coco shouted again. 'Get over here!'

Emmeline's eyes blazed in her bruised make-up. Then she turned, glossy hair flicking like a whip, and stomped off to join Coco and Verity.

Tabitha saw someone else she knew and asked if I wanted to join her as she crossed the room. I shook my head, realising that I was OK on my own, and walked in the direction of the kitchen to get a Coke.

In the pool room there was a loud shout as Freddie dive-bombed into the water. A couple of other people started splashing around. Rollo started chucking balls and floats at Freddie, who was laughing as he tried to dodge the hits. I spoke to one of the Lower Sixth girls from the play, and then Rex from my Art class. Waiters brought round drinks and trays of miniature fish and chips, tiny burgers and hot dogs. Photographers' flashes went off like fireworks. A band started up in the space where the pool room adjoined the conservatory – a group of cool hipsters with a trumpet and sax. They were amazing. The music filled the space, making it impossible not to smile.

I was actually having fun.

It was hard to admit that a tiny part of me kept looking

around for Ezra. Every time anyone tall with brown hair came into my eyeline I got a little spike of adrenaline, but it was never him.

Daniel found me in the pool room, leaning up against the mirrored walls. He was decked out in the swirly gold Versace and sunglasses.

I laughed.

'That's the kind of reaction I aim for. A real good belly laugh,' he said, striking a little pose before he sat down.

In the pool Freddie was hurling huge waves of water over the edge, soaking Rollo's clothes.

Daniel was in the middle of telling me a story about the trials of finding trousers to match his garish shirt when he suddenly stopped talking and nudged me.

Coco was sashaying towards us. Her gold sequins glinted in the pool light. Verity was beside her, boots clicking like bullets on the tiles.

Emmeline was just behind her. Rollo sidled over. Freddie slid himself out of the pool.

I stood up. Instinct telling me that I was her target.

When she drew level, she cocked her head to one side and said, 'Why are you here?'

'I was invited,' I said.

'Shouldn't you be off visiting Daddy?' She looked me up and down. 'Or are you sniffing around for Ezra?'

Out of the corner of my eye I saw Freddie wince and

burrow down into his towel.

I would have liked to do the same. My cheeks flamed at the mention of Ezra's name.

Coco smirked. 'You are, aren't you?'

I felt foolish all glammed up to the max. Vulnerable.

'He's not here,' she said dismissively. 'He's gone to the States. His whole family have. He's left and he's not coming back. But you'd know that, wouldn't you?'

My shock was obviously clear on my face because she added with a gleeful smirk, 'Did no one tell you? Poor Norah. So desperate.'

Behind her Verity sniggered.

Rollo was enjoying the show. Emmeline at least had the decency to look away.

I tried my best to look impassive, aware of the power Coco wielded, remembering the time she'd made me sing in front of everyone in the corridor. But my brain was so distracted by the news about Ezra that I couldn't think straight. How could he have left?

Coco smoothed her hair back and took a step forward, towering over me in her spangly catsuit. She sensed the weakness in her prey. 'You've got to learn when to give up,' she drawled, eyes vicious. 'Get some dignity.'

I knew I was wavering. My eyes threatened tears, I imagined them dragging lines of smoky shadow down my cheeks. I tried to muster some strength but there was only so much I could take. Everyone was watching, feeding off my humiliation. I should never have come. I tried to widen my eyes to chase the tears away.

And that was when I saw the reflection in the mirrors that covered the walls. We stretched on for infinity, Coco and me. She was no taller than I was.

She was just a girl with blonde hair standing opposite a girl with brown. Same height.

I had made her towering. My mind had made her towering. My fear of her.

I saw Verity too in her pink-ribboned bikini top. Realised how dreadful her outfit was, how tacky. I had respected her style just because she had money. I imagined the look of horror on my mum and Jackie's faces if they saw her. My lips twitched.

'Something funny?' Coco said.

I shook my head. 'Nothing.' The threat of tears had gone. I put my hands in the pockets of my white suit trousers and stood, waiting. I had faced much worse than Coco Summers this year. And if that hadn't broken me, there was no way she would. I could feel a confidence rising up in me, the strength Tabitha had opened my eyes to.

I saw it perplex her. Saw her recalibrate.

The others stood mute, the squiggles of swimming-pool water reflected over their faces like she'd trapped them behind a wall of fire.

'Well?' I asked.

'Well, what?'

'Keep going,' I said, knowing suddenly that I wasn't afraid any more. 'Carry on about dignity, Coco.' Just saying her name gave me power. 'You could talk about the time I stole someone's part in a play because I wasn't quite good enough to get it myself.' I frowned. 'Wait, that wasn't me.'

Daniel laughed, then immediately covered his mouth.

'How dare you,' she hissed.

I stayed where I was, hands still in my pockets. If I took them out now, she'd see they were still shaking. I really had deserved the lead part in the play, because my insides were threatening to turn to jelly. Despite the feeling of confidence, the venom in Coco's eyes made her a terrifying opponent.

I willed my voice to come out smooth and flat. 'What are you going to do, Coco? Push me in the pool?' I goaded her with the kind of confident drawl my dad could pull off. Maybe we all needed a bit of the liar in us.

There was a tiny pause. We both had no idea where this would end. I braced myself just in case she did decide to push me in the pool. She looked like there was every possibility. Either that, or kill me with her bare hands.

But I had forgotten who I was dealing with. Coco was the master. She knew she was on the back foot. She suddenly took a step forward and threw her arm round me. 'Don't take everything so seriously, Norah!' she said.

She gave me shoulder a squeeze. I could smell her sugary perfume. 'You should have a little bit more fun!'

All around us people laughed and the atmosphere relaxed. Her friends were grinning.

I had been *that* close – but of course she'd managed to pull it back. Now she was the victor.

Coco preened, like we were posing for a photograph, her arm still slung over my shoulder. Then, glancing round, she said, 'I do like the idea of the pool, though.'

And before I fully understood what was happening, I felt the pressure of her hand against my chest. She whispered, 'You will never win against me,' just before shoving me hard into the glistening pool.

I gasped as my back smacked the surface, warm chlorinated water filling my mouth, going up my nose, my clothes weighing me down. When I resurfaced, coughing, spluttering, hair a mess, I saw people open-mouthed in shocked laughter. Over my head, Coco did a perfect, graceful swan dive into the pool to the whoops and cheers of her friends, successfully trumping any memory of what she'd just done to me.

I swiped the water from my face. Incredulous.

Loads of other people had followed Coco's lead and dive-bombed fully dressed into the pool. Coco the mermaid queen in the centre was lifted high on to Rollo's shoulders in her glimmering sequins.

She was right. I would never win against her. But as I

watched her, blonde hair dripping and head thrown back with a laugh, I realised that I had won against myself. I was no longer afraid. I had snagged one little victory before she pushed me. That flicker in her eyes. I had seen her for who she was, and she knew it.

Daniel was crouching by the side of the pool, all amused pity as I hauled myself out of the water. He handed me a towel so I could dry my face and hair.

'Are you OK?' he asked.

'Yes,' I said. 'Yes, I'm fine.' And it felt like the whole truth.

CHAPTER THIRTY-TWO

I left the party after that, wrapping my coat round my soaking white suit. Standing on the pavement, hair wet and icy cold, I felt like I belonged nowhere, but I loved it. I felt free.

The air was crisp and dry, the sky dark without a single star. A taxi was just dropping off some sixth-form latecomers, so I took their place and sat trying to warm up in the back, staring out at the luscious houses with their elegant lighting and the expensive shops and the people walking in big fur coats.

My brain was running through everything that had happened, fizzing with adrenaline: facing up to Coco, her hand pushing me in the water, the smack of the pool as I fell. The feeling that in some way I had won just by taking her on. But then I remembered what she'd said about Ezra, and why I had an ache in the pit of my stomach. He had gone, Coco had known, and I had never got to say goodbye.

When the taxi pulled up at the jetty, I had never been more relieved to see our boat. The fairy lights twinkling, the scrappy old bunting flapping in the light breeze, the warm yellow glow and the gypsy jazz that meant my mum and Jackie were home.

Out on the river, guests on a wedding boat party were throwing pink lilies into the water. They bobbed like jewels in the frothy wake.

My killer heels had well and truly killed my feet. As I limped down the gangplank, my little toes pinched red, wet and cold, the suit fabric sticking to my legs, I thought about getting into my pyjamas, curling up on the sofa and watching my mum and Jackie giggle as they mixed fresh limes and gin and danced haphazardly to the music.

I could see them through the porthole, ice clinking in my mum's glass as she waved her hand during some story. I could see Jackie throw her head back with a roar of laughter. If this was to be our new normal while we were waiting for my dad to come home, perhaps it wouldn't be so bad.

Then I saw another face, grinning on the sofa as my mum was talking. Laughing along with her. Someone who looked remarkably like Ezra.

I squinted to see better. To check it was him. Oh god, it definitely was. What were they talking about? I wondered if my mum had had a go at him about the play. But then he looked pretty comfortable. Was that a cup of tea in his hand? Why wasn't he at the party? I hurried the last few steps, almost breaking my ankle in my shoes, and threw open the door.

'Oh, hello darling,' said my mum, eyes very bright. Behind her Jackie was grinning knowingly in Ezra's direction. 'You're early,' she went on, clearly a bit tiddly. Then she frowned, registering my appearance. 'Why are you all wet?'

'I –' I started but I didn't finish. I just stared, confused, at Ezra. 'It's too long to explain. What are you doing here?'

Ezra stood up, looking half sheepish, half amused.

Jackie said in a very loud whisper, 'He's been here for hours.' I tried not to imagine what the chat had been about.

'We found him on the jetty when we got here. Poor lad was freezing,' Jackie went on.

It was Ezra's turn to blush.

'Norah, honey,' my mum said, sloshing her drink a bit as she came over with a blanket from the sofa and tried to drape it over my shoulders. 'You need to get changed into something dry, you'll catch a cold.'

Jackie chimed in. 'Shall I make everyone a nice cup of tea? Ezra, one sugar was it?'

I covered my eyes with my hand for a second, unable to handle the scene, the fussing. I needed to get Ezra out of there. 'No tea,' I said. 'Let me just get changed and then we'll go out.'

My mum frowned. 'But you've only just got home.'

Jackie nudged her and looked between me and Ezra with a bit of a giggle.

'Oh!' said my mum as it dawned on her that we might want to be alone. She sniggered. 'Of course.'

I dashed to my room and changed as fast as I could into my

jeans and a jumper. Then I came down the little flight of stairs, pulling on my trainers, one arm in my huge Moomin puffer jacket – the only one I could find at such speed – to find everyone standing pretty much as I'd left them. Jackie and my mum stifling giggles like schoolgirls. Ezra looking increasingly uncomfortable.

'Let's go,' I said.

Ezra was clearly relieved to escape, but still paused to kiss Jackie and my mum goodbye.

'Bye, Mrs Whittaker. '

'Goodbye, sweetheart. Have fun in America,' my mum said.

I was dismayed. When I'd seen him here on the boat, I'd figured that Coco had been wrong, not just premature, about his departure.

'Bye, Jackie.'

'Goodbye, ducks,' she said, giving his shoulder a squeeze.

When Ezra had gone through the door, they both did exaggerated kissing faces at me that they thought were hilarious, flopping on the sofa in fits of laughter.

Outside I gulped in some cool evening air.

Ezra was on the jetty, grinning, hands in his pockets. He had on a marl-grey hoodie and a dark green parka.

It was the first time I'd allowed myself a moment to acknowledge that he was there, on my boat. I had been too distracted. Now I felt the first flutter shoot through me. He must have come for me.

'That's a hell of a coat,' he said, nodding towards my big Moomin jacket.

'It's really warm,' I said, unable to think of anything better to say through the wild thumping of my heart.

He looked like he was holding in his smile. 'I like your boat, by the way.'

'Yeah?' I said, surprised. 'I don't imagine you're someone who's spent a lot of time with two mad women singing jazz on a houseboat.'

'Not that often. It was fun.'

I cringed. 'Yeah, right.'

He laughed. 'It was. They're nice.'

I nodded, looking down at my trainers, my hands stuffed into my coat pockets. He had missed the party to wait for me on the boat. He had spent his evening with my mum and Jackie. It was enough to break down any residual anger I still had.

'Shall we walk?' he asked.

'OK.' I realised I knew his profile by heart, the line of his jaw, the sharp angles of his cheekbone.

We walked side by side along the river, the bridges sparkling ahead of us, the dark water lapping gently against the sides. I could feel a hundred things bubbling up but I didn't say any of them. I wanted to see what he had to say first. 'I'm sorry,' he said, dark eyes momentarily on mine. 'I'm sorry I didn't stand up for you with the play. It *was* gutless.'

I tried to remember if I'd called him gutless. It was all a bit of a blur. I stood by the gist of what I'd said about the play, but there were some things I wished I'd never voiced. 'I'm sorry I told you to take the blame for your brother. That was really harsh.'

'No, no. It was good. It was definitely good.'

I shook my head. 'I don't think it was your fault.'

'But it was,' he said, almost urging me to agree. 'It was, and it's much better now.'

I looked at him in surprise. We were illuminated by a streetlight, crystals of frost forming on the ground around us.

Ezra's eyes were smiling in the lamplight. 'I spoke to my mum. It was hard, but good. Really honest. I think we both felt better after it.' He raked a hand through his hair. 'And I spoke to Rollo.'

'Really?' I was impressed.

'And . . .'

Ezra rolled his eyes. 'Just as spineless as I thought.' He went to lean against the embankment with his back to the water.

'I'm sorry,' I said, going to stand next to him with my hands on the cool stone wall.

'It doesn't matter,' he said. Our hands were almost touching, the river lapping below us, 'I think I just wanted someone to share the guilt with me. But once I faced it, I didn't need him. Does that make sense?'

I thought about going to the island to see Jess. Sitting in the courtroom with my grandparents. Saying goodbye to my dad. I glanced at Ezra looking out at the Thames, the outline of his profile so familiar. 'Yes.'

There were two swans on the river, ghostly white in the darkness. All I could think about was how close our hands were.

Ezra looked at me. 'The play was shit,' he said.

I laughed. 'So I heard.'

'I can't believe I didn't say anything.'

'Neither can I,' I replied, one brow arched.

'And neither can your mum,' he said with a grin.

'Oh god.' I put my hand over my eyes. 'What did she say?'

'She got really cross with me. She can be quite scary.' He laughed, eyes twinkling.

I looked at him through two open fingers.

He laughed again, all white teeth and sparkling brown eyes, and pulled my hand down from my face. 'Don't worry. I could handle it.'

I expected him to let go of my hand, but he didn't. Instead, he wound his fingers through mine. He didn't say anything, just studied our interlaced fingers. Then he said, 'I'm going to the States.'

I felt my chest tighten. 'I heard. Coco told me.'

He winced. 'I wanted to tell you, but you don't have a

bloody phone and you never came back to school. Can you get a phone please? Who doesn't have a phone?'

I smiled. All I could think about was his fingers meshing with mine. Our ice-cold hands threaded together.

Ezra rubbed his thumb against the back of my hand. 'It's for treatment for my brother. If it works, they hope he'll walk again. Everyone's praying for a miracle.' He paused. 'The trials have all been pretty positive.'

I could sense his nerves about the whole thing. I squeezed his hand. 'It sounds good.'

He sighed, the stress and tension visible on his face. 'God, I hope so.'

I knew now why he had to go. 'It'll be good for you and your family to all be together.'

He nodded. There was another pause where he took hold of my other hand. 'I'm a bit gutted about leaving you, though.'

'You are?' I said, caught by surprise.

'Yeah, of course.'

I tried not to let my smile widen, but it was hard. 'When are you coming back?'

'Don't know.'

'When are you going?'

'Christmas Eve.'

I nodded again, trying to quash my sadness.

The street lamps cast tall shadows behind us. The clouds zigzagged to reveal a crescent moon. The white swans drifted past on the water.

'So what d'you want to do?' he asked, pulling me towards him. 'In the time we've got?'

I looked at the pavement, I looked at our hands, I looked up at his face in the moonlight, all pale and sharp. 'I think we should probably work on our kissing,' I said.

He laughed, dark eyes glinting. 'That sounds like a plan.'

So with his hands on my waist under the giant Moomin coat and my arms tight round his neck, the warmth of his body pressed against mine and my fingers in the curl of his hair, we practised like pros under the light of the half-moon and the flicker of a street lamp.

CHAPTER THIRTY-THREE

Later that evening, Ezra and I were sitting cosy from the weather in the window booth of Sorrentos. Outside, frost coated car windscreens, fairy-light starbursts twinkled in branches and Christmas trees glowed through the windows of expensive red-brick houses. In front of us were two Cokes, and we were waiting for two grilled-cheese sandwiches. I had just finished telling him the story of what had happened with Coco at the party.

'I wish I'd been there,' he said. 'I can't believe she pushed you in the pool!'

I could laugh about it now. 'She's crazy.' I shook my head, my hands wrapped round my Coke. 'And what's it going to be like next term? She'll eat me alive.' It was the first time I'd acknowledged to myself that I would actually be going back next term.

Ezra shrugged like it was nothing. 'You'll be fine.'

'You think?'

'Absolutely,' he said. But his expression was a little less convinced than his voice.

I bashed him on the arm. 'I can't believe you're leaving!'

He held up his hands. 'I know, I'm sorry. Come with me.'

'Yeah right.'

His eyes belied a wariness for my Chelsea High future. We all knew what Coco was capable of. Then he reached over and took my hand from round the Coke, toying with my fingers. Around us was the bustle of the café. Orders shouted from the kitchen. The clink of teacups, the bang of the espresso, the ring of the bell over the door.

I didn't want him to leave.

Suddenly there was an icy blast of cold air as the front door opened. I heard, 'I said she'd come here but, oh no, we have to go everywhere else first.' And there was Daniel, arguing with Tabitha as they unwrapped their scarfs and unbuttoned their coats.

I half stood up so I could see them over the back of the booth. I couldn't believe that they had come looking for me. Daniel and Tabitha were walking towards us, him in the gold and white swirl of the Versace shirt and her with her hair still pinned with poppies to match her dress.

Daniel spread his arms wide. 'We've looked everywhere,' he said, air-kissing us with frozen cheeks before sliding into the booth opposite. 'Even had a cup of tea with your mother!'

'I love your little houseboat,' Tabitha said, slipping in next to him. 'It's so adorable. I want to live on a boat.'

Daniel was texting and looked up, scoffing at the idea of

Tabitha ever living on a boat.

Tabitha frowned. 'I could live on a boat. Not forever,' she conceded. 'Maybe for a week or two. For a little holiday. Who drives it? Do you have a driver, Norah?'

I shook my head, holding in a smile.

Daniel put his phone down. 'Are you definitely OK with everything that happened at the party? I feel bad for making you go.'

'It was good that I went,' I said. 'I had to face her.'

Tabitha made a little noise of agreement. 'And I think you sort of got your point across. I mean, it would have been better if she hadn't pushed you in the pool but –'

Daniel rolled his eyes. 'Stop talking please, Tabitha.'

Tabitha went pink. 'OK. Sorry.'

I smiled. 'It's fine.'

Daniel started telling a story that made Tabitha guffaw, then knock over one of the Cokes so it went all over Daniel's Versace shirt and made him spring out of his seat. I was trying not to laugh, watching Tabitha trying to dab Daniel down with a napkin, thinking that maybe it wouldn't be all bad next term, when a cab pulled up outside and someone dressed in slinky black velvet with hair glossy as water stepped out.

I felt myself tense. 'What's Emmeline doing here?'

Everyone stopped what they were doing to have a look out of the window.

'Well, this is where it's at, isn't it?' Daniel said, holding his

Coke-soaked shirt away from his skin. It was clear he'd messaged Emmeline.

'Coco's not coming, is she?' I asked, suddenly worried.

Daniel shook his head. I watched, a bit wary as Emmeline came into the café and walked towards us.

I could feel Ezra's hand resting lightly on my shoulder, his arm stretched behind me along the booth.

Emmeline's black-velvet dress glistened like fur in the low glow of the overhead lights. She'd wiped all her elaborate make-up off so her face was bare and more beautiful than before. She rested her fingertips on the table, flicked her hair behind her shoulders, took a deep breath and said, 'Norah, at the party, I didn't agree with what Coco was saying. And I didn't like who I was when I was standing behind her.'

I bit my lip as she talked. I'd thought she was a die-hard Coco supporter and always would be. When she finished, she looked straight at me with her piercing, serious eyes.

I nodded. 'OK.'

She nodded back, suddenly a little awkward having said her piece.

The grilled cheese arrived, piping hot and gooey.

As the waiter slid the two plates on to the table and was about to walk away, I stopped him. 'Three more of those please!'

And then I smiled at Emmeline and gestured for her to sit down. She smiled back then, visibly relaxing as she took a seat next to Tabitha. Across the table Daniel winked at me.

Ezra squeezed my shoulder.

I took a bite of my grilled cheese and it was the best thing I had ever tasted.

CHAPTER THIRTY-FOUR

It was the first Christmas in my life that it snowed. Only a light dusting that had mostly melted by breakfast, but all the same. My dad would have loved it. I wondered if he had seen it, if his cell had a window. Big Dave's mate had come up trumps, and our visit was secured for Boxing Day.

Today, however, we had been invited, somewhat tentatively, to Christmas at my grandparents'. My mum had flatly refused at first, but I had persuaded her. Something I'd never have imagined doing in the past. The idea of it just being the two of us on the boat alone tipped the balance. She couldn't cook a turkey knowing my dad wouldn't be there in his Santa hat, ready to carve. Her only request was that Jackie was invited too. My grandparents had no objection. They had never met Jackie, though.

We arrived mid-morning and were ushered into the living room by my granddad where my grandmother was waiting, poised by the chintzy settee. Everyone had dressed up for the occasion. My mum looked amazing with her hair up in a complicated knot, her high-waisted wide trousers and a red silk shirt. My grandmother was head to toe in velvet, while my granddad wore a novelty Christmas jumper that I wasn't expecting. The dog wore felt antlers. Harold the butler wasn't there.

'Has to have one day off a year,' my granddad joked.

My mum didn't laugh. It was a bad sign.

We put our presents under the sad-looking Christmas tree, decked with sparse silver decorations and real candles.

'How's your mother, Lois?' my grandmother asked, straightening a cushion.

'I have no idea,' my mum replied. 'Sunning herself somewhere, I presume.'

Everyone was silent.

I cringed.

'Vol-au-vent?' said my granddad, handing round a tray of canapés to break the silence.

The doorbell rang. My grandmother went to answer it, and there was Jackie. I had never been more delighted to see her barrelling in with her usual haphazard chaos. Her weeing poodle Percy shot into the room and bounded excitedly up to Ludo the old Labrador. Jackie was wearing a huge turquoise taffeta gown, red stilettoes and a fake fur coat. She was clutching bags of presents and a bottle of eggnog.

'Hello, darlings,' she cried. 'Happy Christmas! Christ, look at that tree. It's a bit sorry for itself, isn't it?'

My mum had to hide a smile as my grandparents turned to

inspect their limp tree.

My grandmother suddenly laughed, light and tinkly. 'Yes, I suppose it is a little on the sad side,' she said.

Everyone relaxed. Jackie flopped down on the sofa. 'I've got a shocking hangover. Shall we all have a drink?'

'Quite right,' said my granddad, going over to the drinks cabinet.

'It's a little early, isn't it?' said my mum.

Clearly no one else agreed. So my grandmother called, 'Sherry for me,' then handed a plate of hors d'oeuvres to Jackie.

'Don't mind if I do,' Jackie replied, plucking a vol-au-vent off the platter.

The drinks were handed round. They'd bought Diet Coke for me, which my granddad served in a champagne flute. As Jackie was handed her champagne she sat up straight and said, 'Look at your old record player! What a gorgeous machine.' Then she stood up and went to have a better look. 'Shall we have some music?'

The suggestion took my grandparents by surprise. It was so clearly not part of their usual routine. 'Why ever not?' said my grandfather bravely, and joined Jackie by the record player to select some music.

Suddenly Bing Crosbie's 'White Christmas' crooned out, filling the room.

'Your dad's favourite song,' said my mum.

Everyone was silent, except Bing.

Mum looked sad, alone on the sofa. I sat next to her. 'Wherever he is,' I said, 'Dad makes the best of things. He'll probably have them all singing round their Christmas dinner in jail.'

My mum looked at me, all soft-eyed. 'When did you get so wise?'

When my world turned upside down and I had to either fall off or learn to cling on. But I didn't say that, I just shrugged. 'I've always been wise.' And she laughed and squashed me to her.

My granddad refilled her champagne, then added a splosh to my now empty glass and said, 'A small one for you too, Norah, as it's Christmas.'

As the day went on, the chat was awkward at times, the turkey overdone – my gran fretting, 'I never quite get it right!' Percy the poodle terrorised Ludo the old Labrador and the fleeting snow turned to rain, but mostly it was lovely. The present giving especially.

My grandmother gave my mum a brooch that was surprisingly nice and caught my mum visibly off guard. 'Thank you, Veronica,' she stammered.

'You're welcome, Lois.'

My grandmother was equally pleased with her peach cashmere scarf, which had been part of Jackie's job lot. And my grandfather adored his book on the seven bloodiest battles in history, as recommended by Big Dave.

Then from my grandparents I got an iPad. 'Oh my god!' I gasped as I unwrapped it.

'No, it's too much,' said my mum as soon as she saw it.

'She needs it, Lois,' my granddad urged. 'For school.'

'I do need it,' I said, trying to hide my glee with a studious expression.

My mum rolled her eyes, resigned, and I almost punched the air.

Then it just got better. Jackie gave me the star-print cashmere I'd stolen for the play rehearsals.

'Wow, thanks, Jackie,' I gushed.

'Well,' she said, 'I thought you needed a treat this year. If I'd known you were getting an iPad, mind . . .' She raised a brow and I clutched the jumper close in case she decided to take it back.

My mum bought me a necklace from Barbara's stall. It was a tiny gold anchor – a symbol of our boat and our tether – and I knew I would never take it off.

I nipped off at one point after lunch to open the tiny present Ezra had placed in my hand when I'd seen him before he left for the airport. 'Don't open it till Christmas,' he'd whispered softly in my ear.

I had given him a journal. Not fancy or expensive, but inside I wrote, 'There are two ways of looking at everything. See this as an adventure. And when you get home, I want to read all about it. Norah x'

Now, I tore off the wrapping of his gift to me and almost cried when I saw what it was. A snowglobe of Battersea Bridge all lit up, the view from my boat dusted with snow. I loved it. The card read:

> *My plan is that the view*
> *will now remind you of me.*
>
> *Happy Xmas,*
> *Ez xx*

That night I slept with it on my pillow.

CHAPTER THIRTY-FIVE

Nine o'clock Boxing Day morning, the sky was the brightest blue and there was a thick, crunching frost on the ground. My mum was next to me, our arms and the backs of our hands brushing as we walked. Ahead of us were the towering gates of the jail. The sun blindingly bright behind us.

I looked at my mum and she looked at me.

'Ready?' she asked.

I stared ahead of me at the grey prison building. I knew now that life wasn't all black and white. That sometimes good people did bad things. That the world was unpredictable and nothing was forever. Those things scared me. I didn't know if life was going to be OK. But I was going to live it anyway.

I took a deep breath. 'Ready.'

ACKNOWLEDGMENTS

Thanks to all the amazing team at Egmont, especially Lindsey Heaven and Ali Dougal for their support and enthusiasm for all things *Chelsea High*, the fantastic art department, PR, Production, and to Lucy Courtenay for weaving her copyediting magic.

Thanks also to my fabulous agent and cheerleader, Rebecca Ritchie. And to Lucy Gilmour for reading this when it was just a very rough draft and being incredibly tactful and inspiring with her advice.

And finally, thanks to my family for putting up with all the years I watched *Grease* every day after school. I can finally call it research!

COMING SOON!

CHAPTER ONE

Weird to know that my future self would be jealous of this moment.

I was sitting on the soft grass of Central Park, New York City, my head resting on the sun-warmed T-shirt of Ezra Montgomery as we sipped iced coffee and watched baseball players practising their pitches. His chin rested on my head, and I could feel the rumbling in his chest as he talked.

Memories of the night before were still sharp and sweet in my head. Hand in hand with Ezra on the red carpet at the world premiere of Helena Rhys's new film. *The* Helena Rhys, who was the mother of our friend Daniel Rhys. She had flown me and Daniel over first class to New York for the weekend. Their apartment had gold taps and linen wallpaper. I'd overheard Mrs Rhys speaking to my mum on the phone, assuring her in echoey tones that I'd be perfectly well looked after and always supervised by an adult; then she'd promptly gone out, returning only fleetingly over the weekend.

Daniel had invited me specifically so I could see my boyfriend Ezra, who had moved to the States. It still sent a rush through me to say *my boyfriend Ezra*. And to have seen his intake of breath as I walked into the lounge of the Rhys's incredible penthouse in an emerald-green silk gown that was probably worth more than all my clothes back home put together.

Helena Rhys had thrown open the doors to her walk-in closet and told me, 'Pick anything you want, darling. If it's in there, I've worn it already.'

'Mum never wears anything twice,' sighed Daniel with a roll of his eyes.

After a night of grinning at the red-carpet cameras, we had walked the streets of SoHo in the dark eating ice cream and then fallen asleep, all of us, on the giant cream sofas in the Rhys penthouse. The next morning we'd wolfed down stacks of pancakes with maple syrup and fresh juice in a New York diner with low lights and turquoise booth seats.

Now Daniel had gone shopping with his mother, while Ezra and I lay in the haze of summer. I wished this moment could be paused in time. Because right here, right now, I was living the fairytale.

'Don't go home,' he said, arms tightening around me. The sun was golden on his limbs.

I laughed. 'OK, I won't.'

I could feel him smile.

In the distance I could hear the crack of the baseball on the bat in the nets. The traffic. The yapping of dogs. Above us, perfect white fluffy clouds blocked out the glare of the sun.

'It's rubbish here on my own,' Ezra said, frowning.

I felt his deep sigh and looked up at him. 'It'll be OK.'

'Will it?' he asked, expression questioning, verging on hopeless.

If I was honest, I didn't know. No one did.

With straight A's and a college scholarship already in the bag, physics genius Caro Kerber-Murphy knows she's smart. But there's one test she's never quite been able to ace: love.

THE SECRET TO L♥VE IS GREAT CHEMISTRY

THE LOVE HYPOTHESIS

LAURA STEVEN

From the author of *The Exact Opposite of Okay* and *A Girl Called Shameless*

'I guess I better explain how I got to this point: eighteen and internationally reviled.'

'Funny, unapologetic and shameless in the best possible way'
Louise O'Neill, author of *Asking for It*

THE EXACT OPPOSITE OF OKAY

COMEDY WOMEN IN PRINT PRIZE WINNER

LAURA STEVEN

'Funny, thought-provoking feminism.' *Guardian*

Sometimes school
can be a killer.

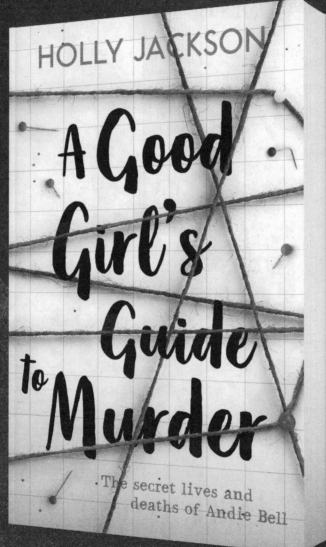

HOLLY JACKSON

A Good
Girl's
Guide
to Murder

The secret lives and
deaths of Andie Bell

How far would you go to
#FindAndie